MAD
COUNTRY

Also by the author
The City Son

MAD COUNTRY

STORIES

SAMRAT UPADHYAY

SOHO

Published by
Soho Press, Inc.
853 Broadway
New York, NY 10003

Library of Congress Cataloging-in-Publication Data
Upadhyay, Samrat, author.
Mad country : stories / Samrat Upadhyay.

ISBN 978-1-61695-796-4
eISBN 978-1-61695-797-1

I. Title
PR9570.N43 U636 2017   823'.92—dc23   2016045127

Interior design by Janine Agro, Soho Press, Inc.

Printed in the United States of America

10 9 8 7 6 5 4 3 2 1

To my family

TABLE OF CONTENTS

FAST FORWARD

The meeting with the minister didn't go well. He was adamant that unless *Fast Forward* printed a follow-up, a retraction of sorts, the magazine would face problems. "If you think you can publish anything you want," Minister Gujrel said, "then you should also be ready to face the consequences."

They sat in the spacious reception area outside the minister's office at the Ministry of Information and Communications. Someone had brought in tea, which Shalini hadn't touched, even though Minister Gujrel, in between threats, asked her in a gentle voice to drink it. Shalini thought that her drinking that tea would be acquiescing to the state's overreach on this matter. "Freedom of the press is essential in the smooth functioning of a democracy," she'd told the minster at the start of the meeting. "Look at how the press functions in Western democracies," she'd said, and that had gotten the meeting off to a bad start.

"Speak less, okay, madam?" Urmila had cautioned her before Shalini left for the ministry. "Let him speak, and you pretend to listen. These old fogeys like it when others listen to them, especially women."

It was possible, Shalini thought, that had she spoken less and been more polite in the beginning, the minister might not be as peeved as he was now. But then she was certain that this fucker had decided to punish *Fast Forward* before she even got here, and nothing she said would have changed that. *I will take you to court,* Shalini thought, *if you do anything to my magazine.* But she also knew that she wasn't going to. A lawsuit would be protracted, with even more hurdles thrown her way, more money sunk in lawyers and whatnot, and she'd not be able to focus on what was important, which was to continue publishing her magazine.

"You think about it," Minister Gujrel said. He was scrolling through his smartphone. "You live in a society, you have to live in harmony with all the elements involved." He looked up. "What do they call it, this living in harmony? Yes, yin and yang. You simply can't print falsities." He pointed to the tea and biscuits. "Won't you drink your tea?"

"Sir, the only falsity in that piece—an error, really—was the location of where the girl's father was imprisoned before he was executed. The girl had heard from several sources that he'd been killed in the district, but now we know that he was brought here to the capital and shot. We have already posted a correction online, and we'll also publish a correction in the next print issue." *Speak less, Shalini.*

"All you have is the testimony of a distraught young girl who has been led to believe by sensationalist journalists like you that her father was killed by the security forces. It's irrelevant whether he was killed in the district or here in the capital—we didn't kill him. What do they say? If a tree falls in the woods and no one is there to witness it, is it still falling?"

"There are witnesses," Shalini said. "We have other sources, sir, you know that, and we have detailed them in the article."

The minister picked up the copy of *Fast Forward* next to his tea and waved it in the air. "Lies, all of them. Making the government look bad at a time when we should all be moving forward. Your magazine should be called *Fast Backward*, not *Fast Forward*."

Shalini had heard that one before. "Moving forward also means ensuring justice for the victims," she said. "Not hiding things, not whitewashing." She said *whitewashing* in English, and wondered if he understood.

Of course he did. "We have neither whitewashed nor blackwashed. Besides, finding what really happened is the job of TRC, not you."

Ah, the ever-convenient Truth and Reconciliation Committee.

The minister's assistant peeked in and said, "We're late for the program."

Minister Gujrel let the magazine drop on the coffee table pointedly. "I've said all there is to say. If you need sources who can confirm that the victim was killed by the other side, by the terroristic forces, I can provide them for you. But this garbage won't stand."

• • •

The three women gathered at Hotel Shakti as they did every Friday. Drinking in the lobby of a popular five-star hotel in the heart of the city was a pointed gesture—they wanted people to see them. The hotel housed three restaurants and two bars, one of which was next to the lobby where the women got their liquor. During the weekends, the hotel saw a steady flow of who's who in town.

"I don't care if anyone thinks I'm smashed," Alina said as she dragged on her thin cigarette. She'd always smoked, but more so since her divorce. There was desperation in her eyes, as if she couldn't get enough of anything, including booze.

"They think you're not only a drunk but a drunken whore, Alina," Priya said softly. She was even-tempered, always calm, always together, married to a husband who encouraged her to go out with friends, a husband who didn't mind caring for their teenage kids. "So what are you going to do?" Priya asked Shalini. "Are you going to print a retraction?"

"Like hell she is," Alina said, then tried to make an *O* in the air with her smoke.

"As my friend says," Shalini said, pointing at Alina, "like hell I am."

Priya took a delicate sip of her wine (Shalini liked beer, Amstel, and Alina whiskey, lots of it) and said, "This minister has a reputation. You remember what he did to Radio Himal? He had the entire top-level staff fired."

"I'll sue him," Shalini said.

"What can they do?" Alina said, stubbing out one cigarette, then lighting another. "They're going to jail her?

Shalini Malla? Editor extraordinaire? Can you imagine the publicity that would generate?"

"When have they cared about publicity, Alina?" Priyanka said. "You remember what our prime minister said to the UN chief."

"They care about publicity," Shalini said. "And this piece in *Fast Forward* is bad publicity for them."

Priya's mobile rang; it was her husband, who couldn't find the scissors that their son needed for a school project. Alina was attempting to flag down a waiter to refill her whiskey. Shalini chided her in a low voice, "Haven't you had enough?"

"Arre, let me, yaar. Life is short."

"Control yourself, please, Alina."

Alina sang a line about losing control and liking it.

"I'm serious," Shalini said. "These days, every Friday I have to take you home totally drunk."

Priyanka was now talking to her teenage daughter, who it seemed was experiencing a crisis. But Priyanka was cool and collected as she spoke on the phone.

"I get sloshed every day now, Shal," Alina said.

"What?"

"I drink every day. In the afternoons. A quarter of whiskey. Half a bottle of wine. Whatever I can get my hands on. Sometimes in the mornings."

Shalini stared at her, then understood: it was an admission, a confession, a cry for help. Shalini had thought on previous occasions that Alina's mouth smelled when she arrived at the hotel, or sometimes when they ran into each other in town, but she'd assumed that her friend was chewing mint or pan paraag to mask her smoke breath.

"How long have you been like this?" Shalini asked.

Alina lit another cigarette, even though her previous one was still burning on the ashtray. "For about six months now."

"Let's talk outside." Shalini signaled to Priyanka that they'd be back in a moment. Priyanka lifted her hand in inquiry but continued talking on the phone. From the snippets of that conversation, Shalini had gathered that her daughter hadn't gotten the coveted acting part in school.

Outside the front entrance of the hotel, chattering because it was a bit cold, Alina said that she was getting worried about herself. "I'm slipping."

"Why don't you stop drinking?" Shalini asked. "Give yourself a break."

"I start thinking about all the things that have happened to me. What Rasik did to me. What life used to be like before we married. Every day I think of how happy we—you, me, Priyanka—were in school. Remember? Smoking ganja, bunking class to go watch movies. Remember that porno we watched at Tuntun's house?"

"Alina, we can't always—"

"What the bloody fuck happened, Shal?"

Shalini put her arm around Alina. "Maybe you should get a job, Alina. Keep you occupied. Right now your mind is too idle."

"He took everything from me. Everything. All the business, gone in his name. And he left me with that boutique shop, a pittance. I don't even feel like looking at that shop anymore, let alone running it."

"You've kept it closed?"

"What's the point of opening? No one comes. But why would anyone come? It's closed most of the time because I'm at home, drinking. It's like that novel we read in school. What the fuck was the name? *Catch* something. It's closed because no one comes, and no one comes because it's closed."

"*Catch-22,*" Shalini said. "Joseph Heller."

"Yes, Heller. My life has become a Heller."

A man walking by the driveway greeted Alina by name, and she gave him a bright, cheery hello.

Shalini was more worried about Alina than she was about *Fast Forward*. She knew what her stance on the article was, to what lengths she'd go to protect her magazine. *Fast Forward* was her baby, and there was no way she was going to let a pudgy-faced minister threaten her with shutdown. She didn't know where all this bravery came from at age forty. She hadn't been brave as a child and throughout her college years in America, she'd barely done anything adventurous or remarkable. The most daring thing she'd done then was attend a Neil Young concert in Cleveland, where she'd smoked dope with strangers and had slept in someone's car.

The idea for a magazine had come about after she'd returned to Nepal and floundered for a few years, in and out of jobs, in and out of relationships. The magazine idea had surfaced while she was chatting with some friends over beer in a Jhamsikhel bar. For the first couple of years, she'd published a glossy magazine focused on celebrity gossip and movie and restaurant reviews. She'd never been interested in such topics to begin with but had been persuaded that there was a market for them, which turned out to be true, at least initially. Soon after the launch of *Fast Times*—that was the name of its glossy incarnation, an echo of the movie *Fast Times at Ridgemont High*, which she'd seen in the dormitory at Denison University—a number of copycat magazines flooded the market: *Fast Life*, *Freaky Times*, *CityMeet*, *Elite Lifestyle*, *The Socialite*. One day at a friend's retail wine shop in Babar Mahal, she saw a number of these magazines spread out on the coffee table and was struck by how remarkably similar they all looked. Inside, the articles also covered the similar topics of fashion, confidence boosters, grooming or weight tips, astrology delivered in hip language. It felt as if you could abandon reading an article in one magazine and open the next magazine and continue where you left off. This realization bothered her to no end, and later, when she was walking home, she saw an Indian magazine on display in the window of a bookstore, a monthly publication focused on investigative journalism she'd heard about but had not read. She bought a copy to take home, and *Fast Forward* was born.

Now in its fifth year, *Fast Forward* had already acquired a reputation as a tough, confrontational journal, and Shalini Malla had become somewhat of a household name. She appeared on TV, was featured on newspapers and style magazines (the kind *Fast Forward* used to be), sometimes with the label "celebrity editor," a title she disliked. *Fast Forward* had by now conducted several high-profile investigations and exposés that had led to scandals and firings and resignations and, once, even imprisonment. There was the case of corruption at the airport: a disgruntled airport worker had come to the *Fast Forward* office one day, which had led to a story on high-level officials at the airport extorting and scamming scores of passengers who traveled to the Gulf countries for work. Another investigation had unearthed fraud and tax evasion schemes in major banks. Prostitution and sexual exploitation in the cinema industry. Nepotism in a premier medical university. It was as though the country could not stop providing her with fodder. The magazine sold so many copies that she was able to pilfer writers and editors from other publications, people with good noses to sniff out wrongdoing, people with sharp eyes and sharper words.

When Shalini took stock of how far she'd come, she was astonished. It almost seemed impossible, what she'd accomplished: she'd single-handedly changed the journalistic scene of the country.

The day after Alina's confession, Shalini received a text from the minister's office saying that *Fast Forward* should be ready for a tax audit. *The fun begins*, she thought. That afternoon she called for an editorial meeting. "Tough days ahead," she said.

Prakash groaned. "Is there anything we can do in this country without these assholes breathing down our necks?"

Chitra was typing on her laptop. She was always working on a story, even during meetings. Shalini had asked her several times to focus on what was being said during the meetings, but it was as if Chitra was helpless. *It's an addiction with her*, Shalini thought. Yet Chitra was the most talented of her reporters, the most stubborn. She appeared not to know the concept of defeat or even frustration. When she returned to the office after a failed attempt at gathering information in the field, she did so with a smile and a near-dismissive "It'll get fixed tomorrow."

Chitra was the one who'd broken the story that had pissed off Minister Gujrel. She'd tracked down the girl whose father had been killed by the security forces during the insurgency. The girl was traumatized, paranoid, and suspicious, but after patient coaxing from Chitra, she spilled everything. Chitra corroborated the girl's information with several sources and wrote a story about the excesses of the government during the civil war that caused an immediate uproar. The article was tweeted and retweeted, and reprinted in several left-leaning newspapers and magazines internationally. At home, too, it had been widely read and commented upon (Shalini had had to order a second printing of the issue within days), but there had also been strong criticism from conservative and government sources.

That was expected with virtually anything that *Fast Forward* published, but the outcry against this article had been particularly strong. The government media called it an effort to derail the peace process. A prominent right-wing commentator wrote, "The article does nothing but open and aggravate the nation's wounds from the civil war that we thought were beginning to heal." There were calls for taking the magazine to court for treason; Shalini received death threats. On social media she was praised by some and blasted by others. A group of men followed Chitra on the bus. When Shalini suggested that if that happened again, Chitra should use her mobile to call the police, Chitra smiled and said that the men tracking her *were* the police.

Now Shalini said, "Chitra, can you pay attention for a moment?"

Chitra looked up from her laptop. "Two minutes."

"No," Shalini said. "This is important enough that everyone should listen."

Urmila came in from the other room. "The tax people are coming tomorrow."

"Tomorrow?" Shalini repeated.

"Yes, they called to say they'll be here by eight o'clock in the morning."

"We don't open until nine," Shalini said. "How will they come at eight?"

Urmila said, "Madam, please don't joke." She was nearly in tears. A nice girl, but fearful. When Shalini returned from Minister Gujrel's office, Urmila had suggested that perhaps Shalini had spoken too boldly with him. "These politicians. All they want to do is bloviate. If you give them enough latitude to do that, then they calm down and are likely to treat you kindly."

"I don't want their kindness," Shalini had said. Urmila was not even a reporter, merely an office assistant hired for her computer and website skills, and here she was, giving Shalini dos and don'ts. "Besides, if we can't joke about these things, we'll all go crazy in this country."

"So what to do about tomorrow?" Prakash asked.

"We simply won't open tomorrow," Shalini said. "You all have laptops. Work from home."

"They'll be really pissed," Chitra said, smiling.

"But doesn't our avoidance signal our cowardice?" Prakash said. He had a fiery temper. He got frustrated easily, and his articles were messy and required much editing, but Shalini liked his sharp mind and his passion. Also his politics. For a young man who grew up in an orthodox Brahmin family, he was progressive and forward-thinking ("You're very fast and forward, Prakash," Chitra often told him). Last year he'd written a scathing piece on the routine discrimination and danger faced by the country's homosexual and transgender population despite laws that seemed to protect them. Shalini suspected that he himself was gay.

"It signals," Shalini said, "that we aren't going to operate on their timetable. They can't simply barge in here and confiscate our documents."

"Yes, they can, madam," Urmila said. "The law—"

"Fuck this law," Shalini said.

That evening as Shalini drove home, she thought about stopping by to see Alina. She hadn't been to Alina's house since her divorce, she now realized. Shalini had always liked Rasik, who appeared to be a happy-go-lucky kind of guy, and it was hard to believe that he'd end up being so unkind to a woman with whom he'd spent so many years. Alina wasn't exactly easy to live with—she was impulsive and disordered—but she'd loved Rasik. She probably still did; that was why she'd taken it so hard.

Shalini stopped in front of the gate and honked. A man peeked out from the guardhouse, then opened the gate for her. *At least the house is still under Alina's control*, thought Shalini. And a palatial house it was, a rarity in the city, a remnant of the old Rana aristocracy, with spacious rooms and a large lawn with a small fountain that didn't work but added allure. Rasik, who had royal blood, had inherited it. Shalini was surprised he'd let Alina have it, although it was clearly too big for a single person. They didn't have children.

She knocked on the door a few times, then called out Alina's name. No answer. She pushed the door open and entered. The living room was a mess, with clothes and magazines scattered all over. The curtains were closed, and there was a musty smell in the air. Shalini called out Alina's name again. She moved through the house, peeking into rooms.

She found Alina in the bathtub with her eyes closed. The tub was filled to the brim, with water threatening to spill out. Alina had her headphones on, and they were hooked to her mobile, which dangled down by the side of the tub. Half a dozen empty mini alcohol bottles were also on the sink and the floor. Alina's head leaned back on the wall, only her chin and nose above the water. Her eyes were closed, and for a moment Shalini thought she wasn't breathing. But her chest moved.

Then Shalini noticed the little red streaks in the water, at times gathering in little pools. Blood. "Alina!"

Alina opened her eyes drowsily. "Shalini," she whispered. "When did you come?"

Shalini kneeled down to grab her. Alina laughed and asked what she was doing. Shalini lifted her friend up by her arms. "Alina, that's blood, isn't it? My god, what is going on?"

"It's nothing," Alina slurred.

"Are you hurt?"

Alina was standing up now, leaning on Shalini. She was in her panties but no bra, and her small boobs looked pointed and hard.

"Where is the blood coming from?" Shalini then noticed the thin, vertical cuts on Alina's left wrist. Blood trickled down her fingers into the water.

"Use that towel," Alina said calmly, indicating the towel on the rack next to her head. Shalini wrapped it around Alina's wrist. Alina looked at her in amusement. "Why are you panicking? Nothing happened."

Unable to speak, Shalini led her toward the bedroom. She had Alina sit on the bed, then fetched more towels from the bathroom and dried her off. "What would have happened had I not arrived?" she asked softly.

"Well, you saved me, didn't you?" Alina said, half-amused, half-ashamed, it seemed.

"Do you have any bandages?"

With Alina's instructions, Shalini found them in the bathroom cupboard. Not bandages, really, but gauze, a strip of which she wrapped around Alina's wrist. Although the cuts were thin, they were long, and the gauze quickly became soaked in blood. Alina laughed. Shalini replaced it with a fresh one, then for good measure, strengthened it with another wrap. The gauze turned pink, but the blood flow seemed to have stopped. She helped Alina get dressed, making sure she wore a long-sleeved kurta that covered her arms. Alina reeked so badly that Shalini, nearly gagging, turned away her face. "What have you eaten?"

Alina looked at her blankly.

"Where's Devi?"

"I sent her home. Can't afford house help anymore."

"So you've been cooking for yourself?" Shalini didn't wait for an answer but went to the kitchen. It was important that Alina get some food into her. But a quick look in the fridge told Shalini that there was nothing, no vegetables, no meat—not that Shalini would have had the patience to cook after a long day. She decided they'd go out to eat.

Shalini had to help Alina get into the car. She kept the windows open so the outside air would help Alina sober up. On the way, Shalini asked, "You let Devi go, but you've kept the guard."

"He won't leave—says Rasik will pay him." Alina laughed.

They went to the new Italian place in Naxal that everyone was raving about, Barolo. The restaurant was filled mostly with Nepalis, some of whom looked at Shalini because they recognized her from her media appearances. Shalini was used to such stares and attention by now. Sometimes people came up to her for autographs. She had a feeling that half these people hadn't read *Fast Forward* and were only vaguely aware of what kind of magazine it was.

She'd also been confronted by unhappy readers. Once she took her staff for a two-day vacation to Pokhara. When the van stopped for lunch at a roadside restaurant, a man approached and began ranting at her, gesticulating wildly about how she was destroying the country. Prakash stood and got in the man's face, and soon the restaurant manager came and escorted the man away. Another time three hooligans, supporters of a minor politician who claimed he'd been "maligned" by the magazine, had burst into *Fast Forward*'s office and thrown stuff around. Luckily, Urmila had called the police as soon as she'd seen them coming, and the police had arrived fairly quickly. The men had not been arrested. The cops knew the intruders—they'd exchanged greetings when they'd arrived—and the situation calmed after the cops talked to them and took them out for tea.

Now, after they'd ordered their food, Shalini asked how long Alina had been cutting herself. Alina said she'd only recently started. "It's the best way, apart from booze, to drive away the pain."

"But you're losing blood, Alina. One day it'll be too much."

"Normally I make small cuts like these," Alina said, then pulled her sleeve up to reveal horizontal cuts right above the crook of her arm. "Today I was going for something bigger."

Shalini gasped, and tears came to her eyes. Afraid that others would see Alina's cuts, she reached across and pulled down Alina's sleeve. She whispered, "Were you seriously thinking about finishing yourself?"

"I don't know what I was thinking, but I wanted to take the next step."

"You should go to a therapist. I know someone."

The food came. Meatball spaghetti for Shalini, mushroom pasta for Alina. Shalini wished Alina would eat some meat, but she'd declined.

Alina said, "Why would I want to pay a therapist so I could think even more about Rasik, torture myself even more?"

The two friends kept up a constant chatter, with Shalini scolding her, counseling her, Alina accepting her counsel, then mildly rebuffing her, then laughing at what she called Shalini's "exaggerated concern." Shalini said it was consoling that at least Rasik had left her the house, at which Alina laughed heartily. "You still think highly of Rasik, don't you? You think that he is a good man." No, the house was also in his name; Alina was living there at his mercy. "Any day now, he's going to kick me out."

When Shalini went to the bathroom and returned, Alina had ordered a bottle of red wine and was already on her second glass—she must have guzzled down the first one. "Don't say anything," she told Shalini. "This is our celebratory drink." She poured a glass for Shalini and raised her own in toast. Shalini almost asked the waiter to take away the bottle, but she didn't want to create a scene, so she took small sips as she watched her friend down the second glass. She couldn't believe she was letting Alina get away with this.

When Alina reached for the bottle again, Shalini snatched it away.

"It's okay when I drink with you, isn't it?" Alina said. "It's only when I'm by myself that it's a problem."

Shalini flagged the waiter and handed him the bottle. "Take it away."

"It's no good, madam?"

"It's fine. We don't want it anymore."

"Two thousand rupees down the drain," Alina said.

"I'm paying," Shalini said.

"Perfectly good wine wasted."

Shalini realized that Alina was still a tad drunk from the small bottles in her house.

The two friends left Barolo and walked through Thamel, arms linked. "Remember when we used to come here after school to smoke pot?" Alina asked.

Shalini did remember. Alina was always the wild one. She had an uninhibited personality that made her popular among her friends and disliked by many others, especially the goody two-shoes at their school. Alina wasn't afraid to talk to boys, get into fights with girls from rival schools, and mouth off to teachers, leading to disciplinary actions or probation. They smoked pot in the back room of a Chinese restaurant they'd named The Dungeon. Alina smoked the most, and by evening she was always in a bad state. Often they went back to Shalini's house, where Shalini called Alina's mother to let her know that Alina would be sleeping over so they could study together. Alina's parents were the uncaring sort, so they didn't seem bothered by their daughter's absence from home.

"How's Mami?" Alina asked.

"Fine," Shalini said. "She's always asking about you."

"She has always been so nice to me."

"Yes, remember one time when your parents kicked you out of the house and you stayed with us?"

"Yes, for two whole weeks," Alina said, laughing, "and I didn't want to go back home."

"Let's go see her," Shalini said.

"Now?"

"Yes, she is just a neighborhood away, in Chhetrapati. You forgot?"

"Oh, yes, she moved here a couple of years ago, didn't she?"

Shalini's mother, now seventy, had abandoned the house built by her husband, who'd passed away not long after Shalini returned from America, and lived by herself in an apartment in Chhetrapati. Mrs. Malla was a small but formidable woman who'd fought for democracy when King Mahendra had slapped the one-party Panchayat system on the nation. During those years she'd spent time in jail, initiated hunger strikes, led protest marches, and gone underground for months. She was somewhat of a legend and still possessed a sharp mind. She read *Fast Forward* cover to cover, occasionally offering her opinions. If she was proud of her daughter, she didn't show it. She certainly wasn't awed by Shalini's celebrity status—it didn't seem to matter much to her that her daughter was now well known.

Her decision to move to Chhetrapati was her idea. She said she wanted to live close to the city center, close to the house of a famous freedom fighter, now dead, who had served as her mentor. She wanted to walk to the vegetable market as well as the markets of Indrachowk and Basantapur. Shalini had objected, saying that Mami was too old to live by herself, that they could look for a house in Chhetrapati so they could live together. "I want to live alone," Mrs. Malla had said, and that had been that.

Mrs. Malla made tea for them, even though Shalini kept saying that it was too late. Mrs. Malla sat next to Alina, held her hand, and asked her to tell everything that was going on in her life. Alina told her about her split with Rasik. Mrs. Malla listened attentively, and in the end she said, "This marriage thing—they make a big deal out of it, don't they?"

"I loved Rasik, Mami," Alina said.

"Love is kind of overrated, too," Mrs. Malla said. "There are so many other important things in life. Your personal independence, for example. Human dignity also."

Shalini had always been grateful to her mother for the way she thought. Mrs. Malla, for example, had defended her daughter when year after year Shalini didn't get married and people began talking. "It's her choice," Mrs. Malla told them. "She has to be happy with her decision." Conservatives who hated *Fast Forward*, however, were quick to seize on her unmarried state as a sign of her moral depravity. "She needs a good fuck" was a constant on Twitter. "She won't be satisfied with one man" was another. Rumors had been spread that she was a lesbian.

Shalini watched her mother. She'd missed her. She'd missed being around her, missed the strength her sheer presence exuded. Shalini would need that strength in the coming days. She'd fought off her magazine's enemies in the past, but something larger seemed to be afoot this time. Yet she noticed at one point in their conversation that her mother had leaned against the sofa and closed her eyes. *Just a momentary respite*, thought Shalini, but seconds later she understood that no, Mrs. Malla had fallen asleep. Alina stopped talking when she, too, noticed what had happened. Shalini wanted to stroke her mother's cheek, but she was afraid of waking her up. Alina took Shalini's hand in her own, and they both gazed at Mrs. Malla.

The next morning, Shalini was bombarded with text messages from the minister's office; then there was a flurry of texts from unknown numbers. Her mobile also rang continuously. She picked it up only when Prakash or Chitra or Urmila called. They were all staying home. Urmila was planning on taking her young son shopping and for pizza, and Prakash was going to a movie with friends. "This is like a vacation," Chitra joked over the phone.

Shalini cooked some khichadi for herself (she'd loved the quick rice-and-vegetable mishmash since she was a child, when Mami was often too busy with her activism to make anything else) and lounged around the house, sometimes walking out to her garden from where she chatted with her next-door neighbor over the wall. A few more texts came in, but none from the minister's office.

After lunch she ended up falling asleep while reading a book. She woke up with drool on her chin; embarrassed, she quickly checked her phone. Nothing. The feeling of grogginess didn't leave her even after she drank a cup of tea. She took a leisurely bath; her overhead shower didn't work, but she enjoyed pouring water over herself from a bucket. After the bath, she got dressed in a salwar kameez that someone had gifted her. It was a bright red one, with an intricate, immensely pleasing design on the front. Viewing the mirror, Shalini got lost in the beauty of the salwar kameez. It made her look younger, as if she were getting ready to go to college.

That college-going Shalini was a Shalini from a different era, naïve and believing in the fundamental goodness of the world. That girl no longer existed. This Shalini dealt with ministers who wanted to silence her to cover up a murder.

Should I take off this dress? she wondered. But it was nice to see herself so bright and cheery, which, given everything that had happened, she no longer felt.

She thought she should get in touch with Priyanka, see if she wanted to get together for the evening. They could discuss Alina, and Shalini could tell her about Alina's drinking and cutting. Priyanka was levelheaded, and perhaps she could come up with a solution.

Shalini called Priyanka, who was home and busy with her children. "Just come on over, Shals," she said.

Shalini drove over to her house, enjoying the long ride to Bhainsepati. On the way she called Prakash. No answer. She called Urmila, who answered but who was in a noisy restaurant and couldn't hear properly. "We'll talk tomorrow, ma'am," Urmila shouted and hung up. Shalini called Chitra, but she didn't pick up despite minutes of ringing.

At Priyanka's place, the two friends sat on the lawn and chatted. Priyanka's son had been caught smoking pot on the roof after school, and apparently all hell had broken loose right at the moment Shalini had called, although looking at Priyanka now, one wouldn't know that anything untoward had happened. Her daughter, who was in the same grade as her son in the same school, had smelled something in her room and wandered up to the roof, where she'd caught her brother.

"So what are you going to do?" Shalini asked.

"He'll need to be punished." Priyanka leaned forward in her chair and whispered. "All the time I was scolding him, I was thinking what my son would say if he found out that I smoke on the same spot where he was caught."

"Smoke? You mean cigarettes?"

Priyanka rolled her pretty eyes. "Do I have to explain everything to you?"

"Ganja khane?"

Priyanaka inspected her well-manicured nails.

"I didn't know you still smoked."

"Both Gaurav and I."

"Also Gaurav?"

"Shals, you look like you're getting ready for a heart attack. It's not like I'm an addict or anything. On weekends, just to relax. Gaurav joins me occasionally when he doesn't bring his work home."

"And where do you get the stuff?"

"There's a guy down the street."

Shalini dialed Chitra's number, but there was still no

response. She called both Prakash and Urmila, but neither picked up the phone.

Gaurav returned from work, and there was pressure for Shalini to stay for drinks and dinner. Priyanka told her husband about their son, and the two of them laughed. They ate on the lawn. Gaurav told stories of his trips to China, where he did business. Shalini's eyes kept drifting toward her phone in her hand. Every now and then she scrolled through her email: mostly junk, nothing from Chitra.

Finally Prakash returned her call around seven-thirty. Shalini quickly stepped away from the table, nearly shouting into the phone, "Where are you? I've been trying to reach you."

"Have you heard from Chitra?"

"No, she's not picking up."

"I've also been trying all evening. I'm headed over to her flat."

"I'm also coming."

On the drive in the night traffic, Shalini realized that Chitra might have moved recently. She called Prakash, who told her that Chitra now lived in Battisputali; he gave her directions.

Battisputali was swathed in darkness—load shedding. She found Prakash waiting for her outside the apartment building. "She's not in," he said. "The door is open, but she's not in."

"Could she have gone to a neighbor's place and forgot to lock the door?"

"That's not Chitra."

"We should ask around."

They went knocking door-to-door in the building. It was one of those ugly concrete structures that had cropped up all over the city when she returned from America, a big single house with about a dozen or so rooms built for renting. Most of Chitra's neighbors didn't know of her whereabouts; it was clear she didn't socialize with them. One young boy said that he'd seen three young men go past his window toward Chitra's flat, which was at the end of the third floor.

Shalini and Prakash entered Chitra's flat. Nothing seemed out of place. Even her laptop was at her desk—she prized it so much she wouldn't have left it there with the door open, even for a short time.

Shalini sat on Chitra's bed. Across from her on the wall was a photo of an elderly woman Shalini knew was Chitra's mother, who lived in Bhotechaur, where Chitra was born. "What to do, Prakash?"

"Ah, that's the big question, isn't it, madam?" His voice was trembling.

Three days later, Shalini filed a police report at the police station. The police had initially told her that only kin could file a report, but Shalini told them that she was Chitra's legal guardian. She'd already contacted the deputy superintendent of police, who had assured her that he'd look into the matter. But the first step, the DSP had said, was to get a police report written so official action could be taken. Shalini hadn't yet contacted Chitra's mother, because she still hoped Chitra would be released after being locked up somewhere.

She briefly closed her eyes every time she thought where Chitra might be, what they might be doing to her.

She had also called Minister Gujrel's office a few times, but there had been no response. She went to his office, planted herself in the reception area. The minister's assistant came and tried to persuade her to leave, but Shalini wouldn't budge. Anger was making it hard for her to speak these days. It was as if her throat and tongue were swollen. "My colleague Chitra has disappeared," she said to the assistant. "I'm going to take you and your boss to international court." But she knew nothing about international courts.

Just then Minister Gujrel, wearing daura suruwal, walked in, chatting with a white man. He glanced at Shalini and said, "You came without an appointment."

She stood. "I came to talk about Chitra."

The minister cast a puzzled glance at her, then at his assistant. "Who is Chitra?"

Shalini tried to speak, but something dammed her up.

"The reporter who wrote that article, sir," the assistant said.

"Right now Mr. Morton and I are consulting about human rights in our country," Minister Gujrel said. "Mr. Morton is the newly appointed deputy chief of the OHCHR."

"How do you do?" the deputy chief said.

"This is the famous Mrs. Shalini Malla," Minister Gujrel said.

"Ms.," Shalini said. "Not Mrs."

"Of course," Minister Gujrel said. "How could I forget?" To the OHCHR deputy chief he said, "She runs a magazine. You must have heard of it. *Fast Forward.*"

"I have the most recent issue on my desk," the deputy chief said. "Still need to read it, of course."

"Come, Mr. Morton." The minister ushered him inside.

Shalini waited. Tea was brought for her. She didn't touch it. She checked her email and tweets. Half an hour, then one hour. Next to her, the minister's female receptionist was working at an old computer. The minister's assistant entered and exited the inner room, careful to shut the door behind him quietly each time. Shalini needed to go to the bathroom, but she was afraid to move in case the minister emerged while she was gone. When the assistant appeared again, Shalini asked him how much longer she'd have to wait. "He's still with Morton sahib," the assistant said apologetically.

The phone vibrated. It was a text from Priyanka. URGENT. ALINA OVERDOSED. COME TO TEACHING HOSPITAL IMMEDI-ATELY.

CAN'T, Shalini wrote back. WAITING FOR A MEETING WITH GUJREL. HOW IS ALINA?

She waited, but Priyanka didn't write back.

After a couple of minutes, Shalini dialed Priyanka, but Priyanka didn't pick up. She found Gaurav's number and dialed. But that number was busy.

The assistant was about to go inside again, so Shalini stepped up to him and said, "Two hours I've waited. Now I'll go into that room."

"Just one minute, please. I'll check. Please, ma'am. He has a very busy schedule. He'll see you as soon as he's free."

Her phone rang. It was Priyanka. "Where are you, Shalini?"

"What happened to Alina?"

"It's not good, it's not good."

"Hoina, what happened? Why aren't you telling?"

"She's in a bad state." Priyanka was crying. Shalini had never known her to cry.

"Okay, I'm coming," Shalini said. She looked toward the home minister's door. It looked monstrous. She wanted to kick it in and go inside and kick the minister, probably even kick the OHCHR chief. But right now she needed to find out what had happened with Alina.

Several weeks later Shalini was in Mami's flat in Chhetra-pati, drinking tea. "I've thought about returning to America for a PhD," Shalini said.

"A PhD in what?"

"I don't know. A PhD in anything. Just to get away from this mess."

Mrs. Malla slurped her tea with her tiny mouth. "I say you go only if you really want to study. Otherwise you won't be happy there."

"I'm only joking, Mami. It's just that sometimes I see no hope here."

"Whatever the case, it's our country, and we need to love it. If we abandon it at the first sign of difficulty, then we're the ones who are hopeless."

Only if it were the first sign of difficulty, Shalini thought, *and not the hundredth, or perhaps even the thousandth.* Chitra had simply disappeared. No sign of her. Chitra's mother had come from Bhotechaur, pounded on a few doors, then returned because she had an aging, senile father to look after. For a couple of weeks, Shalini talked daily with her on the phone, but now the frequency had decreased simply because Shalini had nothing new and positive to report, except to assure Chitra's mother that she hadn't given up on her daughter.

It was true: Shalini was still making phone calls, meeting people, attempting to put pressure on those with power. She was no longer allowed into the ministry; the guards had been alerted not to let her in. One time she had attempted to brush past the guards, but a handful of men whom she assumed were plainclothes police had appeared out of nowhere and dragged her out to the street. When she tried to break free of their gasp, one of them had slapped her and said, "You show your face here again, and I'll break your arms and legs." When she'd used her phone to take photos of the goons, they'd grabbed it, smashed it on the ground, and stomped on it. A bystander had managed to snap a picture of the goons manhandling her, and the next day Twitter was ablaze with a photo of her tussling with the men, accompanied by the caption: *Shalini Malla bitch-slapped by Minster Gujrel's men.* Some had retweeted it as: *A bitch bitch-slapped for being a bitchy bitch.*

When the minister was criticized for the way he treated Shalini, he responded that she had been nothing but a disruptive force since the disappearance of her reporter. "Mrs. Shalini Malla has lost her mind," he said. He went on to explain that his office had nothing to do with Chitra. *Fast Forward* had so many enemies; why wasn't Shalini going after them? He hinted at another suspect, a member of a rival party, one with whom he'd been feuding, whose corruption scandal *Fast Forward* had investigated in the past. A media war erupted between the minister and his rival, with accusations and counteraccusations, and the press's attention shifted from Chitra to their feud.

Fast Forward's office was still open, now managed largely by Prakash. The next issue was going to be a black issue on Chitra's disappearance. Prakash had written a couple of incomprehensible, foaming-at-the-mouth kinds of pieces, hurling accusations left and right, even embroiling some other prominent personalities, including a conservative journalist and a Christian fundamentalist, both of whom, Shalini was certain, had nothing to do with Chitra's disappearance. Prakash's rambling piece traced the conspiracy behind Chitra's disappearance to an event two decades ago, when a prominent left-wing politician had suspiciously died in a car accident.

When Shalini pointed out that Prakash's extreme rhetoric would turn *Fast Forward* into a cheap political rag distributed at the vegetable market, Prakash accused her of not doing enough for Chitra. "Out of sight, out of mind, is that it, madam?"

"Prakash, I have been trying."

"You've given up, I can tell."

She banged the table. "I haven't given up. I never will." But she was tired, she admitted to herself. To Prakash she said, "Who got slapped by the home minister's goons? Not you! So I don't need your lecture."

"Yes, one slap, and now you're the martyr, not Chitra."

"Prakash." What could she say? She wanted to say, *We're on the same side.* But Prakash knew that already. *Let him do what he wants,* she thought. *Let him bring out this black issue and get it out of his system.*

She laughed at her own reasoning. *Get it out of his system*—as though all that was needed was for Prakash to experience catharsis, as though a real, living person with a quick mind and powerful prose hadn't simply vanished from the face of the earth, wasn't in all likelihood already dead somewhere. Perhaps raped before she was killed.

Shalini's agitation was so great that she found herself trembling while driving, while walking the streets, while brushing her hair in front of the mirror in the morning, while changing into her pajamas at night. When she held out her hands, her fingers shook.

One night Alina appeared in her dreams and asked, "Do you miss me?" Shalini had immediately woken up and wept. She'd hadn't thought as much about Alina and her suicide in the past couple of months as she felt she ought to have, so consumed had she been with Chitra. Shalini had gone to Alina's cremation at the arya ghat, consoled Rasik (who appeared devastated, Alina would have been interested to know), and taken part in a memorial held by their school's alumni association. But whenever her thoughts drifted toward Alina, Chitra appeared in her mind, and Shalini became disturbed, felt that she wasn't doing enough for someone who could still be alive. Then she picked up the phone and started calling people and forced herself to get out of the house and knock on doors.

She visited Mami more now, and sometimes mother and daughter cooked in the evenings. Mrs. Malla told her stories about her father and their freedom-fighting days. After dinner they sat on the couch and watched television. Shalini liked to lie down and place her head on her mother's lap, like she used to when she was a little girl. They watched mostly dumb shows like serials and comedies and singing contests because the news and analysis and talk shows now gave Shalini headaches.

Whenever Minister Gujrel appeared on TV, Shalini closed her eyes. Mrs. Malla, oblivious to her daughter's reaction, said, "Look at him, the fool. Look at that pudgy face. Listen to him bloviating about what's good for this country. Ah, what would I do with you if I could get my hands on you, fat face!"

And despite herself, Shalini couldn't help but smile.

BEGGAR BOY

Ramesh pressed through the dense crowd of Chabel. Hardly any room to walk. It was as if the whole of humanity had descended upon this road: starving children and poop on the street and counterfeit clothing and exhaust fumes—and of course the fruits and vegetables that would go bad if not sold by the end of the day. The footpaths were so clogged by vendors that shoppers were forced off the pavements. But a second level of vendors had already spread their wares on the curb, and people had no choice but to walk in the center of the road. The irate drivers yelled at the pedestrians, who cursed the vendors, who in turn blamed the police and the government, who accused the migrants.

Ramesh elbowed people, and people elbowed him. Two young high school boys his age approached, arm in arm, jabbering away. One boy made a funny remark, along with "Hoina?" and the other boy let out a gleaming smile. As they passed him, something was exchanged between the boys and Ramesh: a challenge, a taunt, a bit of condescension that didn't fully register until Ramesh was already a few yards away. He looked back, and above a sea of heads he saw that the boys had also stopped and were staring in his direction, their eyes dark and dangerous.

He moved on. He seemed to be having this type of encounter more and more, and it convinced him that he needed to do what he had been thinking about doing. A soft, tightening tremor passed through him every time he pictured it. He didn't know when exactly, but he'd know when the time came: He'd walk into the bank and pull out his revolver, then wave it into the air. There would be gasps. The fat teller with the enormous lips would be there. He'd go to her window and gently rub the tip of the revolver on her lips.

Would his mother come to visit him in jail after he was captured? Would she feel remorse for what she'd done? He pictured her weakened by guilt, holding the bars of the cell where he'd been kept with other hardened criminals, tears streaming down her face. "It's all my fault," she'd say. "I should have never left you. It's because of me that you've ended up here." He'd console her. He'd clasp her hand between bars and tell her that she shouldn't take all the blame upon herself, that these things happen. "It is my destiny."

It is my destiny. He didn't want to think like this. It sounded as though he was deluded—destiny!—but there was no other way to put it. His mother needed to know what he was capable of. She had to be put on notice.

What happened at the bank with the fat teller a few days ago had further persuaded him that he was being propelled toward an act that would change things forever. She had given him a hard time about his signature. He'd gone to the bank because his father had phoned from The Hague, asking him to withdraw twenty-five thousand rupees and give it to the head servant. Some months ago, Ramesh's father had opened an account for Ramesh, and sometimes when the old man was away for days—he was a well-known diplomat—he asked Ramesh to take out money and hand it over to the head servant for household expenses. Ramesh didn't even know how much there was in the account, except there always seemed to be enough at the time of the withdrawal. His father had also said Ramesh could use some of the money for himself.

But the money didn't mean much to Ramesh. He didn't have friends he could spend it on, and he didn't have extravagant tastes. Once in a while, he liked to go to fancy restaurants, order the most expensive and unheard-of dishes, but he quickly got bored with the food and most of the time ended up watching the other patrons. One time in a Vietnamese restaurant, he ordered a duck egg that still had the embryo inside it, but instead of eating he merely stared at it. Another time, a Japanese fish dish (which he couldn't finish because it stank) cost him nearly three thousand rupees.

That day at the bank the fat lady had taken his check made out to "self" and scrutinized it for a long time. Then she'd consulted a file she had on him. "Your signatures don't match," she'd finally said.

He took out his checkbook, wrote another check, and signed it.

She inspected it and said, "Not the same."

He signed two more, but each time she shook her head. She even stuck out her fat lip.

"Well, it's me," he said. "What do you want me to do?"

"If the signatures don't match, then it's not you."

"I'm here, and I need the money."

She said slowly, "What do you need such a large amount for? A young boy like you?"

"It's me. It's my signature."

"Do you have permission from your father to take out this money?"

Did she know his father? "It's my account."

She shook her head. "Nope," she said.

"Show me how my signatures don't match."

They were talking in low voices, but Ramesh felt as though everyone inside the bank was watching.

"That's not possible," she said.

"Then I'm going to raise my voice."

She stared at him. Her eyes were big. "You think I'm afraid. Afraid of a schoolboy?"

"Where is your manager?" Ramesh looked toward the cubicles to his left, where the other bank staff worked.

She flipped open the folder, pulled out a paper, and thrust it toward him.

Ramesh studied the signature on his account application, then the signature on his check. "They look exactly the same."

She stabbed the check with her index finger. "In this signature, the Y has a loop." Then she stabbed the application. "In this signature, the Y has no loop."

"So I'll make a loop. Or not make a loop."

"Without matching signatures, how do I know you are who you claim to be?"

"I also don't know you are who you claim to be." What he really wanted to ask was, *Are you a fat lady with enormous lips?*

"I'm not the one cashing a check."

"Show me your identification paper so I know you are an employee of this bank."

"I don't have to show you anything."

Ramesh went toward the cubicles and said loudly, "That fatty over there isn't letting me cash my check. Where's your manager?"

The manager came stumbling out of his cubicle. The fat lady was summoned. There were questions and answers and explanations and rebuttals. Ramesh was asked to write his signature on a piece of paper. He did, making sure it had no loop. "Problem solved," the manager said.

The fat lady said nothing, but Ramesh could tell she had become filled with anger. They returned to her station, where she counted the money and handed it to him. He took out a hundred-rupee bill and slid it under the glass partition. "Your tip for a job well done," he said and left.

The gun belonged to Ramesh's father. It was in the cupboard next to the safe in his father's study. Ramesh didn't know where his father bought it, why it was in the house. He didn't talk to his father much, especially since his mother's departure, and he didn't want to ask questions now to arouse suspicion. A silence had descended upon the big house once his mother left. His father had not uttered a single sentence about her. The day after she left, a truck appeared at the big house, and some men came inside and hauled all his mother's things away.

He'd gone to visit her about a year ago, at her behest. She'd called him on the phone and, perhaps feeling guilty, had asked him to come. Driven by his father's chauffeur, he'd gone all the way to her house, where she'd clasped his hands and cried, given him incoherent sentences about why she was in her mediocre house and not in the big house with Ramesh and his father.

A child had appeared from the shadows in the living room where they sat, and Ramesh's mother had pulled her close and told her, "This is your brother. Say namaste to your daju!" Ramesh had instinctively reached out to pat the girl on the head, then recoiled. The girl was older than what she'd have been had she come out of his mother's womb. So she was his stepsister.

Another figure half-emerged from the shadows. A man, her mother's husband. "Hello," he said to Ramesh—in English, as though he fancied himself a foreigner.

"Hello," Ramesh responded. The man was still in half-shadow, so Ramesh couldn't see his face completely, but the body and voice suggested someone much younger than his mother.

When Ramesh first discovered the gun, he had thought that his father had acquired it to shoot his mother. The gun was longer and slimmer than what Ramesh thought a gun would be, at least longer than the ones he'd seen in movies. Its barrel seemed to go on forever. When Ramesh put the gun flat against his cheek, it stretched across his entire face. His father might have bought it when he discovered her affair. Was it an affair? Ramesh didn't know. Until the day she left, he didn't even know she had someone on the side. Where did she find the time? Where did she meet her lover? Ramesh often wondered if his father, too, was hounded by similar thoughts.

On occasion when Ramesh passed by the study, he glimpsed his father staring at the wall. On his desk sat about a dozen tiny bottles of whiskey, the kind they served on airplanes. In Ramesh's mind, there was a melodramatic scene involving him and his father: *One evening Ramesh passes by his father's study, but instead of continuing on, he pauses. His father's gaze falls on him. Ramesh's eyes water. "Aren't you going to come in?" his father asks. Ramesh gingerly steps in. His father observes him and says, "Well, it's just the two of us now, isn't it? In this big old house?"*

It's been the two of us for a while, *Ramesh thinks.*

His father asks him whether he wants whiskey. Ramesh nods. He drinks straight from the bottle, slowly. The whiskey tastes bitter, but it also warms his throat and belly. It's not the first time he's tasted alcohol. He's stolen a few of these bottles before, and one time he went to a local bar to drink with his classmates after school. "We will survive, son," his father says. "We will survive."

The big house sat on a lane that branched off the raucous main road of Chabel, where the bank was located. Some

months ago, a murder had taken place on the lane leading to the big house. No one had witnessed the murder,
but there had been bloodstains on the gravel. Ramesh had
seen it on the way to the school bus stop one morning. The
bloodstain, along with a clump of hair, had sat there for a
few days. Dogs lapped at the spot until all that remained
was the shape of the stain. The servants—there were five
or six servants to take care of the big house's two residents,
Ramesh and his father—had talked about what might have
happened. Then Ramesh's father made the wall higher and
placed big coils at the top. That was the view that greeted
Ramesh when he looked out of his room.

The big house had close to ten rooms, and most of them
were empty now. When his mother lived here, her laughter echoed across the hallways into the rooms. The house
hadn't felt empty. Besides, the servants were always inside
the house, talking, quarreling, cackling, complaining. Now
they did all this in the servants' quarters, which was a separate building.

Often Ramesh sat in his room in the afternoon, listening to the sounds from the servants' quarters. He pictured
himself with them: *He is playing cards, drinking tea, and
chomping on pakodas. They are all very fond of him; they
consider it a privilege that he prefers to hang out with them
in their meager quarters rather than in the big house. He
dismisses their fawning and says that he is no different from
them, that if it weren't for the craziness of fate, he would have
been born in the servants' quarters. "I feel more comfortable
here," he tells them.*

"Really, babu?" they say, their hearts filled with happiness.

"Am I not like your own son?" he asks a middle-aged servant who is about his mother's age.

"Of course you are," she says. "When I look at you, I don't doubt that you are my very own son. Look, even our facial features are the same." She puts her cheek against his.

The others comment, "Indeed! There is a striking resemblance. The same shape of the head. The same chin. Look at the similar eyebrows! My god, how could anyone doubt that these two are related by blood?"

He eats with them; he plays hide-and-seek with their children in the small vegetable garden adjacent to their quarters. He takes his afternoon naps in his servant-mother's bed. It has a thin mattress, but he sleeps soundly on it for an hour or two, until his servant-mother wakes him with a glass of tea. She watches, her eyes saturated with love, as he slurps his tea loudly.

Ramesh's mind had become a source of much fascination for him lately. Some time ago in Chabel, he'd seen a small, pretty girl who was not more than eight or nine and wearing a purple dress, a new purchase from her not-from-the-city parents. The father's shirt was buttoned all the way to the top, the mother wore excessive, cheap jewelry, and the little girl was dressed gaudily: purple frock, shiny plastic earrings in tiny ears, and swathes of kohl around her eyes. *Sexy*, he thought. *Sex-ai*, he mouthed to himself, and his breath whispered *sex-ai* right in front of the parents and the girl, who was sucking on a lollipop as the family stopped in front of a stationery shop. Ramesh didn't find the small girl sexy, so he didn't know why he was saying it. He wasn't attracted to small girls, or girls his age, for that matter.

What disturbed him more was that in subsequent days he'd pictured himself being wedded to the little girl in a village ceremony. *His bride is put in a large doko, with her legs hanging over it, and a man carries her in that basket with a strap resting on his forehead. Ramesh wears a daura suru-wal, holds a bidi in his fingers, and sends the smoke twirling up in the sky. There are a band, crying relatives, excited children climbing walls of houses to watch. Then he sees a group of protestors, led by a well-known bearded human rights activist, standing on the side of the path as Ramesh takes his child bride home. They shout against child marriage, say he should be jailed.*

Ramesh was amazed that he could fantasize about marrying a child when he had no sexual interest in children. For days he played in his mind a scene of him with his child bride on the wedding bed adorned with flowers. *Both sit crossed-legged and play snakes and ladders. He feeds her cake, then puts her to bed with a kiss on her forehead. "Sleep well, okay, nanu?" He goes to his window. "Go home," he tells the human rights activists picketing outside. "Return to your family."*

Until recently, until the bank idea came to him, Ramesh had wondered if he should go to a psychiatrist to sort out his thoughts. Suresh, his classmate who also came from a wealthy family and whose father knew Ramesh's father, had advised him to go to one. Suresh had a know-it-all attitude that irritated Ramesh. Whenever Suresh talked to Ramesh, he seemed to be pitying him, especially when other boys were present at school. *You have no other friends besides me*, Suresh seemed to be conveying. That their names were similar-sounding led the other boys to refer to them as twins.

Recently his classmates had teased Ramesh that he and Suresh had different fathers but the same mother, which was meant as a dig at Ramesh's mother's supposed promiscuity. Suresh had pretended to be offended by this dig, but Ramesh could tell that he was secretly pleased. "What's it to you?" Suresh told his guffawing classmates. "Yes, we are twins, both of the same mother. Why don't you go fuck your own mothers?" He put his arm around Ramesh and led him away from them. He spoke to Ramesh in a muted, cajoling voice, as if he were looking out for the well-being of a younger sibling. "You should not take all of this too seriously. Such things happen. We cannot all have the kinds of mothers we want. What your mother did was very bad. My father tells me that your mother had no right to abandon you. It is abandonment, isn't it? What else would you call it? I know your father is devastated. He might not show it, but my father says that your father has taken it really hard."

Suresh lowered his voice even more. "My father says your father had seen it coming for a long time. Your father told my father that as soon as he married your mother, he knew she wasn't the type to stick around, that she'd leave him after she'd given him a child, which turned out to be you, Ramesh. Isn't that uncanny? My father says ever since your mother left, your father's drinking has increased. What a shame. And how unfortunate for you. Your mother ditches you to go gallivanting around with a younger man, and your father turns incommunicado. Incommunicado. Life is incommunicado, isn't it, Ramesh? People no longer communicate with one another. Look at our country. If only we talked with one another, we wouldn't be in the state we're in today. You know you can communicate with me, right, Ramesh? I am your friend, you understand that, don't you?"

Ramesh nodded, but he knew that as soon as Suresh left his side and joined their classmates, there would be much chortling and thigh-slapping mockery.

Suresh gave him a long look. "You shouldn't really feel ashamed about going to a mind doctor, like a psychiatrist or someone. One of my father's friends is the most famous psychiatrist in the country, Dr. Gopal Man Singh. You must have heard of him."

Ramesh hadn't.

"He's usually booked for six months in advance, but if I make a call, he'll see you today."

"I don't need to see anyone."

"Just a thought. No need to be alarmed."

"I'm not alarmed."

Suresh observed him. "I want you to come to my house," he said. "It'll be just you and me."

"Sure," Ramesh said.

"We need to strengthen our friendship," Suresh said. "We can't do it at school with all this riffraff around. When are you free?"

"Well, I'm—"

"One of these Saturdays. I'll let you know."

A couple of days after that, Ramesh had stopped going to school, partly to avoid Suresh and his gang, but mostly because it didn't seem to matter anymore. Last week when the school called in concern over his absence, Ramesh had pretended to be his father, who was still in Europe. Ramesh adopted a grave, thick voice and said, "Yes, yes, I am aware. Ramesh has simply not been well for a while, especially since his mother left me. Yes, yes, I am heartbroken, too, but I have to be strong for my boy. He will return to school once he recuperates." He had spoken in English, to lend gravitas to his words. The administrators at his school went gaga over English. Even the school sweepers greeted the students in a chirpy Americanized accent: "Gooood *mor*ningggg."

When the school called again after a couple of days, Ramesh said, "My son Ramesh has been diagnosed with a serious psychiatric disorder. I will be taking him to Singapore for treatment. Pray for him."

His father returned home Friday night, and on Saturday afternoon he called Ramesh downstairs. "Why aren't you ready yet?" he asked. When Ramesh expressed confusion, his father said, "We've been invited to the Sapkotas. Didn't Suresh tell you?"

"Oh, yes," Ramesh said. He had to be careful here, as he didn't want his father to know that he hadn't been to school lately. But when Suresh had invited Ramesh, hadn't he said it'd just be the two of them?

• • •

It was a grand party, with more than a hundred people mingling on the Sapkotas' lawn, which was bigger than the Thapaliyas' lawn. A long buffet table offered a variety of steaming food. Waiters in white uniforms carried trays of drinks and appetizers and glided in and out of the throng of guests. A large fountain in the middle gushed water. A band was off to the side, playing traditional Nepali folk songs but with a hint of jazz, perhaps even reggae. Men in tuxedos and women in glittering saris laughed and conversed. Some were dancing ballroom style. Ramesh thought of a scene from a movie starring Robert Redford about people dancing and partying in America in the 1950s, based on that famous novel whose name he couldn't remember.

Ramesh was the only one in jeans, and he wondered why his father, who went off to greet his friends as soon as they entered the gate, hadn't told him to dress more appropriately. He figured his father didn't care enough. Ramesh stood near the gate, his hands in his pockets, wondering what would happen if he left. He could later tell his father that he had developed a headache and had to return home. Suresh would think that he never came, or that he left early. In any case, he didn't owe Suresh any explanation: Suresh had lied to him when he'd said there'd be just the two of them. But this was a full-fledged party, with half of Kathmandu's elites. Ramesh recognized a popular actor who was surrounded

by women. In another group was a well-known socialite, a model-turned-interior decorator who called herself
the Martha Stewart of Nepal. Ramesh caught a glimpse
of a famous banker who was recently in the news for
his ruthless acquisitions. Then he spotted a writer who
had written one lousy book but who was being lionized
as the Himalayan Hemingway for his clipped sentences.
Plastic people, he thought. But he didn't leave, as he was
spellbound by this world-unto-itself appearing before
him while the city raged incoherently outside.

"I was looking for you all over." It was Suresh, standing
before him. "I saw your father, and he said you had come
with him, but I couldn't find you."

"I was just enjoying the view," Ramesh said. *Just you and
me, eh?*

"Isn't it something?" Suresh said, standing next to Ramesh
and observing the party. "The glitterati and literati of our
society."

"The pisserati."

Suresh clapped him on the back. "You have a fine sense
of humor, you know? You should display it more often.
Why hide it? It'll bring out your personality." He put his
arm around Ramesh. "And why haven't you been to the
school lately? You forgot about me, eh? Come, I want you
to meet some people."

Suresh broke into groups, into conversations, introducing Ramesh as though he were his girlfriend, exuding an air
of confidence that Ramesh couldn't help but admire. Suresh
punched a popular actor in the shoulder and said, "Are you

going to talk only about yourself, Pravin dai? You're no Tom Cruise. There are other people in this world, too, you know? My friend Ramesh here, for example."

Suresh tapped young, pretty girls on their cheeks and told them how ravishing they looked. He briefly discussed politics with a former minister, who listened to him attentively, then told the others, "Where does this young boy get his cleverness, I don't know." He pointed to Suresh's father. "Certainly not from his old man, that much is certain. Suresh, you thinking about a career in politics? This country needs an astute dimag like yours."

It was exhausting, and exhilarating. *It's all a big show, only a show*, thought Ramesh.

Yet there was a magnanimous quality to Suresh's social performance. He was not daunted by the big shots at his party—it was as if he owned them, knew who they really were, and could dismiss them with a wave of his hand. In conversations with his guests, Suresh constantly made references to Ramesh such as, "At school, Ramesh and I . . ." Or, "As I was telling Ramesh some time back . . ." He put his arm around Ramesh while talking, or placed his hand on the small of Ramesh's back. Once he even squeezed Ramesh's hand.

By the time they finished doing the rounds, Ramesh felt weak. When Suresh suggested that they go upstairs to his room, he gladly accepted.

Suresh's room was on the other side of the house, in a corner, with windows overlooking a high wall on the back that blocked the view of the neighborhood. "Nice and quiet in here," Suresh said, and he latched the door behind them and turned to Ramesh with a smile. "I told you it'd be just you and me."

Despite the high walls and the barbed wire, the din from the road could be heard in the big house, like a distant yet continuous and unmistakable cry of the country. In between the barbed wires, Ramesh could glimpse the tops of the other neighborhood houses with their satellite dishes and telephone lines running close to their windows. These houses served as the second line of fortification against the racket of the main road.

The phone downstairs had rung a few times since the party, and Ramesh knew that it was Suresh. Once, a servant who was dusting the living room had picked it up, and Ramesh had gone to the landing to observe her. The servant had talked in a low voice—since his mother's departure, the servants talked in hushed tones inside the house, as if his mother had died—and, putting her palm on the receiver, had looked up at Ramesh.

"Who?" Ramesh asked.

"He says he's a friend."

"What's his name?"

"He didn't give it. Shall I ask him?"

"No, just tell him I'm not here."

After the incident with Suresh, Ramesh thought more about why he was in this opulent house with its chandeliers and two living rooms and even a theater room. What made him so special that he was born to this privilege when many boys his age had to wash dishes in restaurants and get whipped for jobs badly done?

One time he'd read about a young Tharu girl who'd been sold as a slave to a doctor's family in the capital. They'd kept her locked in a tiny room for minor infractions, hands tied behind her back with a rope, not giving her food for days on end. Ramesh had tried to imagine being that girl. He put himself in her tiny room, his wrists chafing because of the tight rope, his eyes straining against the dark, his stomach cramped with hunger.

It didn't make sense, Ramesh thought, that he'd be bored with himself in this big house while children scrounged among garbage piles outside. He wondered about the life of the poor, began to fantasize about being poor. He imagined himself as part of a large family that lived in the shantytown next to the Bishnumati River. His parents collected scraps for a living; his brothers and sisters—and he had many of them—played naked on garbage piles.

To accommodate his fantasies, and in preparation for the momentous thing he was going to undertake, Ramesh thought he ought to wear a poor man's clothes. But where would he go to find such clothes? He could find poor people on the streets and pay them to sell their clothes to him. But they would think he was crazy. Or they would think that he was teasing them. He could show these poor people his money, perhaps even hand it to them to gain their trust before they gave him their clothes. He wondered if he could simply buy the clothes from one of his male servants. The problem was that the servants in the big house wore clothes that were cheap but clean and well-maintained. If Ramesh were to wear them, they would neither depict him as poor nor make him *feel* poor. He wanted clothes that, once he put them on, would immediately thrust him into his new reality of poorness.

He considered going to a tailor's shop to have them sew a poor-man's clothes, but even a tailor serving the poor people would sew new clothes for them. After all, poor people didn't have a tailor sew them rags. But one day he came upon a tailor's shop in the market with the sign: "ALTER-ATIONS, BUTTON-SEWING, MENDING, RAFUS, AND SUCH ARE DONE HERE AT REASONABLE PRICES. THANK YOU!" He stepped up to the counter.

In a cramped space inside, a solitary man was bent over a sewing machine. He didn't look up but said, "Yes?"

"I was looking for some clothes."

"Had you dropped them off recently?"

"No, I mean, I want to buy some clothes."

"Well, I don't sell clothes here." The man stopped sewing. "Except these." He pointed to a handful of clothes on hangers, presumably finished clothes his customers had neglected to pick up.

"I'm looking for somewhat older clothes."

"Older?"

"Yes, the older, the better."

Confusion marked the tailor's face.

"I'm looking for clothes that are torn and dirty."

The tailor returned to his work. "Have you come here to joke? Majak gareko?"

"I'm serious. I'm looking for poor-type clothes."

The tailor rummaged through a pile of clothes next to him and showed Ramesh a pair of trousers. "Like this one?" The legs were torn, as though they had become entangled on a bicycle chain. But the rest looked new. The tailor held up a shirt, which had a frayed collar but otherwise looked fine.

Ramesh shook his head and left the shop. He walked toward the Pashupatinath temple. On the way, he saw many beggars sitting by the side of the road, their palms held out for scraps. Now these were the real poor.

As he slowly strolled toward the main temple gate, he scrutinized all the male beggars, especially their build and height. He noted three or four who'd suit his purpose. Once he reached the main gate, from where he could glimpse the back of the giant golden bull that faced Lord Shiva, he made an abrupt turn, not bothering to genuflect.

The beggar he selected was a bearded young man, perhaps ten years older than him. He was wearing a pair of boxer shorts and a tatty T-shirt that had turned brown because it hadn't been washed. The young man sat crouched in front of a dirty towel, where there lay three or four coins of such small denominations even the monkeys who roamed the temple complex would have been mortified to admit them as their day's wages. This beggar's attention was not on his earnings but on a spot inside his own mind. His arms were wrapped around his knees, and he was gently swaying. Ramesh gagged at the filthiness of his clothes, but those were precisely what he needed. As soon as Ramesh began talking to him, however, the beggar became frightened and ran away. The woman who sat nearby asked Ramesh to throw the coins on the towel toward her, "for safekeeping," she said.

Farther up, a boy about his age and build was standing, his palms up for alms. He was wearing trousers that were too small for him, and the zipper apparently didn't work because his underwear was peeking out. The shirt he wore was missing a collar, crumpled, and stained at the front.

Ramesh stopped in front of him. "What's your name?" he asked.

"Naresh."

"Ah, my name is Ramesh. We're practically like twins."

Ramesh was struck by how closely this beggar boy resembled him: the same angular face, the same dull, defeated eyes, the same darkish features and unruly black hair.

"Do you live around here?" Ramesh asked, then realized that the boy, since he was a beggar, probably slept on the streets.

"Here and there," the boy said warily.

"Do you have parents?"

The boy let his arms hang loose and said, "Why are you asking these questions? Are you from a charity?"

"No, no," Ramesh said. He pulled out fifty rupees and handed them to Naresh, who took them sullenly. "Just talk to me for a while, that's all I'm asking."

"I have a father," Naresh said. "But I don't see him that much because he travels to do manual labor around the country. My mother—khoi."

"Tell me. Tell me about your mother."

"She left us a few years ago."

"Where did she go?"

"She went with another man, a young man. I hear he already has a child from a previous wife."

It was difficult for Ramesh to get the words out, but he did. "Is she now carrying a child by this young man?"

Naresh gave him an odd look. "Yes, I hear that she's pregnant with his child."

"I need your clothes, Naresh."

Naresh observed him. "Are you a bit ill? Perhaps touched in the head?"

"I'll give you money for them so you can buy new clothes. I'll give you good money. Plus you can have these clothes I'm wearing. Can we go someplace to swap?"

Naresh took him to an abandoned hut by the Bagmati River. They went to the back of the hut, where Naresh said, "You give me your clothes first, just in case you're playing some kind of sick game."

Ramesh stripped down to his underwear and handed his clothes to Naresh, who inspected them before he took off his own. "Your underwear also," Ramesh said.

"Then what will I wear?" Naresh asked.

Ramesh took off his bright white underwear and handed it to him. Naresh glanced at Ramesh's penis, seemed to become embarrassed, then took off his own underwear, which stank, and gave it to Ramesh, who put it on promptly with his eyes closed. The two boys then finished dressing and faced each other. "You look good," Ramesh said to

Naresh, who said, "And you look like me." Ramesh gave him a few hundred rupees from his wallet. Naresh accepted the money with an expression of disbelief.

The guard at the big house nearly didn't let Ramesh in that day, thinking he was a street urchin trying to get in. "What happened, Ramesh babu?" he asked. "Why are you wearing such clothes?"

Ramesh didn't answer him and went up to his room.

In the privacy of his room, every day for a few hours, he turned into a poor boy. He put on his poor clothes and practiced begging. "Please, sir, can I have some more?" he said, paraphrasing the famous line from Dickens's *Oliver Twist*. He also turned into his father, a rich man on the street who came upon the beggar boy.

"Shameless," his rich man father says. "A healthy boy who should be working. Why can't you go find a job instead of lazing around like this?"

"But sir, I have lost my mother."

"What has that got to do with anything?"

The poor boy becomes silent.

On occasion the rich man turned into someone from Suresh's party: the actor, the politician.

"How did you lose your mother?" the rich actor asks disdainfully. "Did she die?"

"No, sir, she left my father for another man. For other children."

"For other children?" The rich actor laughs. "Why? Were you not good enough for her?"

"That I can't answer, sir."

"Maybe she doesn't love you."

"But sir, I came from her womb. How can a mother not love a child who comes from her own womb?"

The politician slaps the poor boy. "Shameless!" he says. "Begging on the streets. You are the cause of this country's downfall."

"I am so sorry, sir, so sorry, but I can't help that I am poor."

"Of course you can! Lift yourself up by your bootstraps!"

"But sir, I don't own any boots."

Some nights Ramesh slept in his poor-boy's clothes. It seemed to him that those nights he slept a deep, anxiety-free sleep.

Ramesh made sure that he practiced his poor-boy routine only during the afternoons when his father wasn't around, or when his father was traveling, or late at night when his father was asleep. One evening he was practicing when he heard footsteps outside his door he recognized as his father's. The old man must have come home early from a trip. Ramesh held his breath. His father also seemed to hold his breath on the other side of the door.

One afternoon Ramesh dozed off, then awoke, a voice inside him telling him to go to the market. He argued with the voice: it was a hot day, and he was feeling cool under the ceiling fan. But the voice was strong, adamant, so reluctantly he put on his poor-boy's clothes, wore his poor-boy's shoes—his chappals—and left the big house. The servants were in the back, banging away in the kitchen, or dozing in the quarters.

The guard opened the gate and gave him a salute. Ramesh saluted back. He knew the guard thought of him as an idiot, the lonely boy—Richie Rich!—who wore a poor man's clothes to go mingle with the masses. The guard probably had a wife and kids back in the village, plus arthritic parents he needed to buy medicine for. Ramesh thought he could detect the disdain and anger in the guard's eyes, even though his face was impassive.

It shouldn't have surprised him when he saw his mother as soon as he entered the market. Immediately, he knew why the voice had told him to venture out. This was another thing that was happening more and more: his thoughts and inclinations merging with the outside world, a seed in his mind turning into reality. The gun, for example. As soon as he'd held it in his hand, he knew that he was going to do something with it.

Still, when he actually saw his mother at the market with her family, Ramesh took in a sharp breath. The family stood in front of a shop that had kites and balloons hanging above its door. The girl, his stepsister, had grown, and she had a know-it-all look on her face as she addressed her parents in a querulous voice. The young husband was holding a baby who was wearing a tight-fitting bonnet. Even from the distance—Ramesh was a few yards away, across the street—he spotted the black tika on the baby's forehead. Ah! To ward off the evil eye!

His mother was laughing, and her young husband was pointing to a balloon and urging the baby to look. It was a plain blue balloon; there was nothing to look at or laugh and get excited about. And the baby wasn't looking at the balloon but at Ramesh.

Were they actually going to buy something? Or were they merely dillydallying? What was his mother doing so far away from home and so close to the house she'd left behind? Was she on a dare? Was the next step for her new family then to stroll over to the big house, her former family's abode?

Ramesh moved closer, now directly across the street from them, only a few yards away. The baby's eyes followed him, and the father was gently nudging the baby—with the bonnet and its baby face Ramesh couldn't decipher its gender—to look at the balloon. Ramesh wondered if the baby, through some sixth sense, recognized Ramesh as its half brother.

I'm wearing a poor boy's clothes, Ramesh thought, *so I might as well do it.* He lowered his head and held out his palms in supplication. "Please spare a few coins," he said in a pathetic voice to the passersby. "Haven't eaten for three days." The tenor and the tremble of the voice came to him naturally, as though he was a veteran at it.

A coin dropped onto his palm, then another, and after the third coin, he remembered that he ought to be grateful for the alms, so after every *clink* he mumbled, "May God bless you and your family." The coins kept coming, at first slowly, then rapidly. The more people saw the coins accumulated on his palms, the more they gave.

The coins filled his palms so quickly that he had to empty them in the pockets of his trousers. When he thrust out his palms again, the coins at first trickled, then multiplied. His mother's family was still across the street, still engaged with the balloon. After his palms filled for a second time, he emptied them into his pockets and crossed the street. The coins jangled as though he was wearing anklets and dancing across a stage. He bowed before his mother's family, head down, palms held high. "A coin or two. May your beautiful family be blessed." His voice was muffled because his chin was touching his chest.

"A beggar," the young husband said.

"Look how bowed he is," Ramesh's mother said. "Look, children, look at that young boy, begging. If you don't listen to your mother, you'll end up like him."

Ramesh waited for her to recognize him.

"Hello, beggar boy," the young husband said happily.

"Scat!" Ramesh recognized the voice as that of the young girl's. "Aren't you ashamed to be begging?"

"Some money for food, please," Ramesh said. He raised his head a bit, then waited for his mother's exclamation, her cry of distress at seeing her son in this state.

"Don't scold him," the young husband said in a kind voice. "He must not have any parents."

"Young men these days—lazy!" his mother said.

Ramesh raised his head even more.

"Here, baby," the young husband said. "Give the beggar boy this coin."

Ramesh felt warm breath on his head: the young husband had brought the baby close. A cold coin dropped onto his palm. He lifted his chin even more, then moved his eyes up in their sockets so he could see them. But his mother's family had already moved on.

He straightened and scanned the street. They were strolling leisurely, away from the market, down the hill, moving in the direction away from the big house. Watching them, he wondered what his mother would think of what happened with Suresh. His father most likely would not care, or if he did, probably think that it was a one-time thing. His father might conclude that the boys had smoked some pot and fooled around a bit. He might then recall his own boarding school days in the hill station of Dalhousie in India, when things happened in the bunk beds at night that were spoken about only with winks and dreamy smiles the next day. His father would think that there was no harm in that.

When he wondered how his mother would react to what had happened in Suresh's room, Ramesh was flummoxed. He didn't know whether she'd be angry or filled with concern for him. One moment he pictured her furious about what he'd done; the next moment he saw her gently caressing him and telling him that it was okay, that he ought not worry.

That night Ramesh couldn't sleep, even in his poor-boy's clothes. Throughout the night, his mother's face continued to switch from anger to love to distress.

He opened his eyes in the predawn light, triggered into alertness by a pinprick in his consciousness. He propped himself up on his elbow and looked out of the window: the sky had barely begun to be illuminated. In the servants' quarters, a servant was sweeping the floor of the veranda. He watched her. He needed to do something for her. He also needed to do something for Naresh—for his state of existence, which couldn't be allowed to go on. In the greyish light that was now beginning to seep into the room, Ramesh looked down at his poor-boy's clothes. I *need to do something for myself.* The time had come.

He saw himself waving the long revolver in the bank. He saw himself walking out calmly with a couple of sacks stuffed with crisp banknotes, money that he'd then distribute to his servants. He'd then go over to the temple, locate Naresh, and hand him a few thousand rupees. "Here, I want you to start a new life. I want you to forget about your mother. She doesn't deserve you." Then he'd return home and put on his poor-boy's clothes and wait for the police to arrive. The national media would be on the case: The rich boy who dresses in poor clothes. The rich boy who robbed a bank. His photo would be plastered all over the newspapers. The TV reports would probably show clips of him in handcuffs, being escorted out of the big house in his poor clothes into a police van. Across the city, his mother, while feeding her youngest child by hand, would glance at the TV, see his profile, and cry out in alarm, "Why, that is my very own son!"

The bank was in a row of commercial buildings across the street from another row of commercial buildings. It was a popular bank, one that ran radio and TV commercials day and night, and its advertisement jingle was also a hit:

Sano Bank
Our Own Bank
Warm like a home, this bank
Always in service, like a riverbank

Ramesh scoped out the bank. He walked back and forth in front of it, but not so much that it aroused the suspicion of the guard, who stood at the entrance with an old rifle. The guard had an ancient mustache, thick and drooping. He was not scary. The trick was to get the gun in. Customers had to go through a metal detector, but Ramesh knew the metal detector didn't work. On his previous visit, when the fat lady had given him a hard time, he'd been behind a man from whose bag the guard had extracted a small khukuri after the man went through the metal detector. The knife was about a few inches long, the kind one buys as a souvenir, a smaller version of an actual khukuri. The guard had questioned the man, who had become annoyed. "This piddling knife—do you think I'm going to rob your bank with it? If you're that worried, why didn't your metal detector catch it?" Faced with the man's anger, the guard had become apologetic and said that the metal detector didn't work. It needed to be replaced, but the bank didn't have any money. The man and the guard had a good laugh about a bank not having money.

But to this day the metal detector hadn't been changed. The guard still carefully inspected the customer's bags before letting them through. How to get the gun past him? Ramesh finally came up with a solution.

Tuesday was a hot day, with the forecast that it was going to get hotter. Ramesh went to the bank. He carried with him a bag, and wore a tracksuit and tennis shoes. He also carried a tennis racket. The guard patted him down, then sifted through his bag. He extracted a towel, a lotion, and a T-shirt. "What is this?" he asked, his fingers digging deeper into the bag.

"Oh, my tennis balls are in there."

"But why can't I take them out? I can feel them."

"It's a secret compartment."

"I need to see them."

Ramesh turned the bag inside out, unzipped the secret compartment and extracted a tennis ball. The guard took one, sniffed it, squeezed it, then bounced it on the floor, repeatedly, to verify its bounciness. "How much do these cost?"

"They're about a hundred rupees each."

The guard raised his eyebrows. "How much does the bat cost?" He picked up the racket and slammed it against his palm.

"About three thousand rupees."

"How many more balls do you have in there?"

"Five or six."

The guard again dug into the bag. His fingers spent some time there, like he was fondling his own balls. "Why do you keep them hidden?"

"People steal them."

The guard handed him the bag and indicated he could go in.

Ramesh feigned anger. "I come to this bank often after my tennis practice. Will you be harassing me every time I come, waste my time like this?"

"It's my job, babu."

"Well, now that you know what's hidden in that bag, will I have to show you its innards again?"

The guard looked around and whispered, "Now I recognize your face. It's no problem."

Ramesh adopted a pleased expression and took out a hundred-rupee note and slipped it to the guard. "The issue is, dai, I don't have time, so please. Okay? Next time no search, okay?"

Except that on Ramesh's next visit, there would be a gun in the secret compartment.

The guard indicated for him to go in and winked.

Inside, there were four tellers behind the glass partitions at the counter. The fat lady with the enormous lips was there. When their eyes met, something shifted in the fat lady's face. Her expression became focused, like she'd spotted an enemy. Ramesh noticed something else: another guard inside, standing against the wall, watching customers. This second guard hadn't been here the last time. Then Ramesh remembered the recent string of bank robberies in the city. This second guard was sure to put a crimp in Ramesh's plan when he came here on the big day. Ramesh might end up in a struggle with him, which wasn't how he wanted to perform this. This guard was not mustachioed, which Ramesh read to mean that he had no false bravado. He was the real deal. He was lean and thin, with a tough-looking chin. The type who didn't suffer fools gladly, who despised inefficiency, who left no mess. The man didn't drink or smoke—Ramesh knew this instinctively. And judging from his eyes that roved from customer to customer, he took his job seriously.

The guard's eyes landed on Ramesh, then flitted toward the fat lady. Something passed between them. It was as if she'd already talked to the guard about him, given him Ramesh's description.

Ramesh stood in line. There were about five people in front of him. Ramesh felt a change in the air at his back, and without turning he knew that the guard had moved away from the wall and had come closer. There were only three bank tellers today, including the fat lady. Although she was open, she had her eyes fixed on Ramesh instead of the customer at the front of the line, who was looking at her expectantly.

One of the other two tellers left his station, so now there were only two tellers. The customer at the front of the line finally called out to the fat lady, "Aren't you open? May I come?" Without taking her eyes off Ramesh, the fat lady gestured toward the remaining teller, who was engaged.

The customer who'd addressed her turned to others waiting behind him. "Even when they're open, they're not really open. There's a limit to laziness." He was supported by a chorus of voices—"It's craziness, not laziness," "The customer is not a king here but an untouchable"—that became quiet once the third teller returned to his station. Then the line rapidly moved forward, and Ramesh was at the front.

The fat lady called to him, "Please come here." He pretended not to hear and kept his eyes focused on the teller next to her. "I said, please come here."

"She's open now," the customer behind Ramesh said. "Go, go!"

"I thought you were not open," Ramesh said.

The guard was at his elbow. "Please go to her."

Ramesh reluctantly approached her window. The guard went with him and stood a couple of feet behind.

The fat lady was looking at him impassively. "For what purpose have you come?"

"I need to take out some money."

An internal smile passed through her face, like a small breeze that, unless one was a vigilante and knew what to look for, could go undetected. "How much?"

"Five lakh rupees." He didn't know whether the account had that big an amount—he assumed it had—but right now he wanted to throw her off guard.

At his mention of five lakh rupees, he heard an audible sucking of breath behind him from the guard.

Through an image that zipped inside his mind like lightning, he saw them: the fat lady and the teetotaler guard embracing in a dingy flat, he sucking on her enormous lips. These two were lovers. How could Ramesh have missed it? She'd told the guard about the boy who gave her a hard time on what was most likely the guard's day off. "Some Richie Rich," she told him, caressing his bony chest, and he must have said to her, "I will break his mouth." Then they made love. There was a physical connection between the two, the guard and the fat lady—Ramesh could smell it in the air between them, a whiff of animal sex. He'd smelled something similar when his stepfather had emerged from the shadows during his visit to his mother's house.

"Five lakh rupees?" the fat lady said. She looked past him to the guard.

Just let her try to do something funny again, Ramesh thought. *I'm going to bring the house down. I'm going to create such a ruckus that it'll be written up in the papers.* Ramesh might, if it came down to it, even announce that the fat lady and the guards were lovers. *Do you allow sexual relationships between your employees?* he'd loudly ask the manager. *Perhaps you even encourage it?*

"Have you brought your check?"

He took out his checkbook, wrote one to "self," and quickly signed it on the counter in front of her, then pushed it toward her. She picked it up with both hands and lifted it up, even higher than eye level, as though she were scrutinizing it for some invisible ink. She didn't speak. He then understood that she was showing the check to the guard behind him.

"There's no loop in the *Y* today," Ramesh said. "But it's me."

"No problem," she said. She put down the check and smiled at him. "How is your father?" she asked.

"My father?"

"Yes, how is he?"

"Do you know him?"

"Let's say I do."

"What does that mean? Either you do or you don't."

"He's a big man. He might not remember me. But we used to work together a long time ago."

This woman working together with this father. Fat chance. "Where?" he asked.

"Oh, you wouldn't know. This all happened before you were born. Your father and I . . ." She looked at him meaningfully.

"Yes, please tell me."

"Let's say your father and I—how shall I put it?"

"Put it well."

"Let's say we spent some fun moments together. A *looong, looong* time ago."

This woman was half his father's age, and Ramesh couldn't ever imagine his father having fun with a woman, let alone a woman like her. She was goading Ramesh. He couldn't let himself be ruffled.

"How's your mother?" Her voice was softer, lower now, only for his ears, but not too low for the guard, who'd stepped closer to catch her words. Anyone looking from the door would probably see three people in collusion, the teller with her incredible lips, a troubled young man with an impossible amount of money, and a guard bent forward, breathing down the young man's neck.

Ramesh didn't respond to the fat lady's query about his mother.

"So sad," the fat lady said, as though intuiting his emotions, "what happened with her." She looked at him kindly. "Now I hear she has a child of her new beau."

That child wears an evil eye tika, he thought, *probably to ward off bad gazes from people like you.* He wondered if his mother ever put a talismanic tika on his forehead. For some reason he thought she didn't.

"But we knew this was coming a long time ago, didn't we?" the fat lady said.

"We?"

"Your father and I. During our heyday. He'd just married your mother then. You were yet to be born. One evening we were drinking in the lobby of a hotel after an event. Like I said, your father and I—well, what's the point in dwelling on that? But that evening, he said, 'She's not a keeper, this one.' It took me a few seconds to understand whom he was referring to. Your father looked despondent. I prodded him about why he was speaking like that about his wife, and he said, 'Something about the way she laughs when she's with other men. She laughs for no reason. When she's with me, she never laughs for no reason.' I asked your father whether she already had a lover he'd seen her with, and he shook his head. 'Not yet,' he said. 'But she'll get herself someone soon. Maybe she'll even give me a child, a boy, before she moves on.'" The fat lady paused. "And here you are."

"Can you cash my check, please?"

"You know you can talk to me."

"Please give me my money so I can go home."

She lowered her voice. "You know, you shouldn't walk around with so much cash." She beckoned him closer with her hand, and foolishly he leaned into the window so his chest pressed against the counter. "We've had cases," she whispered, "where ruffians loiter outside the bank, sometimes even inside, watching our customers stuff large amounts of cash into their bags, then rob them on their way to their home or office. What you are doing is dangerous." She brought her face very close to him, and for a moment he thought she was going to kiss him with those huge lips. With dismay he realized that a part of him wanted to taste those lips.

Breathlessly she continued, "There has even been a case of murder. A young man. Like you. Throat slit in that alley. The same alley that leads to your house."

Then things happened very quickly. She reached under the counter and pulled out four stacks of banknotes. She endorsed his check with multicolored stamps in rapid succession: clack, dyab, bhyat. "Give me your bag," she said, and like a dolt he did. She stuffed the money into his bag, tightened the strings, then called the guard, who didn't need to be called because he was right behind Ramesh. "Birendra, could you escort this babu home? He's the son of an old friend."

Before Ramesh realized what was happening, his bag with the money was in the hands of the guard, who said, "Follow me," and strode toward the door.

"My bag," Ramesh said weakly and hurried after him.

"Give my regards to your father," the fat lady called after him.

By the time Ramesh exited the main door with its metal detectors, the guard had disappeared into the crowd. "Where did he go?" he shouted at the mustachioed guard.

"Birendra? He went that way," the guard said, pointing toward Ramesh's house.

Ramesh ran down the street. The sun was intense in the sky. He finally saw the guard's head bobbing in the distance, among a sea of heads. Without looking back or breaking his stride, the guard raised his arm and waved him forward. Sweating, Ramesh chased after him.

The guard had disappeared into the chaos of Chuchepati. Ramesh half-ran all the way to Bouddha looking for him, then all the way back to the Ganesh temple. The man had vanished. Ramesh turned around to go to the bank and raise hell.

But as he waited for a break in the traffic to cross the street, he stopped. What did it matter? The phrase *a drop in the ocean* came to him. That money was nothing to him. It was not his money; it was his father's money, and it was a drop in the ocean for his father. His father might not even notice the money gone. Or if he did, he might think that Ramesh somehow spent it. Five lakh rupees! Ramesh could tell him that he lost the money gambling in the casino. His father might get mad, scold Ramesh for being so casual with his money, lecture him about how he, Ramesh's father, became rich only because he conserved every penny he received. Or Ramesh could tell him that he spent the money on a party he threw for his friends, a party like the one he attended at Suresh's house, except it was held in a hotel. "I'd always wanted to throw a big party for my friends, Dad," Ramesh would say in the lazy voice of a rich, spoiled kid, and his father, although outwardly disapproving, would be secretly pleased that his strange son had finally understood what money could do and the moneyed legacy he had inherited.

His father might say, "Son, why didn't you tell me that

you wanted to throw a party for your friends? I would have thrown a grand party for you right here in our big house."

"Would it have been something like the Sapkotas' party, Dad, with liveried servants and a live band?"

"Arre! I would have thrown a party even bigger than the Sapkotas'. I would have thrown a party that would have been the talk of the town for weeks."

Let the guard and his fat girlfriend enjoy the loot, Ramesh thought, as he stood across the street from the bank, human traffic swarming around him. He wondered if the fat lady was still inside, or if she'd already joined her lover somewhere. Perhaps, breathless and giggly, they were already on a bus headed out of town, the bag with the money held tight between them, stunned at how easily this fortune had landed in their laps through the courtesy of a Richie Rich fool. *Enjoy,* Ramesh told them in his mind. *It was never my wealth to begin with.*

Never my wealth to begin with, he repeated to himself as he went home. At home, in the spaciousness of the hallway and the empty rooms, he reiterated, *Never my wealth to begin with.* As if to prove to the world what he'd just said, he put on his poor-boy's clothes. He thought of his mother. Maybe there was a good reason that she left. Maybe things had, for some reason, become unbearable for her, just as—he contemplated his big, cavernous house—they were becoming unbearable for him. Perhaps she was really a poor woman at heart, and had to go away to find her poor-woman's ways.

WHAT WILL HAPPEN TO THE SHARMA FAMILY

The Sharma family's trip to Bombay didn't go well. The Royal Nepal Airlines plane (before the Royal was taken out of it) started acting funny after half an hour—a strange sound choked the left wing, and the plane began to hiccup—so they had to land in Patna, where the passengers were forced to stay in a hotel for the night. The mishap would have been tolerable had not twenty-one-year-old Nilesh sauntered out of the hotel after dinner to "check out the territory" and within two minutes got mugged in an alley, where two hoodlums pocketed his wristwatch, his gold necklace, and the twenty thousand rupees Indian currency stashed in the inside pocket of the coat he had on that warm evening.

"I told you to get traveler's checks," Mrs. Sharma shrieked when Nilesh came back, his face bruised and the arm of his coat ripped off. Mr. Sharma slapped him, for that was what he often did to his children in situations where he felt helpless.

Their eighteen-year-old daughter, Nilima, fat and smart,

said, "Maybe this is a sign we should turn back." She had strongly resisted the trip, saying she needed to study for her A-level exams, whereas everyone knew she didn't want to be away from her Jitendra, who was so stunningly handsome, with a sleek body and a puff of hair on his forehead, that Mr. and Mrs. Sharma often wondered what he saw in their fat daughter. Mrs. Sharma was convinced Jitendra wanted to marry Nilima for her parents' money, which didn't make sense as the Sharma family wasn't super rich. Mr. Sharma thought Jitendra wasn't right in the head, and that the puff of hair hid an anomaly in his brain.

Fortunately, the cash wrenched away from Nilesh wasn't the only money they'd brought for the trip. Mrs. Sharma had another twenty thousand, which they hurriedly converted to traveler's checks at the bank before boarding their plane to Bombay the next morning. Throughout the ride, Mrs. Sharma berated Nilesh, who had recently dropped out of college and spent all his time in cinema halls, dreaming of becoming an actor. "Who will marry you like this, huh? So irresponsible. You'll lose your wife during the wedding procession." She mimicked him, "'Oh, I lost my wife. I don't know how it happened. One moment she was in my pocket, then these hoodlums came and snatched her away.'" Mrs. Sharma laughed loud at her own impersonation, and a flight attendant signaled to her to keep it down.

Nilima was engrossed in a Stephen King novel, ignoring her mother's rantings and her brother's sullen face and timid objections. Mr. Sharma was reading the brochure on emergency steps to be taken should the plane plunge toward the earth. Yesterday's jolts and screams had frightened him. He didn't want to die yet, at least not before making love to Kanti, his neighbor's maid who smiled at him coquettishly and didn't mind his sexual jokes.

At the airport in Bombay, no one came to pick them up. They waited. Mr. Sharma called Ahuja's home, but no answer. Nilima saw this as another indication that they should hop on the next flight back to Kathmandu. Nilesh got into a staring match with two big, unshaven Indian boys who appeared ready to come over and do something to him, had Mrs. Sharma not scowled at them. After two hours of waiting, the Sharmas decided to take a taxi to Andheri, where Ahuja lived. Mrs. Sharma said that they should take the train, but Nilima outright laughed at the idea. She said she'd rather spend the night at the airport than take the crowded, smelly train. So they took a taxi.

Mr. Sharma wondered what it'd be like to visit Bombay with Kanti. They could run away together and live in one of the numerous shacks scattered throughout the city. She would wear skimpy clothes, her midriff showing, and he'd make love to her all day long and into the night. Mrs. Sharma worried about how she was going to get her fat, smart daughter and her stupid son married. A couple of offers had come for Nilima, but the boys had balked once they saw her, and Mrs. Sharma never heard anything further about the proposals. As for Nilesh, he'd acquired a reputation as a no-good loafer, so no proposal had even come his way. In her mind, Mrs. Sharma saw Nilima married to Jitendra, which gave her a shudder, and she saw unmarriageable Nilesh roaming the streets, getting into drugs and fights, ending up in jail.

As the taxi crawled along the congested Bombay roads, Nilesh replayed last night's mugging in his mind over and over, but this time as soon as the muggers approached, Nilesh's left foot shot up like lightning, instantly cracking open one man's jaw; without looking, Nilesh whirled and slammed the back of his right fist on the second hoodlum's nose, shattering it so a fountain of blood sprang forth and drenched a crowd of onlookers, who had miraculously appeared to see this brave young man in action and who now applauded as the two muggers crumpled to the ground. Narrowing his eyes, Nilesh asked, "Anyone else?" Nilesh fast-forwarded and rewound this scene over and over, perfecting his kick, making the muggers beg for mercy, and replacing the "Anyone else?" with a howl.

Nilima turned another page of the novel. The family dog, it turned out, had supernatural powers. But was Rusty going to use it to ward off the evil forces? Or was he going to join the dark side and destroy the family?

Ahuja lived in a nice neighborhood in Andheri, on a quiet, tree-lined street. But no one was home—there was a giant padlock on the door. "They must have gone to the airport," Mrs. Sharma said. "Let's wait."

It was only after they'd waited for nearly two hours that a neighbor came over and told them that the Ahujas had gone on a vacation to the mountainous Nainital for two weeks.

"But that can't be," Mr. Sharma said. "He knew we were

coming. I talked to him on the phone a week ago, and I sent him a message from Patna about our flight's delay."

"You're not the first one," the neighbor said. "The Ahujas do this to their relatives all the time."

The Sharmas dragged themselves into a taxi for a ride to a nearby hotel in Juhu Beach, which they knew would be heart-chillingly expensive, but they were too tired and hot to go hunting for a reasonable hotel.

They stayed in Bombay for only three days, not only because money was running out but also because Ahuja's betrayal had soured everything. Nilima showed very little interest in the sightseeing they did, except for the Hanging Gardens, which she thought were "fabulous." Nilesh became obsessed with the transvestites who roamed the city in groups. He stared at them, commenting upon their "manly" features. One time he laughed loudly as they passed by, and the hinjadas circled the Sharma family and made threatening gestures. Only after Mr. Sharma handed them a hundred rupees did they leave, singing and clapping. Immediately Mrs. Sharma took off her sandal and smacked Nilesh on his head.

On the flight back to Kathmandu, they hardly spoke to one another. The trip had made Mrs. Sharma even more apprehensive about her children's marriage prospects—they were either stubborn or stupid. Mr. Sharma could hardly breathe in anticipation of touching Kanti's midriff, which he knew he had to do the next time they were together alone. Nilima was devouring another book she'd bought at the Bombay airport, a romantic thriller by Danielle Steele.

Nilesh woke up from a short nap, scared. He had dreamed about making love to a transvestite and now had a terrific hard-on. He put the airline magazine on his lap so his mother, sitting next to him, wouldn't notice.

"That's the last trip we'll take as a family," Mrs. Sharma declared as they entered their house. Mr. Sharma immediately went for a walk, hoping that he'd catch a glimpse of Kanti, hanging laundry or dusting a blanket on her balcony, and that he'd quietly approach her. Nilesh went into his room to practice his drums. This was another of his dreams—to become a rock star. He'd tried guitar, but he couldn't change chords fast enough, and his fingers bled. With drums, all he needed to do was bang away, and there was a semblance of a beat. In his mind, women screamed and men danced as he played. The King of Drums, he was called.

Nilima didn't come home that night. She'd gone to see Jitendra soon after they reached home, and the two of them decided they missed each other so much that it was time to consummate their bond. "Let's stay in a hotel tonight," Nilima said. "It'll throw a real scare into my parents. Maybe then they'll stop bad-mouthing you and get us married."

"But they'll be so worried," Jitendra said. He was a sweet boy; he really loved Nilima and, by extension, her parents. But Nilima was too persuasive for him, and they ended up in a hotel in Thamel.

Mr. Sharma did spot Kanti, not on her balcony but outside a shop in the neighborhood. She was talking with a man. Their body language told Mr. Sharma that this was more than a casual conversation. The man was young, about twenty-five, the same age as Kanti. With pangs of disappointment and anger, Mr. Sharma approached them.

"How was Bombay?" Kanti asked when she saw him. Laughter was etched around her lips and her eyes.

"Don't you have work at home?" Mr. Sharma asked sternly. "Why are you chatting here?"

"I just came to buy something," she said.

"Go home, go home," Mr. Sharma said. "Who is he? It's not good to be standing here, chatting. It doesn't look good."

The young man appeared indignant. "I'll see you again," he told Kanti and walked away.

Kanti and Mr. Sharma began walking. He used his soothing, intimate voice, the one he'd never used on his wife, to mollify Kanti's anger. "You shouldn't do these types of things in public. It'll only bring criticism from everyone, and might even get you fired. I'm a good man, so I won't tell your employer. But someone else might not be so nice. I am nice because I like you so much. You're a nice girl. And I'm a nice man. That's what we have in common, and when people have things in common, they can do many things together. I can teach you many things you didn't even know existed. Who is that man? What can he give you that I can't, huh? Tell me, what do you want? Just utter the word, and it's yours."

Kanti, who was no fool, said, "What gift did you bring me from Bombay? I want a gold necklace."

They were nearing Kanti's house. Mr. Sharma had to

think fast. "Is that what you want? You are my queen, so you'll get what you want. But you also have to do what I ask." His hand touched her midriff.

"We'll see," she said. "Let me see the necklace first," and she slipped into her house.

Nilesh knew what his father was up to. His room was on the third floor of their house and commanded a view of the surrounding alleys. He saw his father talking to the maid. Remembering his father's slap in Patna, Nilesh wanted to go down and usher his mother outside so she could witness her husband's desire. But Nilesh also remembered how she had berated him throughout the trip, and he thought, *Let her be ignorant of this; it'll be fun to watch her face when she finds out.* Wouldn't it be spectacular if the maid became pregnant by his father and demanded a share of their property? He envisioned a little half brother looking exactly like his father—the same prominent Brahmin nose, the long earlobes. Nilesh laughed and went back to his drumming.

By dinner, Mrs. Sharma had begun cursing Nilima. "At her age, she should be helping me cook dinner so that when she gets married, she won't be an idiot in the kitchen. We've got to put a stop to this, do you hear me?" she addressed her husband, who was wondering if Kanti would be able to tell the difference between a gold-coated necklace and a real one. He concluded she would, and ate another mouthful of rice.

"I don't trust that Jitendra. What are you going to do about it?" Mrs. Sharma asked her husband, then turned to her son. "And you, loafer supreme, how can anyone call you an older brother when you don't take care of your sister?"

"What can I do?" Nilesh said.

"Leave him alone," Mr. Sharma said. "And leave us alone, at least for tonight. I don't care what our daughter does. Just be quiet."

Mrs. Sharma was going to retort, but she thought the better of it, and they all ate their meal in silence.

At ten o'clock that night, Mrs. Sharma called Jitendra's house, something she'd never done before. When she identified herself, the man at the other end said, "Oh." No, Jitendra wasn't home; neither was Nilima. Jitendra had called and said he was going to a late-night party. Had he gone with Nilima? The man didn't know. Mrs. Sharma didn't ask him who he was—probably the boy's father.

She went to her bedroom and woke her husband, and the two of them made phone calls to Nilima's friends. Then Mrs. Sharma woke Nilesh violently from his sleep, and sent him out to search for his sister in the neighborhood. They talked of going to the police station, decided against it; they talked of skinning Nilima alive were she to appear at the door shamefaced the next morning. Mrs. Sharma called Jitendra's house again and argued with the sleepy-voiced father, telling him to keep his son away from her daughter.

By one o'clock, they were exhausted. Mr. and Mrs. Sharma sat on the couch, Nilesh on the floor leaning against the wall. He really wanted to go upstairs to sleep but was afraid of his mother's tongue-lashing.

Nilima received a slap from her mother when she entered the house the next morning.

"I want to marry him," she told her mother, nursing her cheek. "I don't care what you say—I won't marry anyone else but Jitendra."

Helplessly Mrs. Sharma looked at her husband.

"You're still too young to be married," Mr. Sharma said. "Why don't you finish your A-level exams, and then we can talk about it? But you can't spend nights with him in hotels. People will spit at you, and tomorrow if he finds another girl, who'll marry you?"

"If you won't marry us," Nilima said, "we'll have a court wedding. We've already decided."

Mrs. Sharma stepped forward to dole out another slap, but her husband stopped her. "Wait, daughter, what's the hurry? Finish your exams first, then marry him. That's all we're saying."

Nilima considered. "Okay, but get us engaged now. And we'll marry after my exams."

Mrs. Sharma left the room in a huff. Nilesh folded his arms and watched the back and forth between his father and his sister. He knew he was expected to be angry at his sister, probably even shove her around a bit, threaten to beat up Jitendra, but all he felt was admiration. She had a sense of defiance he himself lacked. She'd really shown their parents that they couldn't push her around.

Later he went to her room. She was sitting in bed, doodling. "What did you do last night?" he asked.

"What business is it of yours?"

"Good, very good. My little sister is really grown up now."

"I'm glad you noticed," she said.

"Did you . . . really . . . ? You don't have to answer."

"You're a strange brother. But yes, I did."

"Just to spite them?" he asked.

"I don't know. Now go and do your stupid things."

Mrs. Sharma called Jitendra's father, Changu, and arranged for a meeting. That evening Mr. and Mrs. Sharma went to Jitendra's house, a nice-looking building in New Baneswor with a large yard and two cars. Mrs. Sharma told Changu what her daughter had said. "Frankly, we don't think she should be married right now," Mrs. Sharma said. Before, she would have added, "Especially to your son," but the family's obvious prosperity had softened her stance toward Jitendra. Instead, she said, "But what to do? Their eyes are fixed on each other."

"These young people," Changu said. "Once their minds are made up, even Lord Indra's dad Chandra can't shake them."

There was silence while they contemplated the mysterious ways of the young. Changu was smoking from a hookah. He took a long drag, then said, "Well, you're a good family, and we also don't have a bad name in town. If they want to get engaged, let them do it. If we don't agree to this and they decide to elope, our noses will be cut." His index finger mock-serrated the tip of his nose as illustration.

On the way home, Mrs. Sharma said, "Well, at least they're not poor. That was a nice house, and he seemed like a nice man."

Mr. Sharma nodded absentmindedly. During the hustle-bustle of the engagement, he should be able to siphon off a few thousand rupees for the gold necklace. *Perfect, oh, perfect,* he thought. That damn Kanti. She had been avoiding coming to the balcony, as if challenging him about his gift. He had to get that gold necklace for her if he wanted to make any progress.

The engagement date was fixed for three weeks later, with a promise from both Jitendra and Nilima that they would spend nights in their respective beds and that Nilima would study for her exams at least a few hours a day. Jitendra had to study for nothing. He'd failed his School Leaving Certificate exams twice, and everyone expected him to fail the third time, too. That her future son-in-law, like her son, was academically inept bothered Mrs. Sharma. "What is he going to become without even an SLC? A peon? How is he going to feed Nilima?"

"She's going to feed him," Nilesh said. Lately, taking courage from his sister's actions, he'd become bolder in talking to his mother.

"Look who is talking," Mrs. Sharma said. "Loafer, good-for-nothing. And what are you going to become? Who is going to marry you?"

"If someone like you could find a husband," Nilesh said, "why wouldn't I find a wife?"

Mr. Sharma laughed, and Mrs. Sharma tried to smack her son, but he made a scary face and said, "Don't you dare." And Mrs. Sharma didn't dare—she was losing control over her family, and she didn't even know about Kanti yet.

The incredibly handsome but SLC-failed boy got engaged to the fat, smart girl. Nilima was already pregnant, a fact she hid from everybody, even Jitendra. What she herself didn't know was that the baby would be stillborn, and that it would break her heart, starting her on bouts of depression that would last a lifetime, and that Jitendra, the ever-devoted husband, would stick by her side until she died. They would not have another child. "I'm dry, I'm dry," Nilima would cry late into the night, and Jitendra would soothe her with his soft voice emerging from those delicate lips. But for now Nilima was pregnant and happy, and she knew she would do well in her A-level exams because she was smart and knew everything.

Mr. Sharma made love to Kanti two neighborhoods away in a small room that belonged to a carpenter who'd done odd jobs in his house. For his "hospitality," the carpenter received five hundred rupees, with a strict warning not to divulge Mr. Sharma's secret to anyone. Kanti had already received her necklace, a ten-thousand-rupee affair he'd found in a shop in New Road. Mr. Sharma hadn't felt so alive in years, certainly not all those times he'd slept with his wife. Kanti was adept at pleasing a man—her tongue did wonderful things to Mr. Sharma's aging body. Loud noises—laughter, coughs, groans, and moans—emerged from his throat that afternoon, and he knew he would do it again and again and again with Kanti, and feel younger and younger. Little did Mr. Sharma know that he'd gotten Kanti pregnant right on that first day (the condom had broken during penetration), and she'd give birth to a baby boy who looked exactly like his father, as the other son had so faithfully intuited.

That afternoon Mr. Sharma also didn't know that Mrs. Sharma would eventually divorce him, something he couldn't ever have imagined. She'd put all their property in her name, then file for divorce, forcing him to live poorly with Kanti and their new son, shunned by friends, relatives, and even the carpenter on whose bed he'd manufactured his look-alike progeny. Mr. Sharma would deal with this ostracism with laughter on his lips and happiness in his heart, even though Kanti's midriff would sag after their son's birth. Mr. Sharma would walk the streets with swagger. He would be proud of this incredible turn his life had taken.

Mrs. Sharma worried about Nilima. The A-level exams were only two weeks away, but Nilima had taken her engagement with Jitendra as license to spend all day at his house. Mrs. Sharma cursed Changu for being so lenient, but she didn't say anything for fear of spoiling the new in-law relationship. In a way, she was relieved about Nilima's impending wedding. Jitendra was foolish and immature, but he doted on Nilima. Despite herself, Mrs. Sharma had grown to like Jitendra, who was always polite and sweet. Not like Nilesh, whose sullen face only aroused her anger.

And Nilesh? What was going to happen to him? Defying everyone's expectations, and surprising even himself, Nilesh would become one of the leading movie actors in the country. He'd haunt the dreams of young girls and boys, who would cover their bedroom walls with his posters and pray to him more than they prayed to Lord Ganesh. He'd ride in a fancy BMW, and he would star in movies that would not only become blockbusters but also win him accolades from even the most bitter of critics. He would end up owning his own production company that would make one hit after another. No one could have predicted this, but this is how the world works. One moment, you are stuck, and then the moment expands, as if God were forcing it open with his pretty bare hands, and you find yourself in another dimension, and you are still you, but the world around you has suddenly changed colors.

Mrs. Sharma's colors would change, too, but right now, wrapped in worries about her children while her husband explored Kanti's body in the carpenter's bedroom, she didn't know that after her divorce, she would discover in the temple of Swayambhunath a swami whose soft words would make sense of the suffering inflicted upon her by her husband. She would see in a millisecond of remarkable clarity (God's hand at work) that she had invited the suffering upon herself, that all suffering was self-induced, and—this is where her spiritual evolution would begin—that all of life was suffering. This insight would lead her to a place deep inside where she would no longer feel her physical self. Her body would turn into air, and she would fly over the city, glimpsing the lives of her one-time family, their suffering: "I want to die," bedridden Nilima would say to her husband; Nilesh would laugh at a film clip in the air-conditioned auditorium in his luxury house, his arm around another man's shoulder; Mr. Sharma would accompany his look-alike son to his first day in school.

FREAK STREET

SOFI

Sofi found a room on Freak Street. She practiced saying the street's real name, Jhonchhe, as the locals called it, but couldn't wrap her tongue around it, and people didn't understand what she was talking about. One person even thought she was speaking Chinese, so she gave up on "Jhonchhe." The hotel was not really a hotel. It was an upstairs room rented out by a family, two alleys away from the street that was the main drag.

The year was 1978, and pot and hashish had already been illegal for a few years now. The American government had paid millions of dollars to the Nepali king to ban them. Gone was the Eden Hashish Center, where hippies used to flock to buy quality hash and grass and receive the gift of a calendar with blue-colored Krishna and Shiva with a snake around his neck. The hashish business had moved underground, and one had to be on the lookout for the cops who roamed the streets, and who on occasion took the especially long-haired and unshaven hippies for an overnight trip to the station. Many hippies had stopped coming to Kathmandu, and restaurant owners in Freak Street bemoaned that the tourist hub had shifted to Thamel, where cleaner, more athletic-looking foreigners with money and trekking gear stayed before they went on their long hikes to the Annapurna and Everest region. The new tourists flew into the city, in contrast to the hippies, who used to travel by land in their beat-up colorful Volkswagens, passing through Turkey then Iran into Afghanistan, from Pakistan into India and, finally, Kathmandu. Still, every few months, a psychedelic hippie van could be seen parked at Basantapur Durbar Square, at the mouth of Freak Street, where peddlers sold statues of gods and goddesses, bells and dorjes and pipes and hookahs for smoking, and where some pot and hashish still passed through furtive hands.

Sofi wouldn't have found the room had she not been looking for something very cheap, and thus away from the main area adjacent to the square. "Hotel, hotel," a man had said to her, pointing down the narrow alley with his cigarette, and she had asked, "Where?" then saw the sign for Buddha Eyes Hotel, and underneath it: "WELCOME TO HIPPYS." The woman who ran it charged only five rupees a day, a real bargain.

Sofi loved the place. She loved the round, pockmarked face of her landlady, whom she called Sahuni. Sahuni ran an eatery on the ground floor, basically a kitchen, with two tables and a few stools, that opened for business in the late afternoons. The eatery, also the family kitchen, was adjacent to the sleeping quarters where Sahuni slept with her old husband and a son who was about twelve. She sold spicy meat, momos, fritters, and strong-smelling raksi and jaand to the locals and occasionally to a drugged-out-of-his-mind hippie who happened to stagger in instead of going to a pie joint on the main street. Sometimes Sofi helped out in the eatery, boiling tea, carrying food and liquor to the customers, and in return Sahuni let her eat for free. The customers, almost always men, loved the idea of being served by a kuir-iney with her flowing skirt, her bare stomach, and a phuli in her nose. They commented on her pale skin, her dirty-blonde hair, her smell of patchouli, and joked about her in their native tongues.

Sofi loved the narrow alley leading to the hotel that usually became filled with puddles during the rains so she had to sidestep them when she walked back and forth. She loved the patch of garden with its radishes and spinach which Sahuni tended to with care. Her room overlooked a neighbor's yard where children played and chanted, "Hippie, hippie," when they spotted her.

She loved Freak Street. She loved hearing the name from her own mouth and from the mouths of the other hippies. The name, the sound, the syllables evoked a place that was more than the neighborhood where she now stayed, the street with its pie cafés, its curio shops, and music stores from where guitar riffs by Jimi Hendrix, who had hung out here some years ago, pierced the air. Freak Street was also a sweet spot in the imagination, a far cry from the color-less town in Ohio where she'd grown up, a town with the impossible name of Coshocton, where her doctor father and housewife mother lived on a cul-de-sac, or a "dead end," as she liked to call it. By the time she finished high school, the town had become for her a miserable hole. Oberlin College was a big relief, and the first step to liberation. Now at the other end of the world, this country, this neighborhood of Freak Street, was so open and free and pulsing with life. The mix of the locals and the hippies, the restaurants with their spicy Nepali food and brownies filled with hash, the temples—ah, the temples!—with their gorgeous carvings and their gods and goddesses that actually seemed to be living with the people. There was something sweetly natural about this city.

One night she dreamed that she was wearing a traditional jyapu dress, typically worn by farming women in the valley. She spoke in Newari with Sahuni, who turned out to be her mother. The dream moved her so deeply that for days Sofi wandered about feeling that she was indeed a native, if not in this life, then certainly in a past one. Her solar plexus radiated an energy that transmitted images to her brain, images she thought were about her past life: working in the fields, cooking on a woodstove, scolding her children lovingly. She remembered that the solar plexus harbored a chakra, either the third or the fourth chakra—she wouldn't be surprised if it was related to one's reincarnated self. She smoked hash to deepen her experience. She climbed to the top of the monkey temple, Swayambhunath, where she and other hippies passed a chillum around while seated cross-legged in front of the main stupa. A young Danish man with rotting teeth and an emaciated face and body played the madal, the Nepali drum. Most days she meandered through the city, sometimes all day, braving neighborhoods where no foreigner stepped foot, pausing by stone taps to splash her face and drink the cool water and to chat with local women in her rudimentary Nepali:

Tapai sanchai? Are you well?
Ma kuiriney keti. I'm a gringo girl.
Pani mitho. Sweet water.
Aakash garmi chha. The sky is hot.
Tapaiharu sundar chha. You all are beautiful.

She rested at roadside stalls, drinking milky tea, saying, "Mitho, mitho" to the shopkeepers, feeling that she must have been born saying *mitho* because the word came to her easily—she couldn't do the hard "th," but she was happy with the soft "th." Besides, the locals understood her; their faces broke into smiles. The word itself seemed to fit this country, its people. Everything was indeed delicious here: the dust that rose around her feet as she traversed the streets; the way unkempt and snot-covered children happily followed her and called her *hippie* and *kuiriney*; the sudden, exhilarating glimpses of sky-touching white mountains; the torrential rains; the shouting and haggling in smelly, colorful markets. This was a mitho country.

She asked Sahuni to give her a Nepali name. At first, Sahuni demurred, saying, through her school-age son who acted as an interpreter, that Sofi was a good name. But Sofi didn't give up. She told Sahuni about her dream, and insisted that as her new mother, Sahuni must give her a Nepali name. The son haltingly and bewilderingly translated, often pausing to understand Sofi's accent, and after a few tries Sahuni understood. Sahuni's family spoke mostly Newari, but lately they had started using Nepali because they were worried that their son needed to be well versed in Nepali, the country's official language, in order to succeed in school and in life. Since Sofi also picked up Nepali from the streets, this worked out well.

Sahuni lightly tapped Sofi on the cheek and said, "Tan ta paagal nai raichhas."

"You are . . . mad," the son translated.

"Kaasto naam chhaiyo?"

"What name you want?" the son translated.

"A good name."

"Okay, okay," Sahuni said. She had picked up a smattering of English from her tenants over the years. "I give you, okay? Good name, okay?"

That evening Sahuni had Sofi dress in a red sari, applied some makeup to her, and took her to the Maru Ganesh temple. People stared at the white girl in her fiery brilliance as she was escorted through the Basantapur Square to the shrine of the elephant-nosed god who loved mitho sweets, especially the round laddoos that devotees placed under his rotund belly. Sahuni crouched down, whispered some mantras, then put a tika on Sofi's forehead and said, "You now Sukumari. You! Sukumari!" The boy was with them, in his school uniform because he had just returned from school.

"Why are you laughing?" Sofi asked the boy.

"Sukumari!"

"Name not good?" Sofi asked.

"Very good, very good," Sahuni said adamantly.

Spectators had gathered to observe the naming ceremony for this kuiriney, and a chorus of voices said, "Good! Good name!"

"Sukumari!" the boy tittered.

Sofi whispered the name to herself. "I like it," she said. "Mitho chha."

That drew chortles from the crowd.

Sahuni pushed her son. "Tell her what it means. Tell her it means 'a soft, delicate girl.'"

The boy told her.

"Like Kumari?" Sofi asked, pointing in the direction of the house that was a stone's throw away, where the Living Goddess resided. Kumari meant "a virgin," Sofi knew, a requirement for the young girl chosen as the Living Goddess.

"Yes, yes." Sahuni nodded enthusiastically.

"Tara ma virgin chhaina," Sofi said. *I am not a virgin.*

But the boy wasn't sophisticated enough to catch the nuance, so he translated that Sofi said she was not a goddess.

From then on Sofi started calling herself Sukumari. When her hippie friends called her Sofi, she corrected them with,

"I'm Sukumari now." They smiled and nodded, a couple of them saying, "Far out." When her friends couldn't say her full name, she accepted their nickname of "Suku," which was fine, since Nepalis frequently truncated the names of their loved ones to demonstrate affection. There were awkward moments when she was introduced to new people at Yin Yang, where she often hung out in the evenings. Yin Yang was in Basantapur Chowk, opposite the old palace with its tall tower. It was a popular joint, always packed, and a large metal yin-yang sign welcomed customers at the entrance. The reaction to Sofi's Nepali name was initially confusion: people thought it was an Italian name. Once understanding dawned, some chose to mock her, some told her it was a put-on. "Sounds phony," an English girl said.

A bald, muscular man who worked at the American embassy—he was rumored to be a spy with the CIA—was argumentative. One day over beers in Yin Yang he asked what she hoped to accomplish by rejecting her American identity.

"I just love this country," she said. A former Marine, this man's biceps were pronounced as his elbows rested on the table. Every now and then, he clenched his fist so that his muscles bulged more. He was a contrast to the thin, weak-looking men in long shirts around them. He was not well liked among the regulars here, as he was loud and aggressive. "Establishment," they called him, but he appeared to relish frequenting Yin Yang, and occasionally he bought food and drinks for everyone at his table.

"What is wrong with you?" he asked, then paused to

accept the chillum someone passed on from the next table. There were low tables scattered throughout Yin Yang, where customers, both local youth and hippies, sat on the floor. He took a deep drag and offered it to Sofi, who shook her head. She tried to recall how she ended up with him: She had smoked some ganja in her room, then had meandered through the streets, stopping for coffee in the Cosmopolitan, which was on the second floor with windows that overlooked the Basantapur area. She'd watched peddlers try to sell their small trinkets to cash-strapped hippies, followed the movements of a cow with a bell hanging from its neck. A lone dog trotted by, briefly paused for some thinking, then resumed his gait. Across the square, she saw people in the small windows of the tall temple whose name she couldn't remember.

She didn't recall how long she sat at the window of the Cosmopolitan—Stevie Nicks's raspy voice on the stereo filled her consciousness—then she was downstairs and now in Yin Yang with the bald man. *He's a drag*, she kept thinking about him—Mac? Mitt?—and there was no reason why she should allow herself to be bullied by him. She looked around the room. A low hum rose from the other conversations, occasionally punctuated by laughter. Today no one she knew was here.

"Sofi," Mac or Mitt said with emphasis. He reached out to grab her hands across the table. "You need to get a grip on yourself."

"My name is Sukumari, man," she said. She tried to pry her hands away, but his fingers were thick as cucumbers.

"I will not call you Shuka—whatever." He lowered his voice, part threat, part caress. "I like your real name. Sofi. It's American, with a European flavor. You should be proud of your heritage. Why are you so bent on going native on us?"

"What is it to you what I do?" she asked, helpless and angry. "Stop trying to be my father, dude."

Not letting her hand go, he stared at her. "Sofi, Sofi, what should I do with you?" He arose and came over to her side and slid next to her, his body quickly pressed against hers. She looked around to see if she could call anyone she knew. She was familiar with the owner, but today he wasn't around. Mac or Mitt put his arms around her and clasped her tight. "I can't simply let you waste away your life among these—these filthy—wastes of humanity." By now he was whispering in her ear. She felt his hot breath and a quick lick on her earlobe. No one in Yin Yang was paying attention to them. A cloud of smoke twirled in the room—a pungent mixture of hash and thick incense. A couple slowly swayed to Cat Stevens in the middle of the room, the girl's hair hiding her face. A bearded man was slouched against the wall in the corner, eyes closed, his mouth half open. A uniformed waiter was standing in the corner, looking bored.

Sofi was caught in the man's grip, and there was nothing she could do. Inwardly she cried out for Sahuni, and the fact that she didn't think of her mother in Coshocton made her realize how far she'd traveled from who she was. She was not even a part of this— Yin Yang's—world anymore. These people were lost in a Shangri-la that didn't exist.

"I'm going to fuck you today," Mac or Mitt whispered. He pulled her up with his arm, threw some money on the table for their beer, and nudged her out of the restaurant. In the glaring sunlight outside, he sniffed her and said, "You've even begun to smell like a Nepali." He hailed a taxi and gently pushed her in. "Maharajgunj," he told the taxi driver, then spoke to him in rapid Nepali. Sofi caught the word *hippie* and something that sounded like *chick* but was not an English word, she could tell. It sounded more like *chickney*. The driver grinned at her in the rearview mirror.

Mac or Mitt lived near the embassy in a gated house with two Nepali servants, young, good-looking, soft-faced boys. As he took her to his room, she knew that these boys were a part of his personal harem.

She trudged back to Freak Street in a daze that night, her hair in disarray and her clothes smelling of sex. *It's rape.* This thought crossed her mind, but she wasn't sure it actually was. At any point in the evening she could have left: when Mac or Mitt began talking to her aggressively in Yin Yang, when he slid over to her seat, when they stood to leave that hashish den, even when the taxi stopped in front of his house opposite the embassy. But she hadn't left. When he pulled down her underwear and mounted her and began to rock to and fro, she swayed with his rhythm, as though urging him on. She gasped and whimpered and cried out; she might even have had an orgasm.

But she knew that she'd gone along with Mac or Mitt

only because she wanted to be done with it. Quickly. She wanted Sofi to be a thing of her past.

SUKUMARI

She didn't emerge from her room for three days. She didn't smoke. In fact, she made a vow that she was not going to smoke again. It was all this nonstop smoking that was screwing with her mind.

Sahuni was worried. Every few hours she rapped on Sukumari's door. "Suku, Suku, what is going on? Are you ill?"

The son translated, "Suku, Suku, health okay?"

On the second day of Sukumari's self-imprisonment, Sahuni and her son heard a faint answer to their queries. "I am fine," she said. "I just need to rest."

The son translated for his mother, and Sahuni said, "A crazy girl she is. She hasn't eaten for days."

But on the third morning, Sukumari did come down, her hair pulled back in a tight ponytail, her eyes thoughtful, unsmiling. She wore a dhoti given to her by Sahuni a while back, one she hadn't worn until now.

"La hera," Sahuni said. "She looks like a pukka Nepali girl now. Only the skin is white. You must be hungry! What happened to you? Did someone do something to you? Bad news from home?"

Sukumari put her head on Sahuni's shoulder, which was slightly awkward as she was half a foot taller than Sahuni.

"Ke bhayo?" Sahuni asked. "What is wrong with my chhori? Everything all right?"

Tears streamed down Sukumari's face, and Sahuni wiped it. She made Sukumari sit at a table in the eatery. "What would my chhori like to eat? You must eat something. Otherwise you can't go."

"Sahuni," Sukumari said. "Ma maas ko bara khanccha."

Sahuni laughed. "It makes me so happy to hear my chhori speak Nepali. But you are my daughter now, so what is this 'Sahuni, Sahuni' business? Am I still a shopkeeper to you? You have to address me as Ma."

"Ma," Sukumari said, unable to stop her tears. "Maas ko bara khanchha."

So Ma cooked the lentil fritters for Sukumari, who ate them hungrily. The boy came from inside the sleeping quarters, and he started laughing.

"Idiot!" Ma said. "What's so funny?"

The boy pointed at Sukumari. "She! She's funny! Look at her. She a kuiriney hippie, but she thinks she's Nepali." He did a brief dance and sang, "I am a kuiriney hippie keti, but I like to act Nepali."

Both Sukumari and Ma laughed. The boy, whose name was Rajesh but who called himself Rajesh Khanna after the screen superstar, rubbed his belly and said, "I'm hungry, Ma. What are you cooking?"

"This is maas ko bara for your sister." Ma asked Sukumari to hold out her plate for more, but as soon as she ladled a steaming bara onto Sukumari's plate, Rajesh Khanna snatched it and ran out the door.

"Stop! Thief!" Sukumari shouted in English and chased after him. Speedily, Rajesh Khanna ran through the alley,

and with equal vigor Sukumari chased him, the boy bit-
ing on the bara whenever he could. The boy took a left on
the main street, toward Basantapur, and the early morning
shoppers looked at the duo in amazement: a chubby Nepali
boy being hotly and breathlessly pursued by a kuiriney
wearing a stay-at-home dhoti and shouting, alternatively in
English and Nepali, "Thief! Thief! Chor!"

Sukumari avoided Freak Street. She mentally divided the
neighborhood into Freak Street, where all the hippies and
the tourists hung out, and Jhonchhe, which was a little bit
inside and where she lived with Ma and Baba and Rajesh
Khanna. This was not accurate, she knew, because the main
street that opened to the chowk and the tower, was actually Jhonchhe in the Newari language. But the geographical
division inside her own mind provided her some solace.
She practiced saying "Jhonchhe" with determination until
it stopped sounding odd, and the locals no longer looked at
her in confusion. When she had to go to the Maru Ganesh
vegetable market, she took a circuitous route through Jai-
sedeval and avoided Freak Street. If she encountered tourists
or hippies, she kept her gaze averted, or didn't smile if her
eyes met theirs. When she needed to go to New Road or
Indrachowk, she circled around through Pako.

One day a former Yin Yang friend meandered into her
path near where she lived. James from Minneapolis had
spent a few months in jail in Indonesia for smuggling drugs
and had now opened up a chakra studio in Thamel. He was
an incredibly thin man, with shoulder blades that jutted

out of the loose kurta he wore. He was startled to run into her, and although she tried to pretend that she hadn't seen him, he leaped in front of her, blocked her path, and exclaimed, "Sofi! Sofi! Man, what happened to you?" And he laughed, slapping his thighs and hooting.

"Nothing happened to me," she said in a clipped voice.

"But . . . but . . ." James searched for words.

"And you know very well that my name is Sukumari now."

James turned somber. "I'm sorry, I apologize. I shouldn't be laughing, but dude, this is a drastic change."

Sukumari didn't want the attention on herself, so she asked him how his chakra work was going, and the two chatted about James's "healing" practice.

"You should come by," James said. "I'll align your chakra, man. I have some good bud from Thailand."

"I no longer smoke." She had fought off the urges. There were days when she would have killed for a high, but she reminded herself that she was no longer Sofi, reminded herself of what happened to Sofi with Mac or Mitt, and gradually, over days, her cravings diminished. Whenever she experienced cravings, she popped a betel nut into her mouth, which Ma also relished and chewed on all day.

James seemed about to say something, but changed his mind. "You live around here somewhere, don't you?"

Sukumari became anxious that he might invite himself to her place, so she said that she was now living and teaching in a school in Jawalakhel.

"But I heard that you are living above that restaurant."

"I gotta go," Sukumari said, and moved away from him.

She slipped into an alley, then took narrower alleys until she was out of his reach.

The encounter with James left her depressed. It was as though her stupid past was determined not to leave her, no matter how hard she tried to leave it. She thought about her parents back in Coshocton—the name of her hometown sounded even stranger to her now, like the name of a distant galaxy. Her mother must be wondering what had happened to her. Sukumari hadn't been to the post office in Dhara-hara to send her a postcard for weeks now. Her mother was not the worrying kind; one of her favorite songs was, "Que sera sera, whatever will be will be." She began humming it once she began on her gin and tonic every afternoon, a ritual that lasted late into the night. When he was not with his patients, Sukumari's father spent most of his time on his boat on Lake Erie.

The memories of her parents came to Sukumari as though they were characters from a novel set in a remote culture. When Rajesh Khanna plied her with questions about America, she was increasingly unable, and often unwilling, to answer them. It felt like such a long time ago since she'd left America, even though it'd only been about six months since she'd boarded the plane to Amsterdam from Detroit. She now found her previous name odd, and when she whispered it to herself, it sounded like the name of a furniture brand. She tried to remember what her childhood was like, but all she saw was a blonde girl whose emotions and concerns appeared unreal to her.

• • •

Ma had her move into the room below where the family slept and lived. The room was next to the eatery and was the same size as her previous room, except upstairs it had been only Sofi, and downstairs in the same space it was the four of them: Ma, Baba, Rajesh Khanna, and now Sukumari. She had wanted to continue living upstairs so she could pay Ma the monthly rent. But Ma said that Sukumari was her daughter now, so she couldn't accept lodging expenses from her. "It's simply not done in our society." Ma was adamant about this, so finally one day Sukumari moved downstairs, fully recognizing that she was adding to the cramped living conditions below. But it would also mean that Ma would be able to rent the upstairs room to someone else, and there was solace in that.

Ma put down a mattress next to their existing mattress on the floor, and now the four of them slept together, the two males at the ends and the females in the middle. Rajesh Khanna was delighted to be sleeping with Sukumari nearby but was not happy when Sukumari tickled him in the morning to wake him up.

Sukumari's Nepali gradually improved; now she was able to converse haltingly with Ma without Rajesh Khanna's help. The mother and the daughter, when the restaurant closed in the afternoon, talked for long hours. Ma told her stories about her past, her own mother who had passed away when she was a young girl, how her father brought in a stepmother who mistreated Ma and her siblings. Ma especially talked at length of one of her sisters, the oldest one, now dead, who had remained strong and protective while they lived under the abuse of their stepmother. Ma shed a few tears, and Sukumari wiped them away. "It's very hard for me to let go of people I love," Ma said. "And now that I have a daughter in you, I pray that nothing will keep us apart. I want to take care of you, I want to see you get married, I want to hold your babies and play with them."

Sukumari blushed.

"What?" Ma said. "Don't think that you'll be able to avoid the marriage question for long. No daughter of mine will remain a budhi kanya."

"Budhi kanya?"

It look a while for Ma to get the concept of "old virgin" across to Sukumari, who laughed once she understood. But she secretly cherished the idea of remaining an old maid in Ma's house. In this culture, old people stayed with their children and often were taken care of and loved, and she looked forward to spending time with Ma and Baba as they aged, making sure that her brother Rajesh Khanna became college educated and married a nice girl from a good family. She was already beginning to think like a Nepali, but she couldn't imagine herself getting married and going to live in her husband's house, living apart from Ma and Baba and Rajesh Khanna. This was her home now, this small house in this narrow alley in Jhonchhe. She had not known that this type of happiness was even possible, this deep belonging. She was already twice removed—twice reincarnated! There was the Sofi who grew up sulkily in Coshocton, then the carefree hippie Sofi who lived in a cloud of smoke in Yin Yang, who pumped her body full of acid and hash, and now the clean Sukumari who spoke Nepali and performed household chores with Ma and tutored Rajesh Khanna in English and served customers chhoila and kachila and raksi. It was as though she had moved to a space that made her former lives empty and superficial, like they were fascinating but ultimately useless dreams.

The guest who ended up moving into Sofi's previous room was not a hippie but a Nepali man by the name of Manandhar. Sukumari soon found out that it was not his first name but his last, that somehow he had always been called Manandhar. He was a relative of Ma, her aunt's sister-in-law's brother, and he had returned to the city after working on a highway in the east. "I don't like him one bit," Ma said. "But what to do? He's a relative, and he says he wants to stay close to the family as he builds a house in the city."

"So he's staying for free?"

"I told him that I couldn't take him because that room is only for foreigners, and that I couldn't charge rent to a relative, but he has insisted on paying rent. And he's insisted on paying me more than the regular rent."

"Eh, ramro!" Sukumari exclaimed. It was a favorite word of hers now, *ramro*—good, beautiful, nice—as it bestowed approval on everything.

"I don't know, Suku. I bet you it's not honest money. I bet you that man didn't work honestly wherever he was. The sooner he leaves this place, the happier I'll be."

Manandhar came down to eat twice a day: in the morning when the family ate in the eatery, and in the evening with the customers. Ma served him with great strain on her face. He was polite, didn't speak much except to say a word or two to Rajesh Khanna, and quickly returned upstairs. He barely acknowledged Sukumari. He appeared aware of Ma's disapproval of him. Most of the time he was not in his room, but occasionally Sukumari saw him smoking a cigarette at the top of the staircase, gazing into the distance. It was hard to tell how old he was. Judging from his years of work on the highway, he should have been in his early thirties, yet he appeared younger, with a lock of hair boyishly covering his forehead that he didn't bother to brush back.

Rajesh Khanna brought the news one morning that Manandhar was gravely ill. The boy said he had gone upstairs for something (Sukumari suspected that the man gave him money for candy) and found him hacking and coughing and delirious.

"I guess I should go up," Ma said. It was the day of the Shivaratri festival, and she had just bathed and put on fresh clothes to visit the Pashupatinath temple.

"Ma, why don't I go up so you can go to the temple?" Sukumari said.

Ma didn't think it was a good idea, but Sukumari said that it'd be okay.

"All right," Ma said. "Just see what's wrong with him, and maybe take him some soup. Don't linger for too long."

After Ma left, Sukumari went up and gingerly opened the door, wishing that Rajesh Khanna had accompanied her and not disappeared to play with his friends. Manandhar was lying in bed, his head propped up on the pillow behind him. His eyes were squeezed shut, and his face was red. He didn't show awareness at her entry, but when she sat next to him, a soft moan escaped his lips.

"Ke bhayo?" Sukumari asked, and realized how silly it was to ask what had happened to a feverishly ill man. So, she asked a question that sounded more logical. "Are you hungry?"

Manandhar opened his eyes, only slightly, and a word escaped his lips that she took to mean *paani*.

She found a jug with water on the table that was against the window, but it was old water, with a fly floating on the surface. "One minute," she said and, suddenly hot and in a hurry, ran down to the kitchen, where she poured some water from the large gagro into a jug, then had a second thought, and boiled that water before she took it up. But the water was too hot, so she blew on it to cool it, then fed it to him with a spoon.

Still delirious, he called her "Auntie," obviously thinking she was Ma. She touched his forehead: he was burning. She didn't have a thermometer on her, and she wasn't sure there was one downstairs, but she knew that she needed to administer cold presses on him immediately. She fetched some cold water along with a handkerchief and applied the wetted handkerchief to his forehead until his body began to cool. When he fell asleep, she went down to make soup.

When she came back up, he was sitting up, propped against the pillow. "Where is Auntie?" he asked weakly.

"She has gone to Pashupatinath for Shivaratri. You must be hungry, so I brought some soup."

She set the bowl of soup on the floor, hoping he'd pick it up. When he didn't, she said, "You should have the soup. It'll make you feel better."

He winced as he shifted; it was clear that even sitting up was hard for him, and after a while he started breathing heavily.

"Shall I feed you?" she asked.

He closed his eyes.

She sat near the bed and began to feed him the soup with a spoon. "La, aan gara!" she commanded him to open his mouth, like she'd seen Ma command Rajesh Khanna, who was still fed by his mother. Sukumari found it endearing how in this culture even kids who were seven or eight years old were fed by their mothers. On the street Sukumari frequently stopped to observe mothers feeding their children in the sun, asking them to do "aan" and inserting dal-bhat into their wide mouths. In the US, even as early as elementary school, she had to come home and make her own sandwiches. On those days her mother was too tired or drunk (or both) to cook dinner, Sofi would find a note posted on the fridge: *Fend for yourself.*

It occurred to Sukumari now that it was more about the attention than about the food.

In between feeding Manandhar, she wiped his chin with the end of her dhoti. When he didn't open his lips, she gently coaxed him. He soon became tired of eating and closed his eyes, falling into a somnambulant state. Yet his right hand clasped hers, unwilling to let her go. She watched his face. He had a mustache, like many Nepali men, and a stubble of beard because he hadn't shaved recently. His eyebrows were thick (*bushy*, she thought), and yet he had a long, slender face. His lips, even in sickness, were rosy and full. Before she knew what was happening, she leaned over and kissed him. She quickly unclasped his hand and stood, holding her breath to see if he'd open his eyes. When he didn't, she exited the room.

Once downstairs, to calm herself she began to tidy up the restaurant, which she usually did after the morning customers left. *I could use a hit right now.* This thought possessed her for about ten seconds with an aggression that made her tremble a bit. She closed her eyes and squashed the thought—she had no intentions of bringing back Sofi—and swept the floor of the shop with renewed ferocity.

Ma returned in the early afternoon, sweating. It was an unusually warm day for February, she said, and the crowd at the temple was large beyond belief. The line to get a darshan of shivalinga crawled at a snail's pace, she complained. She put the prasad tika on Sukumari's forehead, inquired about Manandhar. Sukumari told her about how she'd nursed him.

"Now I guess we're expected to bring him back to health?" Ma said.

"He's very sick, Ma."

Reluctantly Ma went up, then returned in about half an hour and busied herself in the sleeping quarters. After some time, Sukumari approached her and asked, "How is he, Ma?"

"He still has a fever. If he doesn't get better by evening, I'll go fetch the compounder."

Manandhar didn't get better by evening, and Ma, muttering, went to get the compounder. Throughout the time that the compounder and Ma were upstairs, Sukumari stayed below. She'd wanted to go up with them, but had received a warning glance from Ma. Her arms wrapped around herself, Sukumari waited anxiously for them to come down. She didn't understand her emotions. As Sofi she had known enough men in her life, slept with several of them at Oberlin, then throughout her travels, and now she was acting like a truly Nepali girl, untouched, with a tender heart.

"No need for you to go upstairs now," Ma told her after the compounder left with his medicine bag. The compounder had given Manandhar, who was diagnosed as having caught the flu, an injection and some medicines. "He'll be fine now, so no need to administer to him." There was a hint of warning in her voice. Did Ma have sensors? Did she know the pleasurable thoughts that were cruising through Sukumari's mind when she focused on Manandhar?

The next morning when Ma wasn't home, Sukumari sneaked upstairs, her heart thudding. His eyes were closed, but he opened them when he heard her enter. "Sukumari," he whispered when she went to him. Her name sounded good on his lips—the lips she'd kissed. His eyes, she thought, conveyed to her that he knew what she'd done.

"Come, sit here," he said, patting the floor beside him.

"I came to check how you were."

"I'll be better once you sit here with me."

She sat next to him, and his hand searched for hers, found it, and clasped it. "I was sure I was dying."

"You shouldn't say such things."

"Are you from America?"

"Ma Nepali keti."

He observed her. He was not afraid to simply keep looking, and she couldn't counter his gaze, so she looked down. When she glanced up again, she noticed how full and rosy his lips were. "Yes, you are a Nepali," he said. "So beautiful. So . . ." His finger reached her face and stroked it. "So—fair and angel-like." He fingered her hair. "Like gold."

Whenever an opportunity presented itself, Sukumari crept upstairs to be with Manandhar. It took him another week to recover fully, but by the end of that week they had already made love. It had startled her, the quickness with which she'd allowed it. She'd never experienced anything this intense. It was as if all the light of this world had gathered to bathe them together. With Manandhar she couldn't separate her body from her emotions, couldn't separate their limb-to-limb entanglements from the cry that seemed to emanate from her depth. Sukumari was reminded of the city temples that showed carvings of couples in various carnal positions, in a union that was both physical and spiritual, a spiritual merging. She understood this art now, further convincing her that she was indeed Sukumari who belonged to this culture, this thinking, this worldview.

One day as she was tiptoeing down the stairs from

Manandhar's room, she was alarmed to find Ma at the bottom, glaring at her. It was inevitable: she was actually surprised at how she'd been able to hide her liaison with Manandhar from Ma for weeks. She'd tried to be very discreet, had even acted dismissively when Manandhar's name had come up, as though she shared Ma's disapproval of him.

A big argument ensued, her first fight with Ma and her first fight entirely in the Nepali language. Luckily the quarrel took place behind closed doors in the sleeping quarters below, so Manandhar couldn't hear what was being said. Ma demanded to know what Sukumari was doing in Manandhar's room. At first Sukumari denied anything was happening. "I was only checking on him to see if he needed anything," she repeatedly said, her face red with shame. Had her American mother in Coshocton confronted her like this, Sofi would have lashed out, told her to fuck off.

"I know all about it," Ma said. "Rajesh saw you two." Ma was the only one who refused to call her son Rajesh Khanna. He didn't need to be anyone else, movie star or sweeper, she said.

Gradually, in tears, Sukumari admitted that she and Manandhar were in love. She used the Nepali word *prem*, which was slightly formal.

"Prem?" Ma asked. "How can you be in love with someone in two weeks?"

"I know what I feel, Ma."

"That bastard! I knew he'd pull a stunt like this."

"Ma, he didn't do anything!"

But Ma was already out of the room and bounding up the stairs.

Sukumari sat in the sleeping quarters. Rajesh Khanna approached her fearfully. "I didn't want to tell Ma anything, didi, but she slapped me."

"You scoundrel!" Sukumari twisted his ear, then, seeing that he was in tears, embraced him. "What did you see?" she whispered.

"You and Manandhar dai, in bed, kissing."

"Okay, okay."

Ma came down in about fifteen minutes, but she refused to speak to Sukumari and began sweeping the eatery. Sukumari addressed her a couple of times, but Ma didn't look at her, and with a helpless sigh, Sukumari sat in front of the stove to cook. That evening the shop was especially busy, and Sukumari kept hoping that Manandhar would come down to eat. But he didn't. After the shop closed, she considered going up, but it was too risky. Ma's anger hadn't subsided; she still refused to look at Sukumari.

That night, squeezed between Ma's broad back and Rajesh Khanna's scrawny body, Sukumari wondered whether Manandhar, who was right above the ceiling, was pining for her like she was for him. She recalled their sweat-filled lovemaking—it was hot upstairs in his room—and felt an arousal that was clearly inappropriate with Ma and Rajesh Khanna next to her. Yet her hand danced down to her belly. She remembered Manandhar's breath in her ear. "Mero gori Sukumari," he called her. *My fair virgin.*

She kept her hand on her belly. There was something

growing inside her, a seed of some sort, deep in her stomach. Manandhar's seed, she was sure of it.

The next morning when she went up, Manandhar's room was empty. Panicked, she informed Ma, who refused to meet her gaze. Tears came to Sukumari's eyes. "Why did you do it?" she asked. "Don't you love me anymore?"

Ma finally stopped sweeping to look at her. "I love you more than a girl born out of my own womb."

"I bet you if I was your real daughter, you wouldn't have betrayed me."

A flicker of something passed through Ma's eyes, a wounding, which was exactly what Sukumari wanted. She couldn't help what came out of her mouth next: "You did this because you are not my real mother."

Ma dropped the broom on the floor and walked out of the restaurant into the alley. Rajesh Khanna, who had been watching the entire exchange, asked, "Where is Ma going? Now who is going to open the shop?" He turned to Sukumari for answers, but Sukumari silently went in to fetch her purse. Baba was sitting on the bed, his shawl wrapped around him even though it wasn't cold, and he waved Sukumari over. He was usually bedridden, and his speech had slowed down the past month or so. "Ke bhayo?" he asked. "Ama chhori kina jhagada gareko? Jhagada garnu hunna."

She found herself unable to speak to Baba, so she picked up her bag, which had her sunglasses, some money, a lipstick, and a comb, and she left the house.

•   •   •

She needed to find Manandhar. Where could he be? She knew he didn't have any friends in the city—he had told her so. All of his friends had scattered, he'd said, to different parts of the country or even abroad. "You're my only friend here, my kuiriney." She had liked the idea of being his only friend. She, too, didn't have any friends anymore.

She remembered a name Manandhar had mentioned, Ramesh Khatry, a contractor he knew from the east who had invited him to live with him. "He has a big house in Baneswor," Manandhar had said, "but now I have my kuiriney here, and I don't want to leave her."

In Baneswor it was not hard to locate Ramesh Khatry's house. He was a well-known figure, "moneyed," as a man at the nearby shop where she inquired told her in a tone of disapproval. The house was gated, with a guard who asked her what her business was. She told him she was looking for Manandhar. The guard spoke on the phone, and shortly Manandhar appeared at the balcony, looking sleepy. When he saw her, he told the guard to send her up.

A large, shaggy dog came sniffing as she entered the front door, frightening her, but she squelched her fear and climbed the stairs. Manandhar was lying on a sheetless mattress on the floor upstairs. The room was bare except for the mattress and a Bruce Lee poster on the wall, the one with finger scratches on the actor's tummy. The entire house felt kind of big and . . . empty. "Hello, my love," Manandhar said in English, smiling at her as she stood in the doorway. A bottle of vodka was next to the bed.

"I am sorry for what Ma said to you." Sukumari went and sat with him in the bed, leaning against him.

"Poor Auntie. She's so wrapped up in her tiny world." He was slurring. The vodka bottle was nearly empty. "Her little shop, her small family, her little Jhonchhe. I can only wish the best for her."

She lay her head on his lap. "I will persuade Ma. Once her anger dies down, she'll listen to me."

He stroked her head. "And what will my kuiriney hippie say to her ma?"

"I'll tell her that you and I are meant to be together, that we want to—" She regarded his face, his glassy eyes, the trace of a smile on his luscious lips. He was waiting for her to complete her sentence. "I'll tell her that we want to be together, that I want you back in Jhonchhe, in that room upstairs."

He continued to smile.

"I'll persuade her to allow me to live with you upstairs."

"And we can pretend we're in America. In Coshi . . . Cosho . . . in Kashikoton." He chuckled.

"I no longer think about America."

"Why don't you think about America?" Manandhar asked. "Everyone thinks about America. New York, 'Hotel California,' Robert Redford, *Saturday Night Fever*." He finished drinking the remainder of the vodka, then said, "You really think your ma will allow you to live with me?"

"Maybe not immediately, but given time, I can persuade her. She has a soft heart when it comes to me."

A look of mischief passed over his face.

"Manandhar!" she said. "It's true. She loves me. I am her chhori!"

"Do you really believe that? Do you really, really, really believe that you are her daughter?"

"My name is Sukumari. I am born and raised in Jhonchhe. I am Ma's daughter. I have a brother named Rajesh Khanna."

"You must be a white pari who's dropped down from heaven." He extracted a cigarette from its pack and lit it. He blew the smoke to the ceiling and said, "There can't be any talk of me returning to Jhonchhe now."

"Why not?"

"Khatry wants me to live here. I had been planning on moving anyway, even before Auntie discovered our little thing."

For a moment she couldn't speak. Then she said softly, "You never said that you were thinking about leaving. You said we were meant to be together."

He smoked.

"So," she said. Her throat had filled up, and she eyed the vodka bottle, wishing there was a mouthful left for her to swallow, even though she'd never been too fond of alcohol, especially hard liquor.

"Stay with me here," Manandhar said, waving his arm to indicate the large room.

Footsteps sounded on the stairs. Then, a loud voice boomed in English, "So the guard tells me we have a special American guest." Khatry appeared at the door, carrying a briefcase. He was a short, stocky man in a safari suit. He took off his shoes at the door, placed them neatly to the side, and entered. He sat next to Sukumari and Manandhar with an ease that suggested that he'd known both of them for ages. "Sukumari," he said. "Beautiful name, beautiful name. The delicate virgin."

"Ramesh is an old friend of mine," Manandhar said, waving this cigarette.

"You said you had no friends in the city," Sukumari said.

"I'm his friend, but only when he needs me," Khatry said. "Otherwise, I'm his servant—no, no, what's the word? A butler."

"No, he's Richie Rich, and I'm his butler Cadbury," Manandhar said.

Khatry opened his briefcase and removed a plastic bag filled with chunks of hash. "Now this is a friend that'll never betray you." He took out a few cigarettes from Manandhar's pack and with expert fingers emptied them of their tobacco. Quickly he began stuffing them with the hash. Its smell was sharp, dangerous. "Sukumari, are you here to live with us?"

"I will return to Jhonchhe shortly."

Khatry spread his arms wide. "Why? I have plenty of space here." He paused stuffing the cigarettes and flung open his suitcase. "And plenty of bread." The suitcase was filled with cash. "Isn't that what you hippies call money? Bread? Pauroti."

Manandhar laughed. Khatry finished rolling, and handed a cigarette to Manandhar, who took it, and another to Sukumari, who refused.

"Arre!" Khatry said. "What's wrong? This is the best stuff around. From the mountains of Pakistan."

"I don't smoke."

"I thought all hippies smoked."

"I am not a hippie."

Khatry smiled a kind, repentant smile, then stroked her bare arms and said, "Of course, you are our delicate Nepali virgin girl. Sukumari."

Smoke filled the room, occupying every available space, reminding her so much of Yin Yang, where the music on the stereo always sounded like it was part of her own consciousness—Neil Young, Cat Stevens, Janis Joplin. Something was beginning to vibrate inside her, as though a bone in her chest was on its way to becoming loose. She closed her eyes. The hash smelled good, really good. *But I won't, I won't*, she told herself.

She felt Manandhar's face near hers, and, her eyes still closed as she parted her lips to receive his kiss, he injected her with a dollop of smoke he'd been holding in his mouth. Before she knew what was happening, she'd swallowed more than half of it. The sweetish taste of the hashish seeped into her throat, her gullet, and sputtering, she was about to protest when his lips sealed hers. And she just let him, just let him kiss because it seemed to her that this was what she'd been missing all along.

Manandhar placed the joint to her lips, and she sucked on it, thinking, *Only this time, it won't hurt, just once, just today, then once I return to Jhonchhe, everything will be all right. Ma, I miss you, Ma, I swear I won't do it again, Ma, I'm sorry, Ma.* And she sucked on the joint deeply so it went straight to her belly, to her solar plexus, her chakra. *I'll have James, poor, sweet hippie, do chakra work on me so that I am perfectly aligned, so I am clearheaded, so I won't fall into this trap again. A trap! A trap!* Yes, this was a trap. Some of the earlier hurt had now dissolved, but there was still something, a pit of melancholy into which she'd fallen.

"So fair, isn't she?" It was Ramesh Khatry's voice. He was lying next to her, running his finger gently on the surface of her arm. "Like cream, like milk. Dudh jasto gori."

Her throat was parched, so when Manandhar lifted her head a bit and put a bottle to her mouth, she thought it was water and drank, but it was vodka. Where did it come from? Did Khatry's briefcase have more surprises?

Khatry was speaking to her, in a soft voice from far away. "Delicate virgin, delicate virgin, where are you? Are you with me, angel? Are you here on this earth?"

Someone laughed. It could have been Manandhar, or it could have been her. The lap on which her head rested now was smaller: Khatry's lap. She forced her eyes open. Manandhar wasn't in the room. But he was in her mind, wasn't he? He was in her soul. Her soul.

Ramesh Khatry didn't have any shirt on. His chest was like a jungle, and she could see each hair and thought she could even detect each hair follicle. *It's a jungle out there—* this thought, in the shape of a grinning monkey, floated by lazily through her consciousness.

Ramesh Khatry leaned over her, his moving mouth inches above hers. "I have never tasted a kuiriney before," he was saying.

Sukumari sat in Cosmopolitan restaurant, watching the Basantapur chowk. Her mind was still dull from last night's smoking and drinking. She didn't recall how she got to Basantapur; she remembered an altercation with the guard at Khatry's place because he was trying to prevent her from leaving. Then the next thing she knew, she was in Freak Street in the early hours of the morning, even before the sun was out. A fog had enveloped the area. She must have vomited once or twice by the side of the road, but she didn't return to Ma. She wandered around the Durbar Square area, took a small nap in the Kasthamandap temple, where an old man was playing the harmonium and singing some hymns.

Around eight o'clock, she trudged back toward Jhonchhe, but she was too weepy to return home, so she walked up to the Cosmopolitan. She was aware of how she must have appeared to the man who had just opened the restaurant: smelling of pot, her hair uncombed, her face unwashed, wandering through life in a daze, like any other hippie who passed through Freak Street on a journey from somewhere to somewhere.

DREAMING OF GHANA

PART I

He'd begun to dream about Ghana, of all places. When awake, he rarely thought about Africa, and the only time the continent intruded upon his consciousness was when, wrapped inside his large, unwieldy blanket, he watched television in the evening and pushed the buttons on the remote. There was always someone on the screen, often a white person, often with a beard and in khaki clothes, who crouched next to a dark child with a distended stomach and spoke urgently about nourishment and schooling.

Aakash changed the channel to something more palatable, often a Bollywood dance with men and women in bright clothes thrusting their hips at the camera. He watched with fascination, not particularly enjoying the performance—they were all the same, the hero at the front with a grin, the heroine's eyes kohl rimmed and yearning—but finding in the gyrations and the pivots and the synchronized movements a dumb pleasure. He didn't have to *think* when he watched these movie routines, whereas the plea for Africa got his mind spinning about inequalities and poverty and child labor and colonialism and whatnot.

But Ghana? What did he know about Ghana? Nothing. To him one African country was the same as another, except for South Africa, which he knew to be at the southern tip of the continent and also as the country that had imprisoned Nelson Mandela for twenty-seven years. But Aakash didn't know where Ghana was, in the south close to Mandela country, or in the middle, where he imagined the Sahara desert was (or was it Kalahari?), or to the north, near the Arab countries (he knew the north was more Arab; he wasn't a complete dunce when it came to geography). There was a map somewhere on his bookshelf, buried under a stack of books, or folded inside a news magazine, that showed a rough sketch of the world, and he'd probably be able to discover Ghana in there. But what good would that do?

Every morning he lazed around in bed, drinking the steady cups of tea brought to his room by Danny, who lived in the neighborhood and came every morning to help his mother. Then it was time for the morning meal. Even as he ate downstairs in the dining room, he wrapped his mammoth blanket around himself and endured cold stares from his father and mild chastisement from his mother, who said that a young man like him ought to be up at dawn, exercise, take a shower, be energetic and fresh. His mother repeated the word: *fresh*. Aakash ate hurriedly, then went up to his room, which had an attached bathroom, and showered (or not, depending upon his mood), changed, and left for the office.

He worked for a tourist magazine, *Travelite*, in the heart of the city, in New Road, writing articles describing the sightseeing spots in the country. The magazine was handed out to the tourists at the airport as soon as they emerged from baggage claim. Its pages extolled the cold lakes up in the mountains; the airplane ride that took passengers so close to the Everest that they could glimpse their faces on its icy surface, sometimes even observe a tight line of mountaineers on their way to the summit; the lakhey dance that had drunken men wearing colorful masks prancing and cavorting through the city's lanes; the opulent hotel from where one could see spectacular sunrises that painted pink the white mountain summits, which looked like blushing brides. Aakash was sick of working at the magazine—the exaggerations, the fantasies, sometimes the outright false information—all in the name of tourism.

Just the day before, he'd written about a jungle lodge camp that used elephants rescued from the circus. Tourists rode the elephants to venture deep into the forests, where they spotted tigers, warthogs, the many-antlered deer, the lazy rhino, the crocodile, and such. All of it was true, except for the part about the elephants being rescued from the circus. Why he thought of inserting that bit of lie, Aakash didn't know. He wasn't instructed by anyone to do so—not by the chief editor, who mostly sat in his office and drank tea, and certainly not by the associate editor, who had a goatee and foul breath. Did Aakash conceive that falsehood because he figured it'd attract the bleeding-heart tourists? He didn't recall consciously thinking along those lines, but then, his job was to entice the tourists into visiting these places.

I'm an unconscious liar, Aakash thought, at once humored and ashamed by this realization. When he'd showed the article on the jungle lodge to his associate editor, he'd hoped that the man would mildly rebuke him for the falsity. But the editor's eyes briefly lingered on the word *circus* before he moved on to read the rest. "It's all right," the associate editor said, breathing foully at Aakash.

After work Aakash went to restaurants in Durbar Marg or Thamel to spend time with his friend Rahul. Rahul came from a rich family and didn't work; he smoked Marlboro cigarettes all day and drank his Black Label whiskey, sometimes all day.

When Aakash told his friend about his Ghana dreams, Rahul said, "Maybe you were an African in your past life."

That day they were in Haawa, on the upstairs terrace that overlooked Durbar Marg with its overpriced shops.

Aakash laughed. "Yes, I can see myself in the jungles, carrying a spear and chasing after an elephant."

"What? You think all Africans are junglees? There are cities in Africa. Nairobi. Johannesburg. Mogadishu. Harare." Rahul had raised his voice, probably to impress a group of girls, English speaking and silky haired, at the next table.

Aakash felt slightly ashamed at what he'd said, so he told Rahul, "I know there are cities. I was only joking. And what about past lives? You believe in that nonsense?"

"Of course I do," Rahul said, and stubbed his cigarette into the ashtray. He stood and went to the other table and asked one of the girls, who was smoking, whether he could use her light. Then in the next moment, Rahul was sitting with them and relating to them a story about when he lost close to ten lakh rupees in the casino, which, as outlandish as it sounded, was true. Rahul gambled as though he didn't have another day to live. He lived recklessly, driving his car at a high speed through the crowded streets, bungee jumping hundreds of feet over the swirling, raging Bhote Kosi River, getting into fights in dance bars. Aakash was milder in temperament.

The Ghana of Aakash's dreams was always a desert, always with tents; often a furious wind blew across it. Men rode about on camels, their movements slow and deliberate. When Aakash woke up, there was a cold feeling in his chest, as though one of the unsmiling men on the camels had fixed his gaze there. After waking up, Aakash lay in bed, wrapped up in his heavy blanket, his mind sluggish. He wondered if he ought to get up and check out that map that was hidden on the bookshelf. Then he'd know for sure whether there was even a desert in Ghana. He suspected there wasn't; even his dream was a lie, like the circus elephants.

Until now, Aakash hadn't seen himself in his dreams about Ghana. But the day after Rahul's comment about his past life, there he was, riding nonchalantly on the back of a camel that moved its mouth slowly as though chewing cud, a smirk lurking at the corners of its lips. For a night or two Aakash could only observe himself, as one does through a video camera—now he was inside the tent, now he was taking off his turban and shaking out the dust. A woman hovered in the background, and there was a flurry of bright-colored clothes, a shuffling of feet. But Aakash wasn't inside his own skin. He wasn't experiencing what was happening, merely witnessing. Even as he dreamed, Aakash thought to himself, *I want access.* This word came to him: *password.* Then he understood: a password was what he needed. He was required to have a password to become a participant in his own dream, to actually become the person who sat in the tent with a glass of mint tea in his hand.

In Haawa, Aakash asked Rahul for suggestions on a password that could unlock his Ghana dreams.

"Have you tried swapping the letters?"

"What do you mean?"

"Swapping letters of the word *Ghana.*"

Aakash thought. "Like 'anahg'?"

"That's a good one. And of course anahg sounds like a *naag*, a serpent in Nepali, so that makes sense. Are there any serpents in your dreams?"

Aakash shook his head. "I don't think that's right. It doesn't sound right."

"What about 'aangh'?" Rahul asked. He shouted, "Aangh!" which had the waiter scurrying to their table. Rahul ordered some mint tea, and the waiter said the café didn't have it. Rahul dismissed the waiter. "Aangh sounds like a cry for help. Do you feel like you are pleading for help in your dreams?"

"No, but it does feel like I'm about to start on a journey. A very important one."

"To where?"

"I don't know."

"See, that's where your answer might lie. Think more about that journey, and see whether that prompts something."

Aakash thought about the journey, but no image came to his mind.

"Nothing?"

"I'll do it at home, where it's a bit quiet. Not in this ruckus."

And indeed it was noisy and crowded in Haawa, more so in the last few minutes since a well-known painter had arrived. The painter had long hair flowing down to his shoulders. He was middle-aged, with a smooth, clean face, almost like a brushed-up photograph. He was famous for painting violent images of decapitation and dismemberment that critics praised as extraordinary. A group of young people had already run up to him for his autograph, and the painter obliged them with a deprecatory smile. Aakash and Rahul watched the clamor. Rahul asked Aakash what the painter's name was, and Aakash said, "Sambhavana."

"What kind of an asinine name is that?" Rahul asked.

"That's his name."

"Were his parents crazy? Who in their right minds would name their child 'possibility'? If he's born, he's no longer a possibility—he's a reality."

"It's his nom de plume. He adopted this name after he

became a famous painter. Something to do with the infinite possibilities in art."

"Oho." Rahul nodded in an exaggerated manner. "A nom de plume. A meaningful nom de plume. Yes, Aakash? He thought it was significant? No, Aakash? Poetic, eh, Aakash?"

Aakash knew where this was going: Rahul was revving his engines. *Let the tamasha begin*, thought Aakash.

The painter sat two tables away from them. He was dressed in white kurta suruwal, and Aakash had to admit, with his long hair and his smooth, fair face he looked quite handsome. No wonder the autograph seekers, most of them girls, were beside themselves. If the painter wanted to, he could probably pick up one of these girls, take her home, and fuck her, with his paintings scattered around them.

Rahul ambled over to the painter. Without asking for his permission, Rahul sat in the chair in front of him, and said loudly in English, "Mr. Possibility, how are you?"

"I'm fine," the painter said with a soft smile.

"How much money do you make from your paintings?"

Aakash held his head in his hands, unable to look, but he could picture Rahul leering at the painter.

"Enough to get by."

"Oh, you don't want to tell? Are you making a killing?"

The painter laughed humbly, as though he were welcoming Rahul's sense of humor.

Aakash looked up. Some of the people around them were staring at the painter and Rahul.

"You think it's funny, Mr. Possibility?"

The painter merely smiled.

"You see this?" Rahul made a fist and rubbed the fingers of his other hand on his knuckles.

Once Rahul got going like this, it was impossible to control him. Aakash wondered if Rahul was going to hit the painter. All Aakash wanted to do was to go home and think about Ghana, then enter swiftly into his dream.

"Oh, I see, you are the Mahatma Gandhi type," Rahul said. "Nonviolence, my friend?"

By this time, as people sensed that something was afoot, much of the clamor from the other tables had died.

The painter continued his sweet, disarming smile. "Could I buy you a cup of tea?" he asked.

"Tea?"

Rahul stared at the painter for a while, then stood and returned to his own table. The room seemed to let out a collective sigh of relief. The painter, a smile still sketched on his lips, was inspecting his fingers. He looked as unruffled as before. Aakash tried to remember one of his paintings, something he'd once seen in a glossy magazine, and an image slowly pieced itself together in his mind. It showed a field with yellow flowers, and on the surface it appeared peaceful and lovely, a Monet-type impressionistic meadow. One could imagine walking across it, like a new carpet whose softness massaged your feet. But there was something running through the meadow, a streak of something, and if you looked closer, you could see that a red line slashed through the flowers. It took you a moment to notice the red line, but once you did it was impossible to continue to view the flowers as beautiful and soothing. If you gazed at it longer, then the red line seemed to penetrate your own body. Creepy.

"What happened?" Aakash asked, unable to stop the condescension in his voice, once Rahul rejoined him. "He gutted you?"

"I'll get him," Rahul said. His voice was filled with venom.

"How? When?"

"You just wait."

The password came to Aakash just as he'd finished rinsing his mouth after dinner and was on his way up to his room. The marble floors felt cold on his feet, and he was looking forward to crawling into his blanket when the word popped into his mind. It carried a heft that signaled it was the right one: *Sambhavana*. How odd, he thought as he turned off the lights, that the password to his Ghanaian dream life was a Nepali word. Shouldn't it be an African-sounding word, like *buhitoo*, or *gunusti*, or *even* aangh? But *sambhavana*! As he drifted off to sleep, Aakash wondered if the painter was somehow in charge of his dreams.

The password worked. As soon as he entered the landscape of the desert and the whistling winds and the sand getting into his mouth and his nose (what did he think, that it was going to be fun?), Aakash realized that he was a country bumpkin about to leave for the city to search for his daughter, who had run away. His wife—the fluttering, wavering presence inside the tent—was traumatized by the daughter's departure, so she grumbled and complained.

Aakash understood the language they spoke in the dream. The daughter, Hamad's daughter—yes, that was his name, Hamad—had frequently fought with her father, so a part of Hamad didn't mind that she was gone. Another part of him resented her because now he had to go look for her, whereas all he wanted to do was herd camels and come back home and drink his mint tea and smoke his hookah. But when he pictured his daughter floundering in the city, perhaps resorting to prostitution to survive, his heart ached. He made plans to leave as soon as a friend paid him back a loan. He needed money for the trip, and he didn't know how long he'd have to stay in the city looking for her.

Aakash found Hamad's problem awfully dreary, and in the dream he recoiled when he discovered that as Hamad he'd have to ride for days on the back of a smirking camel through the sand and the wind. Although he felt sorry for Hamad, it wasn't enough for Aakash to want to stay in the dream. When he tried to wake up, however, he couldn't; he was *pinned* to the dream.

Hamad's wife suddenly transformed from a muttering shadow to a haranguing presence. She gave Hamad an avalanche of instructions: how to conduct himself during the trip, where to stay, who to seek help from once he reached the city. "Shut up, woman!" Hamad said to his wife, who thrust her index finger close to Hamad's nose.

"I'll never forget how you sided with your brother and his wife against me ten years ago," she said. "That moment is seared into my memory." She jabbed her finger at her temple. "I pleaded with you, I begged you, I told you how it was not my fault, but did you listen? No. Your brother was too dear to you, and his wife, even dearer. I know what you were up to."

And Hamad didn't have an answer for her. Most of what she said was true. He had treated his wife unfairly at that time. He had accused her of lacking civility and decorum toward his brother and his wife, who lived together with them. Later, it became abundantly clear that it was his brother and wife who were uncivil, who vanished one morning without repaying the large sum of money they owed Hamad. But Hamad's wife wasn't right when she insinuated that he had designs on his brother's wife. His wife's insinuations did amplify his guilt now, and more and more he wondered if he did have feelings for his sister-in-law that he'd refused to acknowledge, and more and more he wondered if his daughter had left because he had failed her as a father? Or be because he'd scolded her too often over small things? These questions troubled Hamad.

At the office the next day, Aakash remained depressed. He played chess on his computer, losing repeatedly at the novice level. He tried out a new chase-and-mutilate animated game that was so brutal he half-expected blood to splatter from the screen onto his face. Disgusted, he went to the window and watched the city, riveted by the newspaper vendor under the peepal tree across the street. The vendor coughed and snorted, then ejected his phlegm to the side, where a stray dog lingered, sniffing. The honk of the cars and motorcycles, which Aakash previously didn't mind, got on his nerves today, and he thought, *I should migrate to Ghana.*

The notion surprised him, and suppressing a laugh, he looked back quickly at his colleagues, who were all busy at their computers. Ghana. He had finally looked it up on the map, and had been disappointed to note what a small country it was. And it wasn't remotely close to any desert.

Something was happening below. An agitated crowd had gathered around the peepal tree, right next to the vendor. Loud, angry bursts flew into the air. More people stopped to look. Aakash's colleagues also came to the window. "Is there a procession scheduled today?" one of them asked. The crowd below became larger.

The goateed associate editor appeared in the doorway (his office was in another part of the floor), and said, "Hmmm, don't we have deadlines to keep?" and everyone scampered to their desk, except Aakash, who waited until the editor left, then went down the stairs to the pavement. Even crossing the street was hard because the mass of people had already spread to the main street, now immobilizing the traffic.

He pushed his way to the front of the crowd, and was aghast to see a dark child crouched on the ground at the spot near where the newspaper vendor had shot his phlegm. Naked. Her palms feebly covered her crotch. But, Aakash realized with a start, she was not a dark-skinned Nepali child. She was a child darker than any he'd seen on city streets, so dark that the whites of her frightened eyes shone in her black face. Then Aakash noticed that she was not a child, not thirteen or fourteen as he'd originally thought, but close to eighteen or nineteen. She was a small-boned young woman, looking younger than she actually was because she didn't have on a strip of clothing. Her breasts were the size of small oranges. At first Aakash didn't understand why the group of men around her were so enraged. Then, catching the invectives hurled at her, he understood: they thought she was a witch.

"She's a symbol of our dark age, our kaliyug," a priestly looking man with a toupee said.

"Harey!" a woman said. "What is God thinking when he makes a creature like this one—darker than a buffalo!"

People in the back of the crowd were pushing those in the front, and soon Aakash lost his footing and was hurled forward and down to the ground, right next to the girl. The girl's white eyes bore into his. Then, something like relief seemed to pass through them. A smell, not entirely disagreeable, emanated from her body, a smell of wood and pine and mud. Her skin was immaculately smooth, without a hint of a wrinkle or a birthmark anywhere, like a black model one might see on the pages of *GQ* or *Vanity Fair*. Except her hair was uncombed, and wild. The crowd had tightened around them, casting a shadow over the two of them.

"Who is this idiot?"

"Her lover? Her accomplice?"

"Her aider and abettor."

With the agility of a cat, the girl leaped on top of Aakash and wrapped her arms around him. She clung to him tightly, her breasts pressed against his, her raspy breath against his right ear, her hips straddling his waist, her pubic mound pressed against his navel.

"Look! Look!"

Something whizzed past Aakash's ear and thudded to the ground. A shoe.

"Go!" a woman at the front of the crowd said. "Carry your witch home and fuck her."

The word *fuck* from a woman's throat turned the mob hysterical. They hooted and harrumphed and danced like primitives. Aakash took this moment to tighten his grip around the girl's body like a mother monkey carrying a baby monkey, then dove into the multitude of legs surrounding him. He leaped forward on all fours, pushing and shoving his way through. By the time the crowd realized what had happened, Aakash was already a couple dozen yards away. He continued galloping on all fours, then gradually straightened to his full height. He ran, the girl clinging around his neck, bouncing up and down as he whooshed through the evening shoppers. Ten minutes ago he was playing a computer game in his office, and now here he was fleeing a murderous horde. He was giddy and breathless; the girl was tightly clasped against him.

When they reached the New Road Gate, the girl unclasped herself and slid to the ground. *Oh, no!* Aakash thought; their persecutors were only a short distance away. But the girl grabbed his hand and pulled him across the street toward the Tundikhel parade ground. She was fast. He rocketed forward as though he were made of some light substance like feather or cotton. They ran so fast that the cars zooming and honking past them didn't even need to swerve. Within seconds they were on the other side, sliding through the bars into the parade ground.

Once inside the parade ground, they slowed down. The people in Tundikhel—young men playing football, old people out for fresh air, jobless villagers—stopped to watch them: a dark child-woman, pubic hair and all, traipsing across the historic parade ground holding a young man's hand. The mob was still stuck on the other side, unable to cross because of the traffic.

Once they reached the other end of the field, she stopped and faced him, clearly wanting to know what to do next.

"Where's your house?" he asked her.

She continued to look at him.

"Where is your house?" he asked, loudly as though speaking to someone deaf. "Where can I take you?"

She had nothing to say.

He glanced back but couldn't see whether the mob was still waiting to cross. He and the girl had to keep on moving. Already a small group of curious young children were beginning to gather around them. Even kids were dangerous these days. Just last week, an eleven-year-old boy had slit the throats of his parents as they slept. Later, when the police took him away, he'd declared that his parents were traitors and that he'd killed them because the revolution demanded that he did. Which revolutionary group he belonged to—there were so many of them—no one knew.

Not too long ago a band of children, dressed in rags and

armed with hammers and iron rods, had roamed the city's plush neighborhoods. They'd smashed windows, fought with maids and guards, and looted jewelry and food and electronics. A college girl on her way home had managed to take a photo of one of these small bandits on her mobile phone, and the photo was splashed over all the newspapers with headlines such as, "OUR CHILDREN OF TOMORROW," and "THE CHILD IS THE FATHER OF THE CRIMINAL!"

"Come," Aakash said, and took the girl's hand. They slid through the bars at the other end and emerged on Exhibition Road. They walked past Bhrikuti Mandap, where Aakash had come as a child during festivals and fairs, eaten ice cream, and rode the toy train. Those years seemed too far away to be of any importance to him now. When he recalled events from his childhood, he felt as though he were reviewing someone else's life, not his own. There was no emotional tone to anything he recalled, just brief flashes of pictures that could have happened to any average child, anywhere. *Why?* he asked himself, but didn't have an answer. He had been a happy child, hadn't he? He had. And his parents had been good parents, hadn't they? They had. So why did he feel so removed?

Once or twice he'd deliberately recalled a childhood event and tried to inject some flavor into it. Lying in bed, he'd scrunched up his forehead and tried to remember, for example, the joy of playing hide-and-seek in the dug-up foundation of the new house his parents were building in Baluwatar. He recalled the texture of the mud he and his friends had flung at one another, the sonorous greeting of a neighbor as she passed by, the sprouty end of green onions peeking out from her plastic bag. He remembered the exhilarating feeling of being a part of a neighborhood where each house seemed to hold an element of interest, even mystery: an old, arthritic geezer, a former champion wrestler, who sat on the porch of his house, ogling at the schoolgirls who passed by; a young, mustached, skinny-legged man in another house who was rumored to be homosexual; the housewife in the corner who supposedly had healing powers. Aakash remembered everything in minute details. But the child he saw in his mind's eye was not him. The experiences belonged to someone else.

"What am I going to do with you?" he asked the girl. They were walking fast so that the other pedestrians, who did a double take when they saw a naked black girl, didn't have time to harass them. The girl had linked her arm with his, and was watching his face. "You don't speak English?" Aakash asked. Of course she didn't. He wasn't even sure she spoke at all. But there was no time to ponder her language skills; he had to take her somewhere, away from these prying eyes, find her some clothes, then hand her over to someone. But to whom? He didn't even know which country she was from.

Was there a general consulate who covered the entire continent of Africa somewhere in the city? Wait! Was she even African? Why did he jump to that conclusion? She could belong to an indigenous tribe from Nepal, and, judging from her dark complexion, her home could be in a hitherto-undiscovered pocket of the jungles in the south, where no one was aware of the modern world, like the bunch they found on a Philippine island some years ago.

Putalisadak was teeming with pedestrians and traffic. If Aakash didn't do something quickly, there would not only be a repeat of the earlier mob incident, but also he himself could get killed, bludgeoned to death on these streets. The message would then travel to his father and mother that he'd gotten himself murdered on a busy thoroughfare, his arms wrapped around a dark habsi, a dark boksi, a darkie-dark girl without a strip of clothing; that was how everyone would see it.

He'd noticed the sign for Hotel Evergreen weeks ago when he'd passed through this area, and the only reason he remembered it now was because he'd laughed at its name then. Hotel Evergreen overlooked what had to be the filthiest river in the country, whose stench rippled to the surrounding neighborhoods. The river barely held any water, only a lazy trickle of such gloomy color that it resembled oil. Garbage had accumulated on its banks, mounds that rose high into the sky. Even now some ragamuffin children were romping in and around the filth. A dead dog lay faceup amidst the dirt, its teeth bared as though grinning.

Inside the hotel's lobby, the river's stench was so strong that Aakash gagged. Even the girl's face blanched. A man stood behind the counter. His eyes briefly flitted over the naked girl, then rested on Aakash.

"Euta room chahiyo," Aakash said.

The man nodded, then checked on his computer. "We

have just one room available, overlooking the scenic Tukucha River."

Aakash watched his face, but there was no sign of irony or mirth. "Don't you have a room on the other side of the river?" Aakash asked.

"The hotel is fully booked except for this room. It's our best, the most expensive."

"How much is it?"

"One thousand two hundred."

"Okay."

The room indeed overlooked the river, but since it was on the top floor, it didn't reek as badly up here as it did below. The bed was surprisingly clean, and there was even a fan by the table, which Aakash turned on. The girl sat on the bed and looked around. "You wait here," Aakash said. "I'll go out and get you some clothes."

He shopped quickly: a pair of fake Levi's jeans, a white shirt, and, because he couldn't find panties, male cotton Rhino underwear he hoped she wouldn't mind wearing. *Well, she doesn't have a choice*, he thought to himself as he paid for the items. As he hurried back to the hotel, he realized that she probably hadn't eaten, and he hastily entered an eatery and asked them to pack a plate of steaming momos, wondering if they ate momos in Africa.

She was standing by the window, looking at the river, at the children who were playing in the garbage, at the Kathmandu skyline filled with crisscrossed wires for phone and electricity and at tall, dreadful-looking houses clamoring for space. She was so black. At any moment he expected her to turn around and speak to him in Nepali, say something like *Katti ber layako?* or *Khana-sana khayera ekchin ghumna jaunna,* but of course she didn't say that, and he knew that he wished for that to happen only because he felt so connected to her. The air, foul smelling as it was, had become charged, as though something was about to burst open, inside him or inside her or in the space that surrounded this city or this godforsaken country.

But all that happened was that he stood by the door, the bag with hot momos wrapped in foil in one hand and her clothes in the other, and she continued to gaze out of the window, and he knew that she too felt alienated here, that her home was somewhere else. But where? And how did she get to his city without a single strip of clothing on her back? He was afraid that he'd never find the answer to these questions. Yet here she was, standing by the window, as real as the cries of the snot-filled children who were trampling in the muck below. "Momo," he said limply, and she turned.

First he had her eat. They sat on the bed, her mouth moving slowly to chomp on the meat, as she watched him with eyes that were tender and inquisitive. The achar that came with the momos was spicy, but she showed no signs of being bothered, and although she didn't eat greedily, she did finish the plate and emitted a soft, pleasurable belch. The pants and the shirt fit her reasonably well, and she surveyed herself in her new clothes in front of the smudged hotel mirror, even turned to him like a girlfriend or a wife, seeking his approval. He nodded, gratified at her childlike trust in him but also slightly queasy now that she was fully clothed and looked different—more mature, womanly. "Everything looks good," he said in English. He realized that he spoke to her in English when he remembered, sometimes with a jolting, painful awareness, that she was a black girl from someplace foreign, that he had to get her back to where she belonged. (A line by the Beatles came to him, about getting back to where one once belonged. And he spoke to her in Nepali when momentarily he forgot who she was and who even he was. Now that she sat next to him on the bed, he looked into her eyes and a string of words in Nepali ran through his mind: a lament on how screwed up this city was, a dog-eat-dog city, a city of innuendos and false charges and torch-wielding mobs. Where was love? Had people lost their minds?

"You are such a drama queen," Rahul usually said when Aakash complained like this. "You are a whiner, Aakash."

Rahul. The thought of his friend made Aakash's heart skip a beat. How would Rahul react to this black girl? Aakash pictured his friend's face, the astonishment, the suspicion, the mischief. What would Rahul think? He'd probably tease Aakash about this "girlfriend," even after Aakash explained how the girl ended up with him. Rahul would probably circle the black girl, evaluating her, passing judgment on her. What would happen if Rahul wanted the girl for himself? Aakash pictured himself arguing with Rahul that the girl was his, that Rahul better not get any ideas. Aakash let out a small moan. The girl, sitting next to him, watched him, then placed her hand on his back. "Don't worry," he said to her. "I won't let him touch you."

Another possibility formed a knot in Aakash's heart, making it hard for him to breathe: Rahul could charm his way into the girl's heart, and she'd willingly follow him. Aakash peered into the girl's eyes and said, "You wouldn't do that, would you? Would you leave me for Rahul?"

The girl, seemingly understanding his question, tilted her head and continued to gaze at him, as though she couldn't believe he'd hold her in such low regard. He reached out and touched her nose. Then, lest she become frightened, he quickly withdrew his finger. In the manner of returning someone's greeting, she, too, reached with her index finger and touched his nose. He pinched her cheek, and so did she, and this went on for a while until they both were laughing. That they could converse in the language of laughter surprised him, for until now somehow his mind had been treating her as if she came from another planet, one in which people didn't understand humor. But obviously the emotions she experienced were no different than his. Had he forgotten already the fear in her eyes when she was surrounded in New Road? How close was that fear to his own when, as he went to work in the heart of the city, he saw a mass demonstration taken out by religious fundamentalists, with the demonstrators wielding bamboos sticks, khukris, and nanchakus. One time he'd seen a large trishul in the hands of a teenage boy with a saffron turban. The boy's eyes had met Aakash's as he went by, and Aakash knew that the boy wouldn't hesitate to use the weapon.

Darkness was falling, and Aakash had a home to get to, even as increasingly his parents seemed resigned to the fact that their son often stayed out late, or arrived home smelling of booze. These days his father's jaw was always tight, and he seemed to avoid Aakash's eyes. Aakash's mother constantly reprimanded her son; she couldn't mask her disillusionment with him. But he couldn't fully grasp why they were so dissatisfied with who he was. Yes, he slept late, until it was nearly time to go to work. Yes, he came home late, sometimes with alcohol on his breath. Yes, he didn't show much enthusiasm in visiting relatives with his parents, and when he did he usually sat quietly in a corner. But he was also one of the few young men he knew, especially among his cousins, who not only had a job but who'd held on to it, and had already received one promotion. For a twenty-four-year-old Nepali man, Aakash made decent money, forty thousand rupees, nearly half of which he quietly handed over to his mother every month. Throughout school he'd never gotten into trouble, had never failed a subject, and even in college as his friends went wild, he'd always come home at a reasonable time and didn't do drugs beyond an occasional hit of a joint. It perplexed him why his parents regarded him with such displeasure that bordered on hostility. Occasionally he wondered if the transformation in them had less to do with him and more to do with what was happening in the country—the turmoil, the daily savagery, the constant bickering, the fear, the casual violence, the ugly faces on the evening news. Perhaps their hopes for him had secretly included not only success and happiness for him but for the entire nation. This thought jolted him, made him laugh—what a terrible, and terribly large, burden to place on a young man's shoulders. *Here, the whole goddamn country's well-being depends on you.*

He had to leave the girl overnight by herself in the hotel; there was no other choice. If he didn't go home, his parents would worry and search for him. He considered calling to tell them that he'd be staying at a friend's place, but he couldn't think of convincing explanations for why he'd be spending the night elsewhere in a dangerous city when he had his own home to go to. For a brief, sadistic moment, he pictured taking the girl to his house, to meet his parents as though she were his girlfriend. He could see the shock on his father's face, the distress on his mother's. His father, who secretly considered himself modern and progressive, would barely be able to hide his contempt toward the black girl. His mother—God bless her soul—was someone for whom any dark-skinned girl, whether Nepali or foreign, could never be a possible partner for her son. She'd made this abundantly clear in the past. Once, when she'd expressed this conviction, one of her brothers jestingly pointed out that her face itself wasn't the embodiment of radiant light, and she'd responded that just because the mother-in-law was a darkie didn't mean that the daughter-in-law also had to be a darkie. She'd even managed what Aakash thought was a pretty good repartee. "If both women of the house are dark, then the men would also have to live in complete darkness, no?" she'd said.

"I will come back tomorrow," Aakash told the black girl. Then he pointed to her and made a hand gesture of sleep. Was that a universal sign for sleeping?

The girl grabbed his arm, her eyes showing panic, obviously urging him not to go.

"Everything will be fine," he said, patting her. "I will be here at the top of the morning." He gently freed himself, then left.

At home he went straight up to his room and sat on the bed. He wondered if the black girl would be foolish enough to go down to the lobby, or venture out into the streets. Now that she was clothed, she was obviously safer than before, but her absurdly dark skin would still draw people's attention, especially at this time in the evening when teenage boys would be on the prowl. He should have forbidden her to leave the hotel, told her if she felt bored, to turn on the television. He couldn't remember whether the room had television, and wasn't sure whether she'd know what television was, or how to operate it.

He clicked the TV remote in his room. On the screen was the bandaged face of a well-known politician who had suffered attacks from men hired by his rival. The injured politician said, "Bring it on!" He said he knew where his opponent's children went to school. Aakash changed the channel, but today the dancing girls didn't provide the usual relief, so he turned off the television and lay down in bed.

"Is this all you can do in life?"

It was his father, standing in the doorway. Aakash sat up and hung his head, ready for the lecture.

"What has happened to you?" his father said. "Look at you."

Aakash remained silent. When he glanced up, his father was shaking his head at him. A truck blared past their house.

"Your mother and I," his father said. "How to say this? We are going away for a while."

"Travel?"

His father crossed his arms at his chest. "You could say that. But it's not for days, it's for longer than that. For months. At least."

"Where?"

"To Hong Kong first. Then who knows? Maybe to America. Everyone is going there these days."

"Hong Kong? Uncle Subhash's house?"

His father nodded.

"When did this come about?" Aakash asked, not liking that he sounded querulous. "Why wasn't I told about this?"

His father let out a big sigh. "Son, what can I say? Your mother and I—we have given up on you."

Aakash rose from the bed. "What do you mean? What reason do you have to treat me like this? What have I done?"

His father kept his arms crossed. "Are we going to cover the same territory again? Look at your life. Look at you. Doesn't that answer your question?"

Something was rising in Aakash's throat, and he fought hard to squelch it. "When are you leaving?"

"In a few days," his father said. Then, "Come down for dinner. It's ready."

But Aakash remained in his room, door closed, even after his mother repeatedly knocked. "I'm not feeling well," he said.

In the morning, he quietly got dressed and left the house just as the sun hit the white mountains to the north. The beauty of these mountains always surprised him, particularly during sunrise and sunset, when a pinkish rouge lingered on their tips. He'd written about them dozens of times for *Travelite*, and had used the same combinations of words over and over: "the abode of the snows," "the stunning white peaks," "the looming Himalayas." Yet when the skies cleared and the mountains emerged, it was clear that those words were woefully inadequate to describe their magnificence. Today from the microbus, he watched the mountains all the way into town, his stomach a bit hollow because he hadn't eaten anything last night.

As he entered the lobby of Hotel Evergreen, the stench from Tukucha River momentarily made him dizzy.

Upstairs, the girl opened the door with sleep in her eyes. She returned to bed, and he sat next to her and stroked her hair. Then, he, too, lay down next to her. After a while, she put her right arm on his chest, and they slept. They were jolted awake by the sound of an argument below. He peeked out of the window, worried. But it was only kids squabbling amidst the garbage, hitting one another with plastic bottles, occasionally letting out monkey screams. For a while he watched them, attempting to recall the joys of his own childhood. Once again, he couldn't identify with his own memories. Could it be that he was not who he thought he was? And after his parents left, would he then grow alienated even more from his own childhood?

He'd soon have to find a solution for this girl. He couldn't keep her in the hotel for too long—people would find out. Word would get around. Once he found out where she was from, perhaps he could put her on a bus, or a plane if he could scrounge the money. And if he failed in ascertaining where she needed to go, then he'd have no choice but to take her home, no matter what his parents thought.

Then he remembered that his parents were going to leave for Hong Kong, or America, or wherever they were thinking about going, and he pictured himself ushering this girl into the house as soon as he waved goodbye to his parents at the airport. Yes, ushering, as one ushered a bride. He saw himself walking his neighborhood hand in hand with the girl, whom he'd name Ghana. A perfect name for her. He knew, instinctively, that the Ghana of his dreams and this girl were connected, but he didn't know how. He and Ghana would stroll his neighborhood together, and people would stare. Some would spit on the ground, others would make nasty comments about her dark skin, about the deathly dark skin of the potential baby of this union. They'd wonder why an educated Nepali man who wore a tie to work every day, who spoke English smoothly like a khairey would prefer to court a darkie over a fair Nepali beauty, someone who could cook him aromatic Nepali food and bear him fair Nepali children.

The more he thought about it, the more Aakash didn't know why he would have to wait until his parents left in order to take Ghana home with him. After all, his parents hadn't bothered to consult him before they decided to take off. So why shouldn't he also do as he pleased?

"What do you think about it?" he asked Ghana. "How about I move you into my house and hide you like contraband?" She didn't respond, of course, merely gazed at him dreamily. "I'm a smuggler," he said. "Like Haji Mastan." He stroked her nose. "Do you know Haji Mastan? Are there any Haji Mastans where you come from?"

Of course she couldn't respond to him.

"Come, let's go," he said to her. "Enough of this sitting in stinky hotel rooms running scared. I'm going to take you to my house, smuggle you in." It'd be the kind of thing Rahul would approve of. Maybe once Aakash got Ghana into his house, he'd give Rahul a call and see if he wanted to come over and meet her. It had been ages since Rahul had visited Aakash at home ("I don't think your parents like me," Rahul had said), but the mention of a dark African girl in Aakash's room was sure to galvanize him into coming over. Aakash's earlier fear of the girl falling for Rahul had disappeared, and now it was replaced by a mounting excitement at the thought of Ghana in his room, with Rahul inspecting her, as Aakash's parents readied for their trip below.

He and Ghana walked hand in hand down the stairs to the lobby, where the receptionist was listening to the radio. The Supreme Commander spoke about uplifting the country through capitalist economic maneuvers of Deng rather than the isolationist economic policies of Mao. "But we must distribute the wealth," the Supreme Commander said. "The poor must become rich, and the rich must become middle class." The Supreme Commander was a portly man with a thick mustache and deep-set eyes. People had by now forgotten that he had killed hundreds of people only a few years ago during the insurgency. How people had hated him then, called him a mass murderer, a Hitler, a title that the Supreme Commander had welcomed. But now all those memories had been replaced by the media images of the Supreme Commander in military gear saluting groups of soldiers in army fatigues, or in a dhoti with a tika smeared on his forehead, performing some puja or yagya in the front yard of the palace, throwing rice into a fire burning in front of him. The twin images of a militarist and a religionist had been carefully developed, and now they'd merged and had become inseparable. These days it seemed like the Supreme Commander had always been like this. But Aakash remembered that at the start of his insurgency the Supreme Commander had been rabidly anti-God. He'd railed against the state religion, calling it the "charas of the masses"; his soldiers had dragged out priests from village temples and beat them senseless; he'd banned Sanskrit education in the small region of the country that he'd declared autonomous.

The intersection between Baghbazar and Putalisadak was suffocating. Had the whole goddamn city congregated in this juncture? People gabbled and gesticulated, sweated and farted, walked with aggression on their shoulders, yelled at one another across the traffic. Aakash briefly recalled a time from his childhood, long before his parents built their home away from the city center, when he'd stood at this very spot waiting for his school bus. How spacious this street was then, how sparse the traffic.

He held Ghana's hand and pulled her along, hoping to

find a taxi, which they did once they crossed the street. As the taxi inched and crawled through the thicket of cars and trucks and motorcycles, Aakash slid down farther on his seat. His heart was beating rapidly in anticipation of what was to come. There was no way he'd be able to get Ghana past the front door of his house. The kitchen was steps away from the foyer, and his mother was always in there, cooking, cleaning. The kitchen was her "central command," as Aakash's father liked to call it. "Her fort. From where she fires her missiles." When she was home, his mother kept the front door locked for fear of daylight robbers, and although Aakash carried a key, his mother was sure to come to the door if she heard him unlock it.

The only other way he could try to get this girl into the house was through the window. But his room was on the second floor, a good ten feet up from the ground. There were no ladders lying around that he could use. Aakash thought hard: perhaps he could buy some rope and throw it up, like a lasso in a cowboy movie, and hope that it'd fasten itself around one of the two metal hooks that were used to keep the windows open. Even if that were to be successful, it'd take time, and a neighbor could spot them and, mistaking them for daylight robbers, raise an alarm.

When the taxi slowed outside his house, Aakash nearly told the driver to keep going. But the driver had already killed his engine and had taken out a cigarette, which he held between his lips. Aakash paid him and signaled to Ghana to get out.

He opened the large gate to the house, wincing at the

ostentatious clang it made. The glass of the window in the foyer was misty, so Aakash couldn't see his mother, but he was sure she was there, alerted by the sound. He let go of Ghana's hand and walked down the driveway, aware that a neighbor woman, the one who got drunk at night and argued with her mother-in-law, was watching from her balcony. Any moment now Aakash's mother was going to emerge, her forehead crunched in a frown. He waited outside the main door, going over his explanations.

After a minute when no one opened the door, Aakash used his key to get in. They stopped in the foyer and listened. The kitchen faucet dripped; Aakesh's mother had been pestering his father to fix that faucet for weeks, and now it looked like it would remain leaky even after they were gone. Had his parents already left? Without even saying goodbye to him? Then he saw, as he looked into the living room, a half-packed suitcase on the floor. It was rare for both his father and mother to be gone together at this time of the day. Usually one of them stayed home to guard the house against daylight robbers.

Aakash went into the kitchen and set the water to boil for tea. He gave Ghana a tour of the house, feeling expansive and loquacious as he took her into his parents' bedroom on the main floor, which had a large painting of his grandfather gazing somberly at them. Aakash had her sit on the bed, from where they could see the neighbor woman who was still watching the house. But Aakash knew that the dirty screen on the window prevented her from seeing into the room, or even figuring out that someone was inside. Perhaps she could make out the shadows.

Aakash returned to the kitchen, where the mixture inside the kettle was frothing at the lid and the spout, the tea making smart sizzling sounds as it spilled over the fire. He turned off the gas and poured the tea into cups, which he then took to Ghana. He and Ghana sipped their tea. Then they left his parents' bedroom to go into his, where they fell on his bed and took a nap.

His parents were entering the house. Ghana had opened her eyes, but he hushed her by putting his finger to her lips. He quietly opened the door and went out, gently shutting it behind as he stepped on the landing.

Below, plastic bags in hand, his mother was telling his father that it'd be foolhardy of them to expect to get the visa in a day or two, that they ought to be prepared to change their airline tickets to a later date. She looked up, spotted Aakash, and told him that if he wanted tea, he ought to come down. Then, realizing that her son was home from work early, asked, "What's the matter? You not feeling well?"

"Just a headache," he said.

His father, too, looked up at him and said, "No exercise, no fresh air, always sitting in front of the computer—what do you expect?"

His mother, after she put her bags in her bedroom, returned to the foyer, looked up, and asked, "Did you have a friend over? There are two cups in our room."

"Why does he need to go to our room to drink his tea?" his father said.

"Ask your son. He's right there."

Before his father could come up the stairs, Aakash went down. "My friend's ankle was sprained, and so he couldn't climb the stairs, and we decided to sit in your room." The lie took on an aura of truth before it had even completely left his mouth.

"Who's this friend?" his father asked as they both headed to the kitchen, where his mother had already put the tea on to boil and had samosas on plates for the father and son.

"You wouldn't know," Aakash said, sitting on a chair.

"Enlighten me," his father said, sitting next to him and grabbing his samosa. "Who are your friends nowadays?"

Aakash nervously glanced toward the staircase, which he could partially see from the kitchen. But Ghana seemed to be aware that this was a dangerous situation and hadn't come out of the room.

His mother poured tea and brought it to them. "I have arranged," she said to her son, "for Danny to come every day and cook and clean and do your laundry after we leave, just like he does now. Because Danny has an aging mother at home, he can't live here with you. But he's a good boy. His mother used to work for us when you were small, before her arthritis made it impossible for her continue. You don't remember her, but Danny was born when you were in fifth or sixth grade. Who knew that one day we'd end up doing this, leaving our own son so we could migrate to another country? But son, you have left us no choice."

"Stop apologizing to him," Aakash's father said, then delicately took a bite out of his samosa.

"I'm not apologizing, but it breaks my heart that we've been forced into doing this." She began to cry, and it was Aakash who had to console her, telling her that he was sorry for whatever he'd done.

A thump sounded from above, and the three of them glanced up. "What was that?" his father said. "Is your friend still here?"

Aakash shook his head. "Must be a cat on the roof or something. Perhaps a fiddler." Aakash tried hard not to smirk.

"A fiddler on the roof?" his father said, oblivious to the reference. "Our roof is made of concrete. Even if a leopard were to jump down, it wouldn't sound like that."

His mother, her cheek glistening with tears, whispered, "It could be a daylight robber. He must have gotten in through your window. Did you leave it open this morning?"

Aakash shook his head; his mind was thinking fast. Nothing else had sounded after the thump, and he imagined that Ghana had either dropped something or fell off the bed. "It's nothing," he said. He waved his hand dismissively in the air. "These talks of daylight robbers are highly exaggerated. One robbery in six months, and for the whole year, all people do is whimper about daylight robbers." He knew this was not true. Daylight robbers were striking more often, becoming more aggressive. Last month they'd tied up an old, blind couple in their home and robbed them . . . well, blind. In another case, they'd locked up an eleven-year-old boy in the bathroom for hours.

"I'll go check," Aakash's father said, looking nervous, and stood.

"All right, all right, I'll go," Aakash said, feigning resignation. "Mother, could I have more tea?"

Upstairs, Ghana was on the bed, flitting through a magazine. Her hair was combed back, and her face looked clean: the thump must have happened on her way to the bathroom that adjoined the room. Fortunately the sound of her turning on the bathroom tap hadn't reached below. He went to her and kissed her on the forehead. "Are you hungry?" he asked. Then he made a sign of eating and rubbed his belly. Ghana nodded. "Okay, I'll bring you food," he said, "but you have to be very quiet." He put his finger to his lips again.

"No fiddler, no daylight robber," he told his parents once he joined them. "How many samosas did you bring?" he asked his mother. "Any more left?" His mother brought out one samosa and gave it to him. He held it in his hand and jabbered with his father about small things, slipped the samosa into his pocket when his father wasn't looking, then wiped his mouth with his fingers as though he'd just finished eating it. Perhaps encouraged by his talkativeness, his mother, too, sat at the table. She gave him further instructions about taking care of the house—what to do if the water heater stopped working; what the gardener needed to do before he got his wages; how and where to have Danny do the daily grocery shopping—while his father chewed his samosa slowly and kept shaking his head, as though he'd never understand his impossible son.

"If we had another son, none of this would have come about," Aakash's father finally said.

"Now let it be," his mother said. "We've discussed this enough. No need to mention it anymore. We're leaving." She cried a little more. She was being forced into exile, her tears suggested.

When Aakash went upstairs, he found Ghana asleep on the bed. He took out the samosa and placed it on the bedside table, then sat watching her. The afternoon turned into evening, and after making sure that his mother was in the kitchen preparing dinner, he went up to the roof. To the south stood the big hills he didn't know the names of, to the east the Phulchoki hill, and on the northern horizon, glistening under the slanted rays of dusk, the snowcapped mountains: Ganesh, Manaslu, Langtang, and his favorite, Dorje Lakpa. Birds flew overhead, chirping and cawing.

The sky appeared to be humming, a sound of its own that had nothing to do with the earth; it had a little bit to do with the sun, which was now in the process of slipping away in the west; and a little bit to do with the mountains which would, once the sun left, retreat into darkness. He'd never come up here at night to see what shapes these mountains assumed once night fell. He recalled what Rahul had shown him on the computer the last time he'd been at his friend's house: an image of the earth at night taken from satellites. How brightly lit were the Western countries! America and Britain glittered with small, dotted lights. Even India, to Aakash's surprise, sparkled. But Nepal was bereft of any shimmer—only darkness. So was Africa.

When he returned to his room, the samosa was gone, but
Ghana wasn't in the room. Panicked, he looked down to
the foyer. The kitchen sounds were normal, and his father
was most likely in the living room, playing solitaire with
his cards. Then Aakash noticed that the door to the balcony next to his room was slightly open. He rushed into
his room and out to the balcony, where Ghana was leaning
against the railing. Startled by his sudden entry, she seemed
about to fall, but he reached out and grabbed her by the arm.
He looked down. His father was by the side of the house,
tending to a narrow bed of roses in the dim light of the
evening. His father didn't look up. Aakash put his finger to
his lips, but the situation now appeared comical, and thrill-
ing. The two of them watched his father pull out the weeds
from around the rosebushes, caress the petals of the roses.
He seemed to be in some kind of a trance, for he was completely engrossed in his roses, patting them and whispering
to them, seemingly bidding them goodbye.

Ghana slept cuddled next to Aakash under that large sirak of
his. Her body's warmth made him feel protected, which was
odd, as he had fancied himself as her protector. He woke up
sometime in the night, startled by something. He thought
that maybe she had cried out in her sleep, but she was snoring softly, her mouth slightly open. He listened carefully for
sounds, but there was nothing except for the occasional
barking of the neighborhood dogs. What had awoken him
was his own subconscious fear about being discovered in
bed with Ghana by that mob from New Road.

In the morning, he went down for a cup of tea, which he drank quickly in the kitchen as he listened to his mother talk. Then he asked her for another cup, which he carried to his room for Ghana.

They lounged in bed all morning. Later, Aakash pulled the phone toward him and, placing it on his chest, dialed Rahul's number. Rahul answered in his usual gruff manner.

"You're not going to believe who I have with me," Aakash said. He put his hand on Ghana's forehead, as though checking to see if she had fever.

"Who?" Rahul said. "The Supreme Commander?"

"Someone better. And that someone better is right here on my bed, and my parents are right down there, and they don't know."

The silence at the other end was long and tense. "A prostitute?" Rahul's voice was almost hoarse.

"Come and find out."

"Really? You with a whore? Let me speak to her."

"She's mute."

"A mute whore?"

"Are you coming or not?"

Rahul said that he'd get on his motorcycle and reach there in about half an hour. Aakash's mother was calling him for lunch, and he had no choice but to go down. His mother had laid out a virtual feast on the dining room table. Pulao, curried mutton, eggplant and tofu, aloo sandeko, bhatmas bhuteko, and some sweet curd from Bhaktapur. "What's the occasion?" Aakash asked, and his mother got teary eyed again while his father shook his head at him in contempt.

"Okay, okay, I'll no longer ask," Aakash said. "Can you also put some food on another plate? Rahul will be coming here in about twenty minutes, and I'm sure he'll be hungry. I'll take it to my room."

"Who's Rahul?" his father asked.

"He's been here before," Aakash's mother said. "That rich boy."

"How rich?"

"Very rich. His family owns hotels in the city."

Aakash's father ate the sumptuous lunch in a sullen mood, barely talking. Aakash tried to enjoy the feast that his mother had prepared, but with the impending arrival of Rahul, he couldn't focus on eating. He chewed his food halfheartedly and replied in monosyllables to his mother, who once again cried and said that nothing she did pleased her son anymore, and that was all the more reason that she should get out of the country, go away forever. "You don't need me after all," she said.

"I need you," Aakash said, stuffing pulao and meat exaggeratedly into his mouth.

"Well, we don't need you, that's for sure," his father said. "You're useless."

This worsened Aakash's mother's crying. Aakash, too, experienced a sting at his father's "useless" comment, but he neither had time to dwell on it nor to come up with a repartee because Rahul's motorcycle vroomed loudly outside. Hurriedly Aakash gargled in the sink, wiped his mouth, and, grabbing the extra plate his mother had made, went to the front door.

Rahul came into the foyer but didn't take off his helmet, which meant that he'd been drinking and didn't want Aakash's parents to smell him. "Where is she?" Rahul whispered. "In your room?"

Aakash signaled to him to follow him up the stairs. From the kitchen his mother shouted out a greeting to Rahul, who responded with, "Hello, Auntie."

Outside his door, Aakash whispered to Rahul, "Okay, I want you to really behave. Be gentle with her."

"Gentle with a prostitute? Because she's mute? Come on, man."

"She's not a prostitute. I'll tell you later. Oh, and also remember, this food is for her, and later when you leave, I want you to thank my mother for the delicious meal."

Rahul finally took off his helmet, and the air reeked of alcohol. His eyes were red and bleary: he was thoroughly drunk. "What?" Rahul said. "I was at an afternoon party."

"Remember"—Aakash wagged his finger next to Rahul's nose—"if you do or say anything bad, I'll make your life miserable."

"Where is all this hatred coming from? Chant *Ommmm*, my friend. Life is good."

"Maybe for you. But not for everyone. And especially not for her." Aakash pointed to his door.

PART II

Bajae's flat was in Indrachowk, and so they had to fight through massive crowds that thronged the narrow alleys of this area before they could reach her house. The taxi had to be stopped at the mouth of Asan, which meant that it was about half a kilometer to Bajae's flat, a walk during which Aakash's mother lost one of her slippers and his father lost his temper twice, once with a poor rickshaw puller whose wheel came awfully close to the old man's shoes, and the other time with a small girl who was insistent on selling him oranges.

Bajae's flat overlooked an inner courtyard, one of those smelly, garbage-strewn places that only camera-toting for-eigners found charming. Aakash vaguely recalled the reason why in her old age his grandmother lived here and not with her daughter in her spacious house; it had something to do with her inability to get along with Aakash's father. He had made her life so miserable that she had abandoned the comfort of a two-story brick building with a garden and cool breezes in the morning and the evening and had come to live here in this dump, rooming with another old woman who was also in conflict with her own family.

As they climbed the rickety stairs up to Bajae's flat on the second floor, Aakash wondered about Ghana, what Rahul might be doing to her. No, Aakash was going to think pos-itively, so he tried to recall Rahul's good traits. But he could not think of any, and he cursed himself for his suspicion, his relentlessly critical mind. Finally he came up with some-thing: Rahul was fun, and that was the reason the two had remained friends from their school days. Aakash found Rahul dangerous and exciting—therefore fun. "Yes, fun," he muttered as he and his father and mother stood in front of Bajae's door. And Rahul would entertain Ghana until Aakash got home, which would be soon, Aakash assured himself. He'd stay with Bajae only for a few minutes, then return.

Bajae's room was dark, with only a small, lopsided wooden window to invite sunlight. Her roommate was sitting by the window, trying to insert a thread into a needle, but it was obvious her eyes were poor. "All day long she has been asking me for some Coca-Cola," the roommate said. "Now where would an old woman like me go to get Coca-Cola?"

"You can find Coca-Cola right out there," Aakash's mother said. "In that shop in the courtyard."

"And who's going to give me money?" the roommate addressed her needle.

Bajae was sleeping in her bed, a cot, really, with a lumpy mattress that gave out a smell.

"My mother, look at her!" Aakash's mother said, seemingly choked up.

"Old mother!" Bajae's roommate yelled at her needle. "Wake up! Your daughter and her husband are here."

Bajae opened her eyes, and after they adjusted to the figures in the room, she asked, "Did you bring my grandson?"

Aakash's mother yanked him closer toward the bed.

"Sit here, Aavash," Bajae said.

"It's Aakash," his mother said.

"The old hag is completely gone," Aakash's father said.

"You haven't heard what the old mother says about you," the roommate informed Aakash's father. It was quite

possible, Aakash thought with abrupt clarity, that the roommate had been engaged with the needle and thread business
all day, perhaps every day for the past few days. Or perhaps
she'd been doing it for years. It took him some effort to pry
his eyes away from the roommate, who had licked the end
of her thread anew, and sat on on his grandmother's bed.

His grandmother's hand was old and arthritic as it
stroked his chin, commiserating with him about his parents
leaving. She said that she had never abandoned any of her
children—neither Aakash's mother nor her other daughter
who died in an accident—so she didn't understand where this
daughter inherited this newfangled idea. Bajae proceeded to
lay all the blame on Aakash's father, even after his mother
reminded her that her husband was right there. "What are
you going to do? What are you going to do?" Bajae asked
Aakash, who said, "I'll be fine, Bajae. Can I go now?"

Aakash's father, stung by Bajae's indictment, retreated to
the shadows, but Bajae, smelling his presence, launched a
series of invectives against him that stunned everyone except
the roommate, whose gnarled fingers trembled in the dim
light as they held the thread.

With strength Bajae clasped Aakash's arm and said, "How
can people do this to their own blood is beyond me. How can
a mother do this to her own child is beyond me. How can a
daughter do this"—she tilted her head down a bit to indicate
herself—"to her own mother is beyond me. Do you know
how long I have been living in this foul-smelling place now?
For five years. Five years, and my daughter has come to visit
me here only seven times. Yes, I've kept a tally. What else do

I have to do in my old age? If it weren't for this budhi"—she gestured toward her roommate—"I would have died within a month after I was forced into this place. Does that surprise you, my grandson? I don't know what story they've told you about me, but are you interested in listening? Are you?"

Aakash was only half-listening. He should have never left Ghana's side. But what could he have done? The pressure of the moment was enormous, and he'd found himself caving in before he could think properly. The instant that he and Rahul had entered his room, Aakash's mother had shouted at him in panic from below, "Son, I completely forgot that we were supposed to visit Bajae today. She's called us because we are leaving the country."

Aakash yelled back at her, "So you two go. She's invited you and Father, not me. I'm not needed."

"No, no, she repeatedly said that she hasn't seen you in ages, that she doesn't know when she's going to die."

"I'm not going!"

Rahul was sitting on the bed, his eyes locked with Ghana's. Her facial expression also indicated that she was in awe of him. Rahul hadn't uttered a word since he entered the room and sat on the bed, but now he said, without taking his eyes off Ghana, "Who's Bajae?"

"She's my mother's mother."

"I didn't know you had a grandmother."

"You don't know much about me."

"You should go."

"Why?"

"Family relations are important."

"You saying that? *You?*"

"I've always been a family man."

"You will sell your mother for a bottle of Jack Daniels." Aakash shouldn't have uttered such harsh words about Rahul's mother, but Rahul was getting on his nerves. Was he saying these things to impress Ghana? Did he not realize that she couldn't understand what he was saying?

"You should go," Rahul said. He reached out to grab the plate of food Aakash had set on the side table and placed it in between them on the bed. Ghana dug her right hand into the rice and vegetables, scooped them up, and—lo and behold!—lifted them to Rahul's face. Rahul opened his mouth wide and lovingly took the food in.

"What are you doing?" Aakash asked him. "That food is for her."

"Aakash!" his mother shouted from below. "I can't go to Bajae without you. As it is, she is not happy that we're going to Hong Kong by ourselves."

"Go, Aakash," Rahul said, his mouth full. "We'll be fine here." Now it was his turn to scoop up the dal-bhat and feed it to Ghana.

"I'm not going," Aakash said. He'd reached out to snatch the plate away from between them when there was a loud rap on the door. "Aakash." It was his father. "You might not ever see your mother again, and your Bajae—who knows when she's going to croak."

Aakash moved closer to the door and said, "Father, I have a headache."

"Then take Citamol."

"Go, Aakash," Rahul said. "I'll make sure that she's okay. I'll make sure that . . . no one touches her."

"What is your rich friend saying?" his father shouted from the other side.

"Nothing."

"Are you two smoking ganja in there?"

Rahul smiled at Aakash as though to say, *Well, we could*, but then he said, "Go, Aakash, what's the worry? It's just a matter of an hour or so, isn't it? I'll stay with her, make sure she's well fed, try to talk to her, and you'll be back."

"Why don't you come with me, Rahul? I could use some company. You're a charmer with old women, and Bajae will love you."

"It's a private family matter," Rahul said, his eyes on Ghana. "I don't want to intrude."

"Aakash," his father said, "smoking ganja, are you?"

Frustrated, Aakash flipped open the latch and cracked open the door. "Okay, I'm coming."

His father slid a foot in, preventing Aakash from closing it again. "Is that ganja smell?" His father was strong, and Aakash had to push hard to keep the door from opening farther. He threw all his weight on the door as his father attempted to widen the gap to slide in. Aakash made frenetic hand signals to Rahul, who clasped Ghana's hand and took her over to the balcony, making her crouch behind the balcony door. Aakash motioned to him to leave her and return to the room, and after he did, Aakash slowly let go of the door. His father was panting as he stepped in.

He looked past Aakash and Rahul, saw nothing, smelled nothing—except perhaps the whiff of booze on Rahul's breath—and Aakash challenged him, "Satisfied? Anything else you need to see?"

"If you're not smoking, then why this hush-fush? What do you have to hide?"

Rahul put his arm around Aakash's father as though the two were friends, and led him out of the room, saying, "Nothing, Dad. You are becoming suspicious for no reason."

Strangely, Rahul's touch mollified Aakash's father, and he grumbled, "If you had a son like mine, you, too, would be suspicious."

All three were on the landing now. Rahul said, "Aakash, why don't you go and visit your poor, ailing grandmother? I'll wait for you here."

"I don't know how long I'll be."

"No worries. I'm free today and don't have any other place to go."

"What do you need now?" Aakash's father addressed his son. "A medal for going to visit your grandmother?"

Everything became too much for Aakash, and he told his father, "All right, give me a minute, and I'll be right out."

Leaving Rahul's arm still around his father, Aakash retreated to his room, slamming the door shut behind him so his father couldn't see. Ghana was still crouched on the balcony, tears streaming down her face. "Don't be afraid," he whispered to her. "Rahul will take care of you. I'll be back soon." The softness of his voice seemed to soothe her, and she looked pleadingly into his eyes. He kissed her on her forehead before he left.

Bajae's voice became softer. "You know when I was young, when your mother was still a child, I used to go to the movies. Ashok Cinema Hall—that was my favorite theater. We lived in Baghbazar then, your grandfather and I, and on some Saturdays we walked over to Ratna Park and caught the bus to Patan Dhoka. I used to link my fingers with his, with your mother walking in between us. There were no minibuses then, nor any three-wheelers, only those big buses, and while we waited, my husband bought some amla from a nanglo shop, and we sucked on them. The bus ride was my favorite part. I sat by the window, watching the city pass me by. The bus ride seemed so long—from Ratna Park to Shahidgate, turning around, then onto Singha Durbar, through the wide expanse of Thapathali, crossing the Bagmati Bridge, then the steep climb in Pulchowk toward Patan. By the time the bus stopped at the Patan Dhoka, I would be flushed with excitement at what lay ahead: the walk from the Dhoka to the cinema hall, the small temple on the side of the road that you half-circled before moving deeper into the alley, and—*voilà!*—there it was, Ashok Cinema Hall. You know, in those days, Ashok Kumar the actor was really famous, and I'd watch his movies in that very cinema hall. For the longest time I thought that Ashok Kumar the actor owned our Ashok Cinema Hall, that he was behind the curtains, observing us watching his movies. Ha, ha, ha! How silly I was. But those were the happiest days for me, before your mother began to throw her teenage tantrums and before your dear grandfather passed away and I was left at the mercy of your mother and this man." She thrust her finger at Aakash's father, who was so deep in the shadows that it was hard to tell he was in the room.

"Mother, leave him alone," Aakash's mother said, her cheeks wet with tears.

"They told me I was too old," Bajae said, addressing Aakash. "They said I was losing my mind. They belittled me every moment they got. They told me that I was a bad mother and a dreadful mother-in-law."

Aakash's father mumbled from the shadows that on her deathbed, the old woman had turned into a candidate for an insane asylum.

"Grandma," Aakash said, "I have a friend waiting for me at home. I really have to go."

Bajae loosened her fingers on Aakash's arm and said, "Of course, you, too. What was I expecting? After all, what am I to you?"

The left side of her face was twisted, as though a bone or a sinew inside had slid down. He remembered a photo of Bajae from her younger days, a young, fair-faced woman standing next to her husband and her daughter. Her fingers were entwined with her daughter's.

"Grandma," Aakash said, "you are everything to me." He sounded like an actor in a third-rate Nepali movie. Still, he couldn't help himself, and he said again, "You mean so much to me, Grandma. Seriously."

"Do you mean that, Grandson?" Bajae asked.

"Yes."

"Then don't let me die in this purgatory. Take me somewhere, Grandson, where I can exhale my last breath in peace."

From the shadows, Aakash's father: "Now you want to burden your grandson with your old, rickety bones?"

Trembling, Bajae attempted to sit up on the bed. "I have a right to die in dignity, do you hear?"

"Dignity," her roommate said, nodding at her needle and thread.

"Grandma, I can't look after you," Aakash said. "I can barely take care of myself."

"I don't want to die here!"

Helplessly, Aakash looked at his mother, who chided Bajae, "What are you doing? After so long your grandson comes to visit you, and all you do is add to his worries?"

"Her grandson can wipe her arse when she loses control over her bowel movements," Aakash's father said. "He can feed her soup and wipe her chin. He can give her a bubble bath."

"Hush," Aakash's mother said.

Bajae had now curled up in the fetal position, her leathery feet pulled close to her behind, her eyes clenched tightly shut. Aakash placed his hand on her arm and said, "Grandma," but Bajae had turned into a shy turtle, impenetrable.

"It takes ages for me to coax her back out when she gets like that," the roommate said.

"You should've kept your mouth shut," Aakash's mother said to her husband.

"What do we do now?" Aakash asked.

His mother sat on the bed, jiggled Bajae's arm, and said, "Come on, Mother. Give up such childishness. We came here to say goodbye to you, and I don't see why you can't nicely bid us goodbye. Who knows when we're going to be back next—it'll certainly not be while you're alive."

"She's going to play corpse until you take her away from here," the roommate said.

And Bajae did. Aakash called her a few times, but she remained curled up. Aakash's father began to harangue his wife and son, saying that it was useless with this old hussy, that they'd so much to get done before they left the country. Aakash thought about Ghana, whether Rahul had already made licentious advances on her.

Yet there was something heartbreaking about his old grandmother coiled up like this. He had to make things right. After all, it wasn't to her daughter and son-in-law that Bajae had appealed; it was to Aakash, her grandson. He couldn't simply walk away from her! But he didn't know how to appease her. He wasn't used to dealing with old people, and he was certainly not skilled in the art of mollification. "Bajae," he tried again. Then, thinking of something, he turned to his parents and said, "You two leave now. I'll handle her. Can't you see that she's traumatized?" He addressed the roommate, "You, too. Go now, please. Leave us two alone for a while."

"But this is my house," the roommate said. "Where will I go?"

"Take her to that shop down the street," Aakash instructed

his parents. "Feed her some sweets, some tea. Then you can leave to finish your packing."

"You think we have money flowing out of our pockets?" his father said. "If we spend money on toothless old ladies in Nepal, how will we survive in Hong Kong? Or in America, if it comes to that?"

"Here," said Aakash, and handed a five-hundred-rupee bill to his mother from his wallet. "Please leave now."

"All right, Bajae, we're going," Aakash's mother said, but Bajae remained motionless. Her roommate finally set down the needle and the thread by the window and stood, her spine bent. She was even smaller than he'd thought—she barely came up to his mother's waist as she exited the room with her palm on her hip.

Aakash sat on the bed and massaged his grandmother's back, gently rubbing his fingers along her spine. The movement soothed him, but he was uncertain it was doing her any good. Still, he continued to rub her curved spine with his fingers until it straightened a bit. Finally, she stirred, opened her eyes, and turned toward him. "Why are you still around?" she asked. "Why don't you, too, leave me to my fate?"

"Grandma, I don't want you to think badly of me."

"After I croak, no one will have to worry about me anymore. Your mother may even dance in the streets."

"You know she won't."

"And your father will celebrate with a goat sacrifice."

"They're leaving the country, and there are no goats in Hong Kong."

Bajae sighed, then took his hand. "You need to look after yourself, my grandson."

"I will, but I can't look after you, Grandma. I wouldn't know what to do with you, and I'm afraid that you'll suffer even more with me than you will here with your room-mate."

She watched him for a while, then smiled. "Then will you do one thing for me?"

"What?"

"Take me to the Pashupatinath temple and leave me there. Someone I know lives in a house inside the temple complex, and I'd rather spend my last days there than in this room."

"Who is this person?"

"It's someone from my past. A man who I once thought I was going to marry. When I didn't, he became celibate."

"Have you been in touch with him all these years?"

"No, but he'll take me in. I know him well."

Aakash looked at his watch.

"It's my death wish, Aavash. Other people ask for water. This is what I am requesting."

He helped her pack a few things in a bag—nothing more than a dhoti or two, a few photos of gods and goddesses, and a couple of necklaces. But when it came time for her to walk, she couldn't. She stood up, then sat right back down again; her legs couldn't hold up her body. He had no choice but to hoist her on his back. She was light like bamboo, and he carried her down the stairs with no effort, although he had to ask her to watch her head as the ceiling was quite low. The bright sunlight outside dazzled his eyes. He paused for a moment, getting his bearings as people walking by the busy alley looked at them curiously. It was not a common sight in the city; in the hills and mountains people still carried the sick and the old on their backs to health posts miles away. He had to find a taxi, and he had to find it before his parents and the roommate returned. He found a taxi idling in the chowk, and he helped Bajae into the backseat and slid in next to her. As the taxi pulled away, he looked back and spotted his father and mother and the roommate emerge from a tea shop, not too far from the mouth of the courtyard where he and Bajae were only a moment ago.

As they approached the Pashupatinath area, Aakash realized that if his parents decided to return home before he did, it was quite likely that his mother would go up to his room with tea for Rahul, and she'd discover Ghana, unless Rahul didn't open the door for her. Aakash had to move: he had to find Bajae's celibate friend quickly, deposit her there quickly, then head on back home quickly. The taxi stopped near the temple and they got out. With Bajae on his back, he loped toward the big gate of the temple, he in Calvin Klein jeans, she in a tattered dhoti. People stared, some laughed, some gestured in awe. His arms were numb by the time they passed through the gate and came upon the giant buttocks of Shiva's bull, Nandi, who was gazing tenderly at her lord in the main shrine.

Aakash swiveled left, where on raised platforms some sadhus and monk types were reciting prayers. He asked

Bajae what the name of her monk was, and she could come up with only his first name, Gopal. With her on his now-throbbing back, he asked around. Some said there was no monk named Gopal living in the complex; others said complainingly that there were too many monks named Gopal.

His arms aching, Aakash exited the main temple area and crossed the footbridge across the Bagmati River to the east. As a college student, he'd smoked hash here during Shivaratri, when ash-smeared naked sadhus from all over flooded the temple to pray to Shiva. A few tourists, making awed sounds, were snapping photos of burning corpses on the funeral pyre across the river to the left. An old sadhu, his eyes red, sat in a pavilion and smoked a chillum, and it was to him that Aakash turned with his query.

"Gopal Shivakoti?" the sadhu asked. A small cry escaped Bajae's mouth, and the sadhu said that Gopal had shifted to the Gueswori temple, a short walking distance to the north.

Aakash observed the steps up the hill that he'd have to climb to take her to Gueswori. He looked around to see if he could hire someone, perhaps an idling laborer, to carry Bajae, but was overcome by the notion that it was his filial duty to transport his grandmother on his back. This was the least he could do for her. He recalled the Hindu myth of a young man who carried, in two baskets balanced by a wooden bar on his shoulders, his feeble, blind parents for a pilgrimage across the Gangetic plains. But the myth's high-mindedness soon dissipated, as after only a few steps up the hill he was breathless, and his calves burned. "You can rest for a while," Bajae said, but he continued, now each step weightier. At one point he did stop, and they both sat on a step. Bajae used her dhoti to wipe the sweat from his forehead. "Poor grandson," she said. "You never thought you'd end up doing this for your grandmother, did you? Don't worry. Lord Shiva above is watching all of this. He'll remember when it comes time for you to get to heaven."

"Grandma," Aakash said, "I'm not doing this so I can get to heaven."

A few temple monkeys gathered around them. Aakash shooed them away.

"Hanumanji," Bajae said.

"Filthy, disease-carrying monkeys, Grandma," Aakash said. "Don't be fooled into thinking that they represent your monkey god."

"Hanumanji carried an entire mountain on his palm because he was so devoted to Lord Ram, did you know that?"

"Yes, yes," Aakash said impatiently, all too familiar with that story. An hour had passed since they left Bajae's room, and he doubted whether his parents were going to wait for much longer, if they hadn't left already. And he shuddered to think what might have happened in his room between Rahul and Ghana. When he reached the top of the hill, his whole body was burning with exhaustion.

Once more they rested, then proceeded again, passing by a group of youngsters in yoga postures. Fortunately, the ground was level here, and a bit farther up, the stairs descended to Guheswori. "You know what *guhe* means,

Grandson?" Bajae asked. "It means a woman's private parts. So Guheswori is a temple of a woman's private parts."

Since the temple of the goddess was in a fairly small courtyard, it didn't take them long to find out that a sadhu named Gopal lived in one of the houses surrounding the main shrine. Bajae, suddenly energized, stood on her own two feet and repeatedly shouted the man's name. Children gathered around them.

A man appeared at a window. He was bearded, with grayish hair tied at the top of his head. It was hard to discern his age; he didn't look as old as Bajae. "Anuradha?" the man asked in disbelief.

"Recognize me, Gopal?" Bajae cried. "Did you ever think you'd set your sight on these old bones?"

The man withdrew from the window, and Aakash thought that the man, the celibate sadhu that he was, wanted nothing to do with this woman from his past. But there he was, at the door. Aakash saw that he was indeed older than how he'd appeared. His head was big, but his body was small and his back slightly bent. He leaned against the doorframe and smiled at Bajae. "Anuradha, you are as beautiful as ever."

Bajae's cheeks were moist. "And you have completely changed. Look at you. You've turned into a sadhu-santa, renouncing the world."

"What else could I do? You . . . life dealt me such a blow that I had no choice but to retreat."

"Well, we can't change what we've done, can we? But here we are, after so many years."

"Won't you come in, Anuradha? I don't have much, but I can offer you tea."

Bajae turned to Aakash. "Grandson, you can go now."

"Are you sure, Grandma?"

"Yes. Now I've found Gopal."

Aakash embraced her and kissed her forehead. "Call me if you need me."

But her full attention was already on Gopal, who was also gazing at her rapturously.

As Aakash exited through the northern entrance, where he'd be sure to find a taxi, he glanced back. Both of them stooping, Bajae and Gopal were entering the house, and Bajae was holding Gopal's arm for support.

Everything looked normal as he approached his house—the front gate was shut, all the windows were shut, as they always were, in fear of daylight robbers. He opened the main gate and slipped in quietly. Rahul's motorcycle wasn't there. Aakash knew that an empty room awaited him upstairs. With a breaking heart, he trudged up and opened it. He thought he could detect a faint smell of romance, a crushing kind of infatuation.

He lay down on the bed. Within minutes he heard his parents come in, and suddenly wondering whether he'd been mistaken, whether Rahul had left by himself, Aakash jumped up and rushed to the balcony. But Ghana wasn't there.

"Aakash," his mother yelled as she climbed up the stairs. "Where did Bajae go? Where did you take her? We waited and waited, but neither you nor Bajae returned. What did she have you do?"

Aakash lay down on the bed again. His mother spoke to him from the doorway. "Where did you take her, Aakash?"

"I took her to meet her old lover."

"What shameless talk! Why are you speaking about your grandmother that way?" his mother said. "I don't know what has happened to you these days. It seems like you are bent on hurting us, even in our last minutes here."

Aakash turned away from her.

PART III

There were moments when Aakash thought he didn't know anyone in the city. And in one sense it was true: with his beard and his uncombed hair—he was beginning to resemble the lead singer of Jethro Tull, one of his favorite bands when he was a teenager—he himself had become unrecognizable. He hadn't shaved since the day Ghana went missing, and now nursed a filthy, unkempt beard. On the streets where he meandered all day, acquaintances passed by without recognizing him, or they scrunched their noses, thinking he was a beggar. Some of them did double takes, exclaimed, "Aakash! Is that you?" They tried to carry a normal conversation, asking about his parents, his work, as if it weren't abnormal for them to find Aakash in crumpled clothes, his body reeking, a semimaniacal expression on his face.

One relative was aghast when she came upon him. "Just

because your parents have left, does that mean that you simply let go of all of your faculties like that?" She pointed to the dirt caked on Aakash's feet (he was wearing slippers). "No, no," she said. "I won't let it happen." She dragged him by the hand and took him to her house, where she fed him. He ate rapidly and hungrily, slurping and licking his palms; he ate so much that his stomach became distended. She pushed him out to the yard, where he crouched in his underwear as she angrily scrubbed his skin. As she bathed him with water spurting out of a pipe, she continued to rebuke him for his self-neglect, and briefly he wondered if she'd now commence to beat him with the pipe. She forced him to wear her husband's clothes and threw his smelly clothes in a basket for the washerwoman. "You're staying with me for a few days," she said, but he managed to sneak out when she visited the bathroom.

Since Ghana left, he'd been experiencing a stabbing kind of pain in his stomach. These days he didn't go to work and meandered all over, from Badikhel to Budhanilkantha, peering into alleys, knocking on people's doors. Occasionally in the middle of the street he bent over with stomach pain, especially when he imagined what Rahul was doing to Ghana. He likened himself to the figure in a painting he'd seen in a book once, titled *The Scream*, or was it *The Silent Scream*? A baldheaded person—a man or a woman?—stood on a bridge, holding its head, its mouth open wide in a scream. It was an image Aakash's mind had summoned for more self-pity. Wait. He was talking as though his mind was a separate entity from him: there was Mind and there was Him, and the two were involved in a complicated, vexing relationship.

"Mind," he addressed his mind in exasperation. "Just stop."

One afternoon it occurred to him that thus far he'd assumed Rahul and Ghana were in the city. What was the basis for that assumption? Couldn't Rahul have taken her out of here, perhaps to Jhapa, where his family owned big properties? Aakash could picture the two of them, in the heat of the south, on their porch chewing on corn and slurping on mango while a coterie of servants catered to their needs, brought them cushions and soft drinks and little stray puppies to play with.

Or—and this possibility made him numb—Rahul could have flown her out of the country. He could have taken her to Bombay. Rahul frequently talked about Bombay. "I'd like to live in a house by Juhu Beach," he'd told Aakash. "Hire a couple of actresses to be my concubines. Maybe I'll get a role in a movie, huh, Aakash? Maybe old man Amitabh Bachchan himself will take a liking to me and plead with me to join him in a buddy movie, like a sequel to *Sholay*. Maybe I can get you a small role, as a joker with a two-second appearance, you know, the type who makes a clown face in the background?"

"Yes, you and Amitabh Bachchan," Aakash had said. "I can see the two of you riding trains without tickets, jumping into hay with buxom village girls."

"Or I'll get a flat by Marine Drive and eat kulfi on Chowpatty Beach."

Rahul could have taken Ghana even farther away, like Hong Kong. Aakash visualized his parents running into Rahul with a dark African girl on Hong Kong streets. Rahul could have taken her all the way to America—he had that kind of money—and they could be in a hotel in New York City's Times Square, gazing at the neon signs.

But she was here, she was here—he could feel it in his bones.

The Supreme Commander appeared on television. "My enemies are after me," he said. "They want to chop my body to pieces; they want to feed me to the vultures." In the background flashed images of various beheadings, not just of Nepali workers in Iraq: a cat's head severed as it continued to meow; a bull being slaughtered during Dashain in Hanuman Dhoka, a giant khukuri coming down swiftly on its neck and the head bouncing off toward the alarmed spectators.

One morning instead of entering his office building, Aakash crossed the street to the peepal tree and loitered there, remembering that day he'd met Ghana. The phlegm-shooting newspaper man now also sold tea, which he boiled in a supersized kettle, and Aakash crouched next to him until five o'clock, drinking tea. This became his ritual: convince himself that he was going to work, then veer at the last moment to cross the street. At five his colleagues left the building across the street, filing out one by one, laughing and talking. It wouldn't be too long before he'd be terminated. Already the associate editor had left him several messages, demanding to know why he was missing work.

One day in Thamel, Aakash spotted the long-haired painter. For some reason Aakash became immensely happy at running into him. The artist was, after all, Aakash's only connection to Ghana. The painter was the one who'd introduced him to her. Wait! What was he saying? It was Aakash who'd found Ghana on the street, ready to be mauled by a mob. The painter merely allowed him access to his dreams. But this painter knew something about Ghana—of this Aakash was convinced. He couldn't remember the painter's name as he lurched after him, so he cried out, "Painter sahib, painter sahib."

The painter turned around just as Aakash reached him, breathless. "Do you recognize me?" Aakash asked.

He didn't. He wouldn't have recognized a dapper, clean-shaven Aakash, and here was a filthy-looking young man with manic eyes.

"No, I don't," the painter said. "Where have we met?" He tossed his head to throw back his hair like a woman.

Aakash launched into a description of the day at Haawa, then quickly realized how absurd he sounded.

"Do you need some money to eat?" the painter said. "Is that what you want?" He patted his pockets and extracted a wallet.

"Do you know a girl from Africa?"

The painter paused. "Who?"

"An African girl."

The painter observed him. "What's your name, young man?"

"Aakash."

"Do you know an African girl?" the painter asked.

"I used to. But she's flown the coop."

"Come with me," the painter said, and led him into a nearby shop, which, Aakash realized, was his gallery, filled with his paintings. The painter led him to the back corner, where a small painting hung. It was an African girl. Ghana. "She came to me in a dream a few weeks ago," the painter said.

Ghana's eyes were slightly lowered, as though she was contemplating a decision.

"I need to find her," Aakash said.

"Where are you going to find her? She is a product of my imagination." The painter bunched his hair in his palms, then let it fall down again in a beautiful cascade.

"She exists. I have met her."

"Certainly you're not suggesting that our dreams are real? If that were the case, then all of these would have to become real, too, wouldn't they?" The painter gestured toward his paintings. Covering an entire wall, one piece illustrated the decapitation of a Nepali migrant worker by an Iraqi insurgent. The hooded insurgent was holding the head aloft by its hair. In a garish manner blood spurted from the neck like fireworks, with extra large drops threatening to leap off the canvas. The eyes on the head were closed, and a smile adorned its lips, as though a prank were being pulled on the viewers.

Riots had broken out in the city when the Nepali workers

had been executed in Iraq, Aakash remembered now. Muslim establishments had been attacked; people had scorched tires on the streets and smashed shop windows. Rumors had floated that gangs of men were about to be unleashed on the Muslim population in the city, with instructions to capture them and behead them in public with khukuris, symbols of Gorkha warrior pride. When he'd first heard the rumor, Aakash was in Haawa, smoking a joint with Rahul. He'd felt a cold breeze on his Adam's apple, as though someone was indeed brandishing a khukuri close to his throat.

There were other paintings: a fly-ridden body decomposing on the sidewalk, a woman carving out an eye from a monkey's face in the Swayambhunath temple, vultures eating a child alive on a mountaintop. There was no subtlety here; everything was glaring and blaring. How did this man become so famous through his art? Even his depictions of the gods and goddesses were tasteless: Lord Ganesh fornicating with his conduit rat; Goddess Kali in a dance bar, twirling around a pole; Shiva drunk and vomiting in a gutter. A thought cruised through Aakash's mind: a man who lived by the sword died by the sword. He turned toward the painting of Ghana, an oasis of calm in this assault of images.

"Do you want her?" the painter asked.

"I need to find her."

"The painting, I mean."

"What will I do with it? It'll make my heart ache even more."

"Take it. You can have it. It has no monetary value for

me. This is where my bread and butter is." He pointed toward his other paintings.

Aakash hung the painting in the living room, right in between the solemn portraits of his parents, and was pleased at giving Ghana a place of such prominence. His parents' expressions seemed to turn even more somber at finding the dark African girl separating them.

The day before his parents were scheduled to leave, his mother had asked whether he wanted to go to the airport to see them off, and he said, "It doesn't matter to me." She took that as a further sign of his uncaring attitude and spent the next half an hour crying and complaining to her husband, who came to Aakash's room, stood in the doorway, and said, "Can't you show enough character in these final days to at least pretend to be a son to us?"

"What do you want me to do?"

"Be nice to her!"

"Do you want me to tell her that I'll go to the airport to see you two off?"

"That is the least you can do."

"What else do you want me to do, Father?" Aakash asked with no malice. "What else can I do that'll make you and Mother happy?"

His father glared at him from the doorway. "Figure it out for yourself."

Aakash went to the kitchen, where his mother, sad faced, was flipping through a magazine, and he told her, "Mother, I'll go to the airport with you tomorrow."

"Good," she said in a clipped voice.

"And tonight why don't I cook a nice dinner for you two?"

His mother looked at him sharply, then smiled. "That'll certainly give me happy memories on my journey."

So Aakash went to the market and bought all the groceries he thought he needed. On the way back to the house, he imagined, cruelly and briefly, what'd happen if he were to put some rat poison in what he was about to cook. He could see the headlines tomorrow: "YOUNG SON MURDERS HIS PARENTS FOR TRYING TO ABANDON HIM."

That evening he cooked. He chopped the meat, he sliced the vegetables; he poured oil into pans, he transferred oil from one pan to another; he rummaged in the cupboard for spices; he opened the window to let the smoke out and heard the neighbors quarrel; he threw a piece of meat to the stray dog that stood outside the window; he hung a towel over his shoulder like a real cook and dipped his index finger into the gravies and the sauces to ascertain their tastes and textures; he talked to himself in the course of the cooking: "Maybe not enough salt in this one. Hmm, I wonder if the jackfruit needs five more minutes. This must be the best-tasting spinach in the country." All the while his parents sat in the living room, now and then commenting favorably on the ruckus he was making, and the extraordinary aromas that had filled the house.

"We should take him with us," his father said. "He'd make a good cook for us in the strange lands."

"We should buy him a chef's hat," his mother said, "and pretend we're royalty."

It took him three hours to get everything ready. He overwhelmed himself with everything he'd concocted: apart from chicken and mutton dishes, he'd cooked four vegetables and prepared two achars. Like a true chef, he'd tasted his fares as he'd cooked, but he didn't know whether they'd be up to the standard of his parents, who were now standing slack jawed at the entrance to the kitchen. His father came and embraced him. "Even if this meal tastes horrible, you have proven yourself to us, son." And his mother cried. Then they sat down and ate like hungry animals.

"Who knows whether we'd be able to eat like this again, or ever?" they wondered loudly. Uncle Subhash had a Chinese wife, they said, and the Chinese were all about noodles or pigs' ears or frogs' legs. "How will we survive?" Aakash's father asked, and his mother said that she'd have to do all the cooking herself. "But won't Subhash's wife get offended?" his father countered.

"She most likely will," Aakash's mother admitted, and for a while they pondered this problem.

The next day they flew out of the country.

Aakash woke up with a jolt. He had dozed while the evening had descended. It was dark in the room now, and he could no longer see the painting, but he felt its presence. A neighbor's radio was on full blast, and he heard the chirpy voice of a radio deejay speaking in a mishmash of English and Nepali: "Ani tyo Radisson Hotelko beauty contest ke, dai, it was a well-attended affair, hoina? Ani tyo radical Maoist-haru le protest program hotel kai lobby-ma gareta pani, the beauty contest chanhi successful consider garnu parchha. Ani hamro listeners harubatapani hamilay nikkai feedback paisakyaun, there is no room for old-fashioned thinking in Nepal anymore, bhanera. Understand garnubho, dai?"

I have to find her, Aakash thought. *I have to find Ghana.*

At moments he was certain he'd come upon her, some-where unexpected, just like that time when he'd chanced upon her cowering before a mob under the peepal tree. As he wandered through alleys and lanes, Aakash suspected that Rahul, being Rahul, had already abandoned her. She must be lost and bewildered again, like she was before. He hoped he would reach her in time for her rescue.

His foolishness made him smile. Ghana herself was surely not the same person anymore. Rahul could have even taught her some Nepali by now—the boy was good at these things. In fact, Rahul was magical in many ways. He'd been the smartest one in school, stunning the teachers with the carelessness with which he solved the toughest of math problems, wrote the most inspiring of essays. One time he'd given such a stirring performance of Mark Antony's soliloquy during Caesar's funeral that the principal had contacted a well-known filmmaker, an alumnus of the school, to come and speak to Rahul about career possibilities. But Rahul had sniggered through the meeting, and the filmmaker had left in frustration.

A vision flashed across Aakash's mind, forcing him to pause along the banks of the Bishnumati River that was now a shantytown: Ghana in a bright red bridal sari, bejeweled, circling the groom, Rahul, who was sitting in front of the wedding pyre, the priest reciting his Sanskrit chants. *Surely not?* Aakash thought. *Surely, surely not?* In all likelihood Rahul abused her for a night or two and then left her in the streets.

But this made Aakash pause: He recalled a conversation he'd had with Rahul. Aakash had joked that he could see Rahul in his old age, like the *Playboy* magnate Hefner, with two dozen sex kittens about him. Rahul had laughed, pleased by the projection, then said, "You underestimate me, Aakash. Deep inside I'm a one-woman man. I'm waiting for the right one to come along. All of what you see about me is only a play, an illusion." When Aakash had asked him how Rahul would know when his right woman had appeared, Rahul had snapped his fingers and said, "Like this. I'll recognize her instantly."

The possibility of Rahul and Ghana tied in matrimony turned Aakash into a heavy smoker, a pack-a-day man, his fingers constantly fumbling with the pack, lighting up, taking deep drags. His room reeked of smoke, and the smell crept to the other parts of the house—his parents' abandoned bedroom, the kitchen, the downstairs bathroom with its bidet.

On the street, whenever he caught his reflection in the mirror inside a shop, he surprised himself by how unfamiliar he looked. If observed from a certain angle, he thought he resembled a renunciate who had given up all of his worldly concerns. But that was far from the truth. If anything, he was now immersed in a sadness that had collected like a deep pool inside him. He had no hopes of finding Ghana, yet once in a while in a courtyard deep in the innards of the city he couldn't help but glance up at one of the crumbling houses, hoping that he'd see her sticking her head out to watch the street.

Once, when he was climbing the three hundred sixty-five steps to the Swayambhunath temple, he spotted a dark woman descending, and he froze. A monkey circled him, looking at him expectantly. But when the woman came closer, he saw that she was a tourist.

The dream returned, this time with a vengeance. Aakash was fully inside the dream, experiencing Hamad's life. He was in a teahouse, sipping mint tea. His fingers went up to his face to touch the bruises he received from thugs in a dark alley the night before. The young men had beaten him, then taken off with his money, laughing as they called him a country bumpkin.

Luckily he had kept some cash in the side pocket of his tunic. It would be just enough for him to survive for the next two or three days. He had to find his daughter soon. He looked around the tea shop, which was filled with men drinking tea, smoking hookahs, or talking quietly. Some of them were laborers—he could tell by their stained and worn-out garbs. He was not like them, he told himself, not poor like them. He had property in the village; he'd never have to migrate to the city to work as a laborer like these people. But he wasn't sure anymore. Anything could happen in a person's life. People's fortunes changed. Tomorrow he could lose his house and his land, and he'd be on the streets. Then he'd have to find a job, and he might even be forced to migrate to the city.

Family. First he had to make sure that he had a family. His thoughts returned to his daughter. He hoped the city hadn't forced her into prostitution. Girls from his village had ended up in the city brothels. If indeed his daughter had joined a brothel here and word reached his village, he wouldn't be able to hold his head up again. His wife wouldn't forgive him.

Hamad finished his tea and ambled back to the lodge where he was staying. *She's not that kind of girl*, he told himself. But what if some shyster had managed to seduce her, then sell her to a madame? Hamad paused under a street lamp, weary. Moths frolicked around his head. Two beggars crouching in a darkened corner heckled him.

In the lodge he lay in bed, listening to the evening noises outside, his cheeks still smarting from the bruises. His stomach was growling, and he knew he ought to go out to eat, but he didn't have the energy. He closed his eyes and slowly drifted to sleep, his dreams frequented by his daughter.

At home Aakash's mother had left a series of messages for him on the answering machine. Her voice was chirpy, young, filled with laughter and possibilities. She said that they were in Hong Kong, had visited many tourist sights, and were so impressed with everything they saw—the cleanliness, the orderliness, the skyscrapers—that they had decided to settle right there instead of moving on to America. Uncle Subhash was in the process of finding Aakash's father a job, any job, possibly even a job as a rifle-toting guard at a bank. "Don't laugh now, Aakash," his mother said. "Here it's not like in Nepal. There is nothing shameful about working as a guard—here, no one insults you as a paaley. As for me, I don't know what I'll do. I need to find a job, too, although I don't know what. This is an expensive place. A Nepali woman I met has opened a hair salon, and she was saying she would be willing to train me without pay for a few weeks. She says that cutting hair is easy, and you get to meet interesting people. You know how social I am. I like talking and mingling with everyone. So I am seriously considering it."

She continued on in the next message: "How are you, Son? How come you're never home to pick up the phone? You haven't changed a bit, have you? Always roaming around like a lafanga, hanging out with your no-good friends." Her voice cracked. "That's why we left you, Aakash. That's why we're here in this foreign land, listening constantly to the chatter of these Chinese people going *ching-chung-chang-fung* all day long."

Next message: "I miss you, Son. I wish you could join us. You'd like it here. But I don't think your father would approve of the idea. He's very disappointed in you. Whenever I mention your name, he puts up his hand and says, 'Enough.' That's what he says, Aakash: 'Enough.' And how can I convince him otherwise? You've broken our confidence. You've broken my heart."

In the following message, his mother launched into a detailed description of how to cook the cauliflower that was growing in the garden. She asked, "And how is Danny doing? Is he making you happy with his work?" Little did she know that the very first morning that Danny had appeared for work, Aakash had paid him a month's wages and asked him not to come by anymore. The boy had looked at him, aghast, and Aakash had said, "This is not a good place to work. You won't like it here." When the boy didn't look convinced, Aakash added, "You won't like me. I am not a good man. I don't like young boys. When I see them, I feel like smacking their heads inside out, like this." He lifted his hand as though ready to strike the boy, and Danny ran out the door.

"Aakash! Aakash!" his mother's plaintive cry from the answering machine rang through the house.

What prompted Aakash to try out Rahul's house in Balaju, he didn't know. Surely Rahul would not be brazen enough to take Ghana home? Rahul's relationship with his parents was even stranger than Aakash's was with his. At least Aakash could claim that his parents showed affection every now and then, and that they displayed awareness that disappointments and accusations weren't the only way parents and children could relate to one other. But Rahul's parents barely spoke to him. And that was how it always had been, as far as Aakash could remember. The first time he went to Rahul's house—the boys must have been in fifth grade then—Aakash saw his parents in the

living room, playing cards, and they didn't look up when
the boys went in. Rahul took him upstairs to his room,
where shortly a servant brought them some snacks and
milk. The servant stood around, watching with soft eyes,
asking them whether they needed anything, asking Rahul
about school, until Rahul forcefully pushed him out.

Whenever Aakash asked Rahul about his parents, he
merely grunted, or he seemed to be thinking about something else. The few other times Aakash visited Rahul, his
parents barely acknowledged his presence. It had occurred
to Aakash that for Rahul's parents, their son simply wasn't
a major factor in their lives. It was the servant who had
raised him.

Today, the same servant, now with wrinkles on his face,
opened the door. "Is Rahul in?" Aakash asked, more curtly
than he had intended.

"Oho, Aakash babu!" the servant said. "I didn't even
recognize you with your beard." His gaze fell on Aakash's
grimy feet. "You look like you're sick. Everything okay?"

"Everything is okay. Is Rahul in?"

The servant shook his head.

A female voice from inside asked who it was, and when
the servant said that it was Rahul's friend, the woman, who
sounded like Rahul's mother, asked, "What does he want?"

"Auntie, I was just wondering if Rahul was in."

Rahul's mother asked him to come in. She was standing at the bottom of the stairs that Aakash had climbed
in the past to reach Rahul's room. It was slightly dark
there, so her face was in the shadows, but immediately

he could tell that she was an alcoholic. There was a smell, something minty that was an attempt to cover the smell of liquor.

One of her arms was holding on to the balustrade, as though she were afraid of falling. "What's your name?" she asked him.

"Aakash."

She was silent for a while, then said, "He's not been home for the past couple of weeks."

"Three weeks," the servant said from the doorway.

"I was just wondering whether Auntie knew where he was." He felt awkward standing a few feet apart from her, unable to see her face.

"My son never gave me a chance to know him," Rahul's mother said. "But I heard that he's somewhere in Bouddha, living with a girl."

Aakash's heart skipped a beat. "What kind of a girl, Auntie?"

"Who knows? One of my relatives told me this the other day. Isn't it true, Harka?"

The servant said, "That relative also has a penchant for gossip."

"Is the girl dark, a habsi?"

Rahul's mother went silent. He asked again, and when she didn't respond, he knew that she had drifted into her own world now. He said goodbye and turned. At the doorway, he asked Harka, "Where in Bouddha is he? Did the relative say?"

Harka shook his head.

Aakash knew he was being impudent, but he couldn't help asking, "Auntie is always like this?"

The servant didn't seem to mind Aakash's question. "It's gotten worse since Rahul's father passed away. Before, always together they used to—" He signaled drinking with his hand.

"When did Uncle pass away?"

"About six months ago."

Aakash thanked the servant and left. So Rahul's father had died not too long ago, but Rahul hadn't told Aakash. Nor had he shaved his head and worn white, as was required of a grieving son. Was Rahul's mother also wearing white? He couldn't even tell.

Aakash hadn't been in Bouddha in years—he'd been to the opulent Hyatt, a mere stone's throw away from that neighborhood, a few times with Rahul, but hadn't visited Bouddha itself—and was surprised to see how much the area had grown. Previously the entrance to the temple was discernible even from a distance, but now so many houses had cropped up around it, with so many shop signs obscuring what used to be the gate's distinctive sign, that Aakash had to keep his eyes wide open to locate it. But as he was about to enter the temple, it occurred to him that Rahul's mother had simply said Bouddha, which could have meant the entire neighborhood, and not just the enclosed temple area. He thought he'd try out the neighborhood first, so he walked about the main street, looking about him alertly. But it was a hopeless venture. The street was packed with people, and the likelihood of him spotting Rahul or Ghana, if she indeed had taken to strolling the streets, was far-fetched. He asked a few shopkeepers whether they knew anyone named Rahul. When the shopkeepers shook their heads, Aakash said, "He may be living with a very dark girl, a habsi."

When they heard that, the shopkeepers' eyes gleamed with curiosity. "A habsi?" they asked. "You mean like a habsi from America, or Africa?"

"Yes."

"A Nepali boy living with a habsi?"

"Yes."

At this point some of the shopkeepers laughed, and others shook their heads in disbelief. Aakash walked on. Once again he was outside the temple entrance, and he decided to go in, even though the likelihood of Rahul and Ghana being in there was slim. The temple compound was a small community in itself, with a side temple that held a large Buddha statue in it, and many shops and restaurants that catered to tourists. Buddhist nuns in wine-colored robes were circumambulating the giant stupa, and small children were running around it, chasing one another.

For a while Aakash just walked about, peering into shops, fingering some beads here, inspecting a mask there. One shopkeeper asked him, after seeing that he had been holding a brass Tara in his hand for a long time, "Are you only going to look or are you also going to buy?" Aakash put the Tara down, then continued.

From the upper platform of the stupa, tourists were taking

pictures of the surrounding houses, of the mountains visible between rooftops. Aakash, too, climbed up the stupa, dodging a couple of beggar children as he did so. He sat on the platform. The sun was on its way down, and the evening air had amplified the noises of the neighborhood, and he felt like he could, apart from the conversations and laughter and prayers and haggling around him, also hear distant voices, sounds from houses far away. Near him a couple of tourists, an elderly couple, were pointing to the pink hue the setting sun had thrown at the houses surrounding the temple. He watched the excitement on their faces, and for a moment he was also transfixed. Then the corner of his eye caught a movement to the right, in the third floor window of a house near the stupa. It was the figure of a dhoti-clad woman, bent down to do something—sweeping, he determined. He couldn't see the face of the woman because she was bent over, and the lighting inside the room was dim. When the woman straightened up to adjust her dhoti, a groan escaped Aakash's throat, causing the foreigners to look at him and nod approvingly because they thought that he, too, had been awestruck by the sunset. The woman in the window, apparently done with her work, turned off the light and left the room.

Aakash stood and went down the steps to the street level. On the first floor of the house was a tourist shop selling masks; on the second floor was a restaurant. He opened the door on the side of the house and went in. Behind the stairs was a motorcycle, which resembled Rahul's, but it was too dark for him to be certain. He climbed the stairs, pausing briefly outside the second floor, where a sign saying "PEACE RESTAURANT" hung outside the door. Aakash went up to the third floor. Perhaps because of the sound of his steps on the stairs, someone was already opening the door.

Hamad packed his belongings from the lodge, paid the lodge owner money for the remainder of the week, then went about town to say goodbye to the few friends he'd made in the past months. He laughed, smoked a few cigarettes with them, and didn't decline when they offered him wine. After a few drinks, his mind turned toward his daughter again. He'd always had a strong connection with her, even since she was a child. It was only once she'd turned into a teenager that father and daughter had drifted apart. He couldn't talk to her without adopting a stern voice, and she either avoided him around the house, or even when she obeyed him, she did so with her shoulders tight, and sometimes an openly defiant look in her eyes that brought a reprimand from her mother. *Daughter*, Hamad addressed her in his mind, *may you be happy wherever you are, if you are indeed alive.*

Hamad went to the bus station. The bus journey would take him about six hours to a large village, where he'd fetch his camel from a distant relative and begin his two-day journey back home.

"Dai?" she said. She was wearing a red dhoti. There was a bright tika on her forehead. Her wrists were covered with colorful bangles.

"Ghana?" he said softly.

"Dai, it's so good to see you. Just the other day I was telling him that we should invite you home."

It didn't surprise him that she was speaking to him in Nepali, albeit with an accent. In fact, apart from her very dark skin, she looked like a regular Nepali hill girl—large, beautiful eyes; a slim nose; a narrow face. With a sharp stab to his heart, he saw the red vermilion powder that adorned the parting in her hair—the sign of a married woman.

"Won't you come in?"

Gingerly he stepped inside.

"I'll make some tea," she said as she motioned to him to sit on a small sofa.

"No need," he said, unable to mask his disappointment.

"It won't take a moment." She disappeared into a side room, where he imagined the kitchen was.

He lit a cigarette and took deep drags. This room was the one where he'd seen her earlier; now through the window he could see the stupa and the tourists who were lingering on its upper platform. The elderly couple was still there, now only as silhouettes because the sun had already gone down. He looked around the room. On the wall opposite was a large photograph of the late King Mahendra and his wife, and next to it a photo of Satya Sai Baba. He was struck by all these photos: Rahul was never one to pay respect to the king, especially an old one. And Sai Baba? Who would have thought that Rahul would even tolerate the image of a self-declared demigod like him in the house? Or were the photographs there because of Ghana, who'd latched on to them as the symbols of a dutiful Nepali middle-class wife?

Ghana entered, carrying a tray with two cups of tea. "Dai," she said. "You've started smoking."

"Occasionally."

"It's not good for your health, you know," she said, but after she sat down, she passed a saucer for him to use as an ashtray. He accepted it gratefully, his eyes again traveling to the Sai Baba photo. She noticed his gaze and said with what he perceived was a hint of embarrassment in her voice, "I don't know why, but these days I have developed a great shraddha for Sai Baba. He is truly a divine being, an incarnation of Shiva. He can work miracles."

Aakash wanted to ask her whether Sai Baba was behind her fluent Nepali, her demure housewifey demeanor, but all he said was, "So you two are married now?"

If she was aware of the sensitive nature of his question, she didn't reveal it. Instead, she answered shyly, "Yes, we went to the Manakama temple to get married."

"When?"

"Soon after we left your house."

"How long have you been living here?"

"Right after our wedding. He knew someone in the area who helped us find this place. I love it here. All day long we get to see devotees circling the stupa. We get to see the tourists. I feel like I have been given my own personal god."

"Don't you miss . . . home?" Aakash sighed because he himself didn't know what home was for her.

She studied her hands. "Home feels very far away now.

Even when I remember, it feels like it happened to someone else, not me."

"Where is Rahul?"

"He's at work."

"He's working now?"

She nodded. "He found a teaching job at the Stellar School."

The Stellar School was an elite, expensive school. Both old-time aristocrats and the nouveau riche vied to get their children admitted to Stellar. It was no surprise that Rahul got a job there—his family name had pull, and he was very smart. What was surprising was the idea that Rahul had been transformed enough to want to go get a job (and a teaching job at that), where all day he'd have to deal with mouthy brats—youngsters exactly like him when he was in school! *I have to see this new Rahul,* Aakash thought.

"Shouldn't he be home by now?" he asked. "Schools have been out for a couple hours."

"There's a football tournament at the school today. He's coaching a team, so he has to stay."

Aakash fell silent.

"The students love him, dai," she said. "He's so good with them. So patient."

"Rahul?"

"Yes. I know you probably don't believe me, but he has changed." She smiled. "He's told me stories of what he was like before he met me. How did you two even remain friends for so long?"

He drank his tea. It had turned lukewarm during the conversation. "I have to go now," he said.

"You can't go now!" she said, alarmed. "You have to wait for him. Otherwise he'll never forgive me. You have to stay for dinner."

"I have to be somewhere else."

"Dai, please don't." The disappointment on her face was clear, but he couldn't stay. He couldn't face Rahul, observe his transformation, then try to decide whether any of it was real, whether this was just a phase that'd pass in no time and then he'd abandon Ghana.

"We will meet again," he said at the door and waved.

Aakash went back to the upper platform of the stupa and sat in a corner, half-hidden, so that she couldn't spot him from the window, but he could see what went on in there. She had turned off the light in the living room again, and had presumably returned to the kitchen to cook dinner.

He waited. After nearly an hour, the light in the living room came on again, and he saw Ghana at the door, welcoming Rahul. Yes, it was him. Even from the distance, Rahul's lanky frame was unmistakable. What was different was that he had grown a beard and was wearing a kurta, like an intellectual and a poet. Rahul embraced Ghana, and after a quick glance toward the window, kissed her. Yes, he kissed her, even with the living room light on and with this city fully able to see them, and in the compound of their "personal god." The kiss wasn't long, but it was full of feeling, which Aakash could discern even from that distance.

• • •

A couple of days later in Durbar Marg, Aakash sat in a street-side café and ordered an Americano. He had shaved, and wore decent enough clothes, but hadn't returned to work, and had acquired the habit of mumbling and chuckling to himself. Teenage girls and boys in designer clothes sauntered past him. The Ghantaghar clocktower sounded its discordant ding-dong, as though a goblin up there was banging away haphazardly. Droppings from birds flying above him landed on his table.

In about an hour, a demonstration was supposed to pass through Durbar Marg, and the Supreme Commander, who now lived in the palace where the ousted king used to live, had said that he was personally going to use his shotgun on those who dared to move toward the palace beyond what had now come to be known as the Laxman Rekha, that invisible line running across the street, from between the chic clothing shop and the police station. Aakash was fairly certain that the Supreme Commander himself was responsible for the term Laxman Rekha. The man had invoked a well-known Hindu legend, one that spoke of do-or-die loyalty, of chastity, to protect his newly confiscated asset, the palace. In the ancient story, Laxman drew a line on the ground for Sita, his brother's wife, asking her not to go beyond it so she'd remain protected. But she ended up violating his dictum, and in the end an entire war, filled with monkeys and giants, was launched.

A faint roar was sounding in the distance, and gradually it became louder. The procession. The noise seemed to be rumbling across the sky toward the palace, like rolling thunder. Rumors had been floating around that the demonstration today was going to be large, but such rumors were attached with every antigovernment activity, so Aakash had discounted them. But this one obviously was meant to do some real damage. The shops had begun closing their shutters one by one. Some people were visibly angry at the way their morning was becoming disrupted. "It's always something, isn't it? When is it going to end?"

"When that pseudo-king is out of that palace," someone said.

Aakash heard someone nearby say that the demonstration was now at the Tri-Chandra College. *Here we go*, thought Aakash, and he stood. Before the very large crowd could enter the wide boulevard of Durbar Marg, Aakash made his way toward the tourist district of Thamel, but here, too, the shops were shutting down. "Someone was murdered a few moments ago," one shopkeeper informed Aakash. "A celebrity. Right here in Thamel."

As he continued snatches of conversations floated to him:

"Religious zealots."

"The Supreme Commander's men, for sure."

"That painter, the fool! Why touch anyone's religion? Paint flowers, for God's sake!"

"He's merely an excuse, a scapegoat."

"Now the SC can go after his enemies, to protect our ancient heritage."

A restaurant or two was open for tourists, but waiters were anxiously peeking out for signs of trouble. Then Aakash heard it: a faint chorus from a few streets beyond.

The chants came to him in waves: "Must do . . . must do," and "Our religion, our culture." People were evacuating the streets; doors and windows slammed shut. But for Aakash there was something entrancing about the collective cry that was emanating from a short distance away. Now the crowd was in the next street, and he was the only one walking, willfully in that direction. People shouted at him from windows: "Eh, paagal, get off the street, quick!"

"He has a death wish," someone said.

But what had Aakash to lose? He felt numb, as though whatever happened could not damage him more than he already was.

Around the bend they came. It was not just a posse of men—it was an entire mob, at least a hundred of them, some of them in saffron colors, headed toward Durbar Marg to confront the demonstration. The man in the front with a freakish expression was holding a bamboo pole, on top of which was the severed head of the painter, his long hair swaying.

AN AFFAIR BEFORE
THE EARTHQUAKE

The earthquake was yet to come.

She promised him before she left for America that she would return in two years, and they'd be together.

"Will we marry?" he'd asked.

"That I don't know," she'd said. "What good would that do?"

What good would marriage do! Well, marriage would keep us together, he'd thought. *It'd tie us in an official bond, and never would we be apart! Or something like that.* But he would have felt foolish uttering these words, so he hadn't.

When she first told him that she was going away, he'd known it was coming. They'd been walking in the city center, holding hands, moving from Thamel through Asan, then Indrachowk toward Kathmandu Durbar Square. Soon they'd pass the giant drums to the right, statue of Hanuman the Monkey God to the left, then, to the right, figures of Shiva-Parvati leaning out of a temple window. On to the square and the nine-stage platform that led to the base of the Maju Deval temple, which was more than three hundred years old, where tourists and locals (now increasingly young lovers) hung out and watched the scenery. In front of the temple she'd say, "Shall we?" and they'd climb the steps, linger for some time as they watched the people below, and then they'd come back down. The next stop was the Kasthamandap temple, where they'd observe the Gorakhnath statue (both of them were not particularly religious), and she'd say, "This temple was made out of a single tree." He was aware of the legend, of course, and he recalled that this structure was nine hundred years old, serving as a resting pavilion, a sanctuary, for merchants who traveled the ancient trade routes. "Our city gets its name from this temple," she said, every time, as though he was unaware of it. And he'd take note of "our city" because that meant that she considered the city to be theirs, theirs together.

Our hearth, he thought. They'd circle the small shrine of Ganesh, still holding hands, and he'd feel that they were consecrating their togetherness.

But she was a free spirit. He knew that. If he'd chosen to ignore it, how was she to blame? Before they became lovers, he'd watched her from afar, and he'd admired her and thought, *Now there's a free spirit, and I'm not.* It was strange, identifying oneself as an unfree spirit. But he'd felt a constriction inside himself ever since he could remember, since childhood. Shy, they used to call him, but he'd always known that it was more than shyness. He was trapped by his own thoughts, which, it became obvious to him by his teen years, went around in circles, or repeated the same patterns—which meant that his life followed the same patterns, over and over. He was free to go wherever he chose, and he traveled quite a bit in the early years of his profession—China, Germany, Australia—yet he was moving within this circle of entrapment.

But she was not restricted to her body or her mind. Even her laughter (and she laughed often) came from a different, liberated place. She used to work at an INGO, in the same office building as his, one floor below, and her laughter reached up to him from her veranda, where she gathered with her coworkers for breaks. He would be on his own veranda, and he'd lean over so he could see her. He'd see her hair, the top of her head, a part of her face, perhaps the nose and a cheek, and she'd appear beautiful to him in this partial profile. He'd passed by her a few times on the staircase, and she was always with a coworker, never alone, and she was always smiling or laughing. When their eyes met, he thought she acknowledged him as a person of interest.

For him she was more than a person of interest: she had become, by that time, his lover in his dreams. How could it be? he'd asked himself late at night in his apartment as he lay under his blanket. How could she become his lover so quickly? He didn't know her name, where she lived, whether she was a vegetarian, whether she had family here in the city or elsewhere. He didn't know—he bolted upright in his bed—whether she was married. Why had he assumed that she wasn't? Because she didn't look married, that was why. She didn't wear sindur in the parting in her hair, she never wore a sari (it was always kurta suruwal). Her face looked young: no blemishes, eyes quick and smiling.

He reminded himself that there were plenty of married women who looked young, and that sindur and sari no longer signaled married women. In this modern city, many women who had husbands went to work in trousers and shirts and kurta suruwal, often without applying the red powder to their hair. *Okay*, he thought late at night. *I don't know her name, where she lives, who is in her family, whether she has a husband or children, yet she is my lover. Good job.*

She would come to him in his dreams. They'd hold hands and walk through the city center, the same path they'd take once they became lovers for real, the same path where she told him she was leaving for America. As dream lovers, they'd make bulging eyes at the fearsome Kal Bhairav statue, watch pigeons coo and flutter next to the Monkey God temple, amble to the main square where they'd climb up the steps of the Maju Deval temple and watch the action below.

She continued to be his dream lover even after she became his real lover. And becoming her real lover also happened quickly, easily—too easily, he thought. It all happened in the course of one afternoon and evening, so effortlessly that he wondered if he'd dreamed it. But one afternoon as he stood on his office veranda, leaning to catch sight of her side profile below, she looked up at him and with laughing eyes said, "Hoina, what is your name, sir? I see you all the time, but I don't know your name."

He'd shyly given his name, and then she asked him whether the Lipton Instant Coffee Machine was working in his office, for the one in her office was broken and she was craving some coffee. "Am I not?" she asked her two coworkers, whom he couldn't see but who he could hear were tittering.

"Oh, yes, broken," her coworkers said loudly. "Yes, yes, badly broken." He thought one of them said, "Broken like a heart that's broken," but he couldn't be sure.

The next moment, she was upstairs and they were drinking coffee and swapping mobile numbers.

After they became lovers, their conversations from his dreams bled into their real conversations. When she sucked on an ice cream on the steps of Maju Deval, he wasn't sure if it was the dream she who sucked on a kulfi or the real she.

"I promise," she said, sometimes in his dreams and sometimes in the real world where the earthquake was yet to come. Sometimes just, "Promise." She loved using the word, as if simply saying it made her feel good about everything.

"Promise?" he asked. "We'll be together?"

"I swear I promise," she said.

She liked to sing Nepali songs. She had a soft voice she used to her full advantage. She would start singing without a prompt. "Out of the blue"—that was how he described the abruptness of her singing to a friend to whom he'd confessed how badly he'd fallen in love with her. He'd gone to the friend's house after work, loosened his tie, and paced the room, and his friend had watched him as though he were a performer auditioning for a coveted part. It had been an hour of nonstop confession.

"And she starts singing out of the blue," he told his friend. "Out of the blue, I swear. We'll be sitting on the steps of Maju Deval, and I'll be talking to her softly about something, persuading her about something—it seems as though I'm always persuading her, pleading with her—and she'll appear to be listening. I think that I'm beginning to make some headway when suddenly she'll start singing. And it's always a very Nepali song, often the oldies, from the previous generation, like Narayan Gopal, Aruna Lama, Gopal Yonzan, Prem Dhoj, sometimes even the oldie folksy ones like Kumar Basnet. Even the plowing-on-top-of-the-green-hills guy, what's his name? Yes, Dharma Raj Thapa. The surprising thing is that when we talk, half of her words are English; she can barely utter one full sentence that's unadulterated Nepali. But when she sings her words are so pure, so Nepali that it's almost as if a different person is singing. What's happening, you think?"

But he wasn't really interested in an answer from his friend, and his friend knew this. The friend also knew what the answer was: she was a different person when she sang. Her singing was a deep, yearning subconscious desire to go back to a time when the Nepali identity wasn't sullied by external forces.

"I'll never meet anyone like her," he continued. He was sweating, so he took off his jacket and went to the window. There was no breeze, but he could now look out and talk. The city was straining with tightly packed houses, its inhabitants crammed together like insects. In that moment, he knew that he wouldn't get to share the city with her, even though she'd said "our city" when she'd talked about the Kasthamandap temple, even though it wasn't until a few days later that she'd tell him she was going away. This was how he knew: when he looked out, he saw only himself in the city. He saw himself walking the streets alone, sometimes late at night, perhaps after a rain when the air was fresh. He walked very slowly, pausing every now and then. He watched shopkeepers closing their shops. He moved through the center toward the Durbar Square. A lone woman was bent over the Kal Bhairav statue, praying hard. A couple of drug addicts and drunkards passed him. He looked up at the Maju Deval temple. In the darkness he saw two figures at the top of the platform—two young lovers. He knew they were looking at him, hoping he'd not come up so they'd remain undisturbed.

After seeing himself alone in the city after the rain, he stopped his monologue.

"What happened?" his friend asked. "Go on."

But now the words didn't come.

"Is something wrong?"

He shook his head. "It's time for me to leave now," he said.

"But I thought we were going to do some drinking tonight."

"I'm no longer in the mood."

A few days later she told him her plan to go to America, to a large university in the Midwest where there was a lot of greenery.

"When?"

"Next month. I'll return in two years. This degree is a must for me. I need to move up. I need to be the director of my company."

"But what if you change? What if you become like an American?"

She smiled. "How?"

"What if you start talking like an American? Acting like an American?" He talked to her in an exaggerated American accent, or what he thought was an American accent, with wide vowel sounds and hard consonants, all delivered in a nasal twang. She laughed like she was going to drop dead on the street.

He laughed with her, then held her arm and said in a soft, persuasive voice, "But seriously, what if you change?"

At the top platform of Maju Deval, she began to sing. It was drizzling, enough to make people pick up their pace but not enough to cause panic, and it was nice to watch others hasten as they themselves were protected by the temple's awning that displayed erotic carvings. "Our ancestors were dirty, dirty folks," she'd said a while ago when they'd spotted a scene of bestiality right above their heads.

She sang an old Narayan Gopal song: "Yeti chokho, yeti mitho, dulia timlai maya, birsanechan saraley purana premka katha." Basically: *I will give you such a sweet and pure love that people will forget the love stories of yesteryear.*

He didn't hear from her once she left for America. He emailed her, called her, Skyped her, Vibered her, contacted another Nepali at her university and had his message delivered to her and received confirmation that his message was indeed delivered to her in person. Nothing. He came upon a photo of hers at a university party that someone had posted on Facebook; she was holding a glass of wine, looking happy.

She didn't return in two years. Soon thereafter he, too, left for Australia. So, he wasn't there when the earthquake struck and the Maju Deval temple came tumbling down. The Kasthamandap temple, too, was reduced to rubble.

Before he left for Australia, he took the route that they used to take, from Thamel to Asan, to Indrachowk, then on to Durbar Square past the ridiculously fearsome Kal Bhairav and the pigeons, the giant drums and the statues of Shiva-Parvati surveying the square from their tiny window. He carried on imaginary conversations with her as they walked. "You think it's going to rain today?" he asked.

"It always drizzles when we come here." She briefly squeezed his hand. "But I like light rains." She twirled in the middle of the square, watched by garland sellers and rickshaw pullers. To his surprise, she sang an old Hindi number this time: "Aaj fir jine ki tamanna hai, aaj fir marney ka irada hai."

Basically: *Today I want to live again, and again today I want to die.*

MAD COUNTRY

I was phoned at work by Ramesh's teacher, who asked me to come immediately to the school because the police had been called. In all likelihood they'd take Ramesh to jail, he said.

I was in the midst of an important meeting in my office—I ran a well-known construction company—and that day we were about to strike a deal with a heavyweight industrialist who wanted a housing complex built near his largest factory.

"They can't take a sixteen-year-old boy to jail for merely threatening the principal," I informed the teacher.

"The principal is chummy with the chief of police, whose son also attends our school."

"What difference does that make in a free society?" I was annoyed because I had been forced to step out of a meeting with Mr. Hari Pathak, owner of Global Concern, which ran textile and cigarette factories. He was flying to Biratnagar early the next morning, so it was crucial that I finalized the terms. We were negotiating a transaction involving fifty crore rupees, no small change. I would have been happy with a verbal commitment from Mr. Pathak—he was a man known to keep his word. If I could just have him say yes, that was all I needed. But here was my son's teacher, telling me that my son was about to be hauled off to jail.

In the hallway, where I had stepped out to answer my mobile, I glanced worriedly toward the meeting room, where I was sure Mr. Pathak was surreptitiously checking his watch to see when I'd return.

"If you don't come now, Gurung, madam," the teacher said, "I don't know what'll happen to Ramesh. That's all I'm saying."

"But I'm in an important meeting."

"Well, I've told you what I need to, madam."

When I returned to the meeting room, my manager was regaling Mr. Pathak with details about the proposed apartment complex—reinforced concrete to withstand earthquakes, the emergency measures installed, the health dispensary, the twenty-four-hour security—but I knew that my manager was merely stalling until my return. I sat down with a smile and said, "Forgive me for the interruption, Mr. Pathak, but I had to take that call. Now at this stage, all we need to do is say yes."

"Everything all right, Mrs. Gurung?"

"Everything is perfect. Now let's talk about the contract."

"There's no bad news, is there? You look a bit frazzled."

"It's just the wrong time for it, but apparently my son is in some kind of trouble at school."

"Then you should go."

"Let's finish our talk."

"Well, we're obviously not going to conclude it right now. There are still some financial points we need to get clarity on."

"I was hoping that provisionally if you gave your assent, we'd be set."

"If I wasn't provisionally committed, would I be here? But at this moment you need to take care of your son, and I'd like our discussion to be full and complete."

"Perhaps Mr. Sapkota here can take over for me, so you are completely satisfied before you leave?"

"Mrs. Gurung, what's the hurry? Go take care of your son. Family takes priority over business."

I had no choice but to let the matter drop. I cursed my son as I headed toward his school. The imbecile! Didn't he realize that his mother was an important woman? Did he think that I was at his beck and call every time he got into trouble? But as my car neared the school, I hoped the police hadn't already taken him away. I worried how he'd do if he had to spend a night or two in jail. They most likely wouldn't feed him well. They might slap him around—for what? For threatening his principal? I was being paranoid; the recent political arrests and tortures had corrupted my mind. In all likelihood, the most that would happen to him was that he'd be behind bars for a few hours, harassed and bullied by cops, then let go.

There was also a traffic jam in Kupondole that held me hostage for about half an hour, during which any remaining molecules of anger had evaporated, replaced by motherly concern and anxiety and indignation at the actions of the school.

By the time I reached the school, the police had him in handcuffs and were on their way out of the principal's office to a waiting van in the driveway. *God almighty*, I thought. That teacher who had called me, and who now was accompanying the police as though he himself had orchestrated the arrest, was right about how serious this was. But I knew how the system worked: the louder you raised your voice, the more righteous you sounded and the more legitimate your grievances became.

"Arre, arre, arre," I shouted, barring their way. I was not a big woman, but I was slightly heavy, and I could project a thunderous voice when I wanted to, a voice I occasionally used on my office staff. "Who do you think you are? And where do you think you're taking this child?"

At the sight of me, a small smile appeared on my son's face. Mama had come to his rescue, as usual. I could see the principal in his room, through the open door, standing next to his desk, his arms folded, watching. The sun was behind him, so his face was somewhat in the shadows.

"Please move out of the way," said a policeman who was escorting my son. "This is a police matter."

"Police matter, my foot!" I said, my arms stretched wide. The teacher who had phoned was looking at me placidly. "What did the child do so you have to handcuff him in front of the entire school and haul him off like this?" I asked.

"We don't have to answer you," the policeman said. "If you don't get out of the way, we'll take you to the station."

"On what grounds?" I asked. "What reason would you have to arrest me when all I'm doing is asking a simple question as a mother, as a citizen?"

"Hire a lawyer, who can ask all the questions in court. Now move!"

I was not used to this type of treatment. Usually men with small powers, like these police here, learned quickly who I was—a businesswoman with considerable capital and clout—and I'd start getting "Hajur," and "Yes, madam," and "Of course, Gurung madam." Things were smoothed, doors opened, and I was offered tea by deferential hands; conveniences magically appeared, and inconveniences disappeared. With upper echelon male figures, I would adopt a gentler approach, my voice becoming more naram, saturated with sugar. With Mr. Pathak today, for example, I had sweetly inquired after his wife and three daughters, and offered my heartfelt condolences on the passing away of his mother (a factoid I had mentally noted when the news of his mother's death had appeared in the papers). I was also not averse to using my feminine charms with these higher-level men (although I didn't do this with Mr. Pathak). I threw them coquettish smiles and asked them how come the more they aged, the more youthful they appeared? I fingered their suits and made appreciative noises, or I adjusted their ties.

I was, however, always very careful: I never gave the impression that there was anything more than mild flirting. One time there was this Indian industrialist with whom I was sitting in the lounge of a luxury resort in another city. We'd each had a martini or two. "So what are you doing tonight, Mrs. Gurung?" he asked.

"I'm heading to bed after this," I said, lifting my glass.

"How about you and I go disco dancing?" he said, and wiggled his hips on the sofa. He had rings on all of his fingers—and I mean all—and he was slow to smile, but when he did, his brilliant white teeth gleamed. I had complimented him earlier on these white teeth, saying he could easily model for a Colgate commercial.

"Disco?" I said. "Didn't disco stop with *Saturday Night Fever?*"

He gave me a befuddled look, not catching my reference. "There's a band playing in the hotel tonight."

"I have an early flight tomorrow." I also had to call my dear husband, who I knew would be waiting.

"Come on," he said. "Just a dance or two, after which I'll let you go."

I pointed out that it was already ten, past my bedtime, but he grabbed me by the hand and insisted. "Okay, okay," I said. "Just one dance." He didn't let go of my hand as we made our way across the labyrinthine lobby of the hotel. I had to pry myself away with the excuse that I needed to dig into my bag for a tissue.

The dance hall was dark because they were playing a slow number—"How Deep Is Your Love?" by the Bee Gees, a song I had taken pleasure in when I was a teenager—and a few couples were close-dancing. There was no way in hell I was going to close-dance with this man, but before I could say anything, he had pulled me to the floor, and there I was, holding hands with him, smelling his booze breath. "You should come to Calcutta," he said. "I'll show you around."

"Calcutta is hot."

"Not in winter. It's perfect in winter."

"In winter I'm busy with my family."

He had moved closer to me, and I could feel his bulge poking me. I gently pushed him away.

"You are a beautiful woman."

"Thank you." I was barely audible.

"No, I mean it. You are gorgeous." He slurred on "gorgeous," and I realized that he was drunker than he looked. He must have had a few even before he had joined me tonight.

When was this song going to end? The high-pitched voice of the singer, a Gibb, I vaguely recalled, grated on my nerves. The song's title should have been "How Long Is Our Song?"

"A gorgeous woman like you needs to be treated better," he said. "I will show you around India. We will travel the world."

"I travel plenty on my own."

His right arm, which was around my waist, pulled me against him. "What I mean is you shouldn't be shackled to . . . chained . . . you know what I'm saying? What kind of a life is this? Having to take care of an ailing partner day in and out?"

"Are you married, Mr. Chatterji?"

"Yes, but my wife doesn't mind what I do outside of home. She's not an educated woman."

The song ended, and I disengaged myself from him,

quickly grabbed my bag from the table, bade him good night, and left. He followed me until the lobby, then realized that it was no good and gave up.

In my room I dialed Kathmandu. After the fourth ring, my husband's sleepy voice answered.

"Kailash, already asleep?" I asked.

"I waited and waited."

"I couldn't get away. How is your stomach?"

"I still have the runs."

"Ramesh asleep?"

"He hasn't come home yet."

"Oh, that boy!"

"And you? How was the meeting?"

"It went well." I didn't want to tell him about Chatterji. Normally I didn't hide anything from Kailash, he being my beloved and all, but I didn't want his feelings hurt by what the businessman had said about me being shackled to him.

"You shouldn't have to do this," Kailash often told me when I gave him a towel bath, or when I changed his soiled underclothes. "No woman should have to do such demeaning things," he said. "This is humiliating for you, offensive, I know it." When I told him that I didn't consider caring for him humiliating at all, he didn't believe me. When he became depressed, he said he wished he were dead, and I had to stroke his chin and smooth his hair to calm him.

Those nights I was away on business trips were hard for him because he missed me in bed. I had hired a nurse to look after him when I traveled. She was a reliable worker, a woman from the hills who had fallen on hard times (her husband and children had been killed by the rebels during the civil war). She slept on the floor in our bedroom when I was not at home.

"Where is Narbada?" I asked.

"She went downstairs to eat."

"I can't wait to get home."

"One more day," he said.

"Do you miss me?"

"Is that a question to ask?"

We had always been like this, very lovey-dovey, ever since we had fallen for each other decades ago. I had fought with my parents to marry him; he had disowned his parents because they had disapproved of me. In the end, we went to court, got our marriage certificate, and invited a few friends over for a party. We drank and danced all night long. We grooved to Donna Summer and mouthed "hot stuff" to each other. We crashed a bar where we smoked hash and got drunk on milky-white tongba that we sipped through bamboo pipes.

In the school's driveway, I dropped my arm and used my naram voice. "Look, bhai, he is my son, what do you expect me to do?"

The policeman shoved me aside and pushed Ramesh into the van. The boy appeared to be enjoying himself. He wore a pained, yet laughing expression. "Ma," he cried, and I cried back, "Don't worry, son. I'll come and get you."

The van sped away, and I went into the principal's office and chewed him out. He was defiant, told me that I had no idea what a troublemaker my son was, that I was living in a cocoon. I told him he should return to where he came from—he was from Darjeeling, or Bhutan or someplace like that. "The nerve of you foreigners," I told him through gritted teeth, "coming to my country to lecture me. I will drag you to court," I said, and left.

I thought that they'd take Ramesh down to the station, knock some sense into him, and then let him go. Even in the most autocratic of societies, how would threatening a principal warrant more than a couple of hours in jail? But when he didn't return home by seven o'clock, I worried. I made some phone calls, found out that he was being held in Hanuman Dhoka. The man who answered the phone couldn't tell me when my son would be released. "I just have the name in the register in front of me."

I employed my authoritative voice that wasn't going to brook any nonsense. "What kind of a wahiyat talk is this? How can you not know? You must have a system."

"System?"

"A system that lets people know when they can expect their loved ones back. Is that too much to ask?"

Did I hear a soft chuckle at the other end? "I don't have any such system."

"Then find me someone who has."

"I'm not allowed to leave my desk, madam."

"Then give me your name and rank. In a loktantric society, your answer is not acceptable. I intend to report you."

"Bhagirath Lamichhane is my name. Police constable."

I switched to my honeyed voice. "Bhai, I'm just talking.

There will be no reporting, you know that. I'm well aware you are just doing your job, and I know that people like you are slogging your butt off for the good of this country. I salute you. I am just a poor mother trying to ascertain the well-being of my son. Is that too much to ask?"

He hung up the phone.

I would have gone to Hanuman Dhoka that evening, but then I heard Kailash's cries. I hurried upstairs to our room. He had fallen off the bed. My immediate worry was that he'd broken a bone, for his bones were weak and brittle. "Any place hurting?" I asked as I lifted him by his arms and put him back on the bed. Until a few years ago, such an act on my part would have been impossible, because Kailash, I swear, had weighed twice as much as I, and had been, despite his age, muscular and brawny. My handsome Kailash. He was a wrestling champion when he was growing up in the terai, and a swimming marvel in Roorki where he went to college. There is a photo of him standing on a bridge, ready to plunge into a raging river, biceps gleaming, his face sculpted like a Roman statue's.

Now his arms resembled bamboo sticks, and the skin on his body had become translucent—if I gently pressed my thumb against his cheek, its imprint remained on it for a minute or so. His cheeks had sunken so much that they looked as though he was deliberately sucking on them. Now I could no longer gaze into his eyes for long without something clogging my throat and me thinking how unfair this world was. His eyes had sunken in, too, floating in their own liquid. "You should leave me," Kailash had started saying recently. "I'm becoming too much of a burden for you."

When he said this, I put my finger on his lips and said, "Hush!"

After I put Kailash back on the bed, he began coughing, so I stayed and rubbed some ointment on his chest, his throat, thinking that I should go down to Hanuman Dhoka, then hoping that soon I'd hear the door creak and it'd be Ramesh, announcing his entry like he always did. I hadn't yet told Kailash about Ramesh's arrest. He was fond of Ramesh, thought of his son's troublesome ways as youthful peccadilloes. "He's only a boy," Kailash liked to say. I didn't argue with him, didn't tell him that I was the one who had to deal with our son's "youthful peccadilloes" and that I was beginning to get tired of it. The boy had brought nothing but trouble to us. Even at an early age, say eight or nine, he used to get into ugly fights at school, then come home grinning with a black eye or a chipped tooth.

In eighth grade, he got into what he called "a gang fight" in the neighborhood and ended up with a broken arm that required surgery. He flunked ninth grade, then accumulated so many absences the second time around that he was in danger of flunking again. He'd have failed again, had I not made a reasoned and fervent appeal on his behalf to the principal (the previous one, not the buffoon I had to deal with today). Basically, I asked for a third chance, and in a shameless moment, I even brought up my husband's deteriorating condition as a reason for Ramesh's performance.

• • •

I awoke at 11 P.M., my palm still on Kailash's chest, the light on in the room. I had fallen asleep! Kailash was snoring softly. He had been sleeping well at night since he'd started taking pills for his depression. Briefly, I contemplated going down to Hanuman Dhoka to check on Ramesh. But that would be madness. I'd have to drive the car myself, and I didn't see well at night. If I got into a car accident, what would Kailash do? Even if I were to make it to Hanuman Dhoka, where would I park? New Road? Indrachowk?

Since the Hanuman Dhoka police station was in a prime tourist spot because of the ancient temples nearby, I wasn't sure I'd be allowed to drive all the way to the jail. I'd probably have to do some walking, and who knew what kinds of characters lurked after darkness? Besides, I wasn't sure that the jail would be open to visitors at this hour. It was not some five-star hotel where a well-groomed receptionist would check me in no matter what time I arrived. That Bhagirath Lamichhane, the police constable I'd spoken to in the evening, had a home to go to, I was sure, possibly to a wife and children. Right now he might be sound asleep, cuddled against his family.

I didn't sleep for a couple of hours, entangled in my thoughts. At one point, in a semidreamy state I had the distinct impression that Anamika Gurung—I had retained my maiden surname, just to aggravate my conservative in-laws—was someone else, that I was looking at her objectively, and that her life, as significant and important as it was to her, was indeed quite pathetic. An educated, smart, married woman who got propositioned by lewd, hairy businessmen in the lounges of lavish hotels; whose husband, once the envy of her friends for his good looks, was wasting away; whose son, at the age of sixteen, was already a jailbird.

Ramesh was not in Hanuman Dhoka when I went to see him the next morning.

"Well, has he been released?" I asked the men in the front room. Its walls were damaged; there was an odor of a drain—sewage?—coming through the windows.

"We'll have to check," they said, but then they all got busy talking.

I waited patiently. They continued talking. I waited some more. Nothing. Something surged inside me. I banged the table around which they were seated. "I am asking a simple question. A citizen of a democratic country that you men have vowed to serve. Have you not vowed? Am I not a citizen? My question is simple: Where is my son?"

There was silence, then two of them stood and grabbed hold of me. One handcuffed me, and another one slapped me, not very hard but enough to leave a sting. Before I could say anything, I was frog-marched to a cell, where there were other women prisoners, and shoved in.

"Arre, arre, arre!" I said. But the men had already returned to the front.

I was stunned. It happened so speedily. *Do these fuckers know who I am?* But instantly the anger evaporated, and I knew I hadn't acted wisely. I should have used my naram voice and appealed to the kindest face in the room, an appeal from a mother instead of a strident citizen.

I consoled myself: this was a temporary punishment to teach me manners, like forcing a mouthy child to squat with knees up to her chin. All I had to do was be silent for a while, then call them sweetly. I could do that. Before Kailash's health failed, he and I had attended a meditation camp or two, and I recalled some of those instructions. *Say Om on the outbreath. Don't force your awareness. Simply be cognizant of your breath. Feel the in-and-out of your belly. In and out.*

I stood against the cell door, eyes closed. Then my thoughts ricocheted inside my head—Kailash; Ramesh; the company; my older, married daughter, Priya, who had drifted away from me.

"Have you fallen asleep, madam?" A woman's voice startled me. I had barely looked at the other prisoners in the room, as I was convinced their offenses were graver than mine. There was a strong odor in the cell, and I saw that a clothesline ran from one wall to the next where some panties and a petticoat were hung. Now I could tell that the women in the room were of the lower class, laborer-type village women. So was the woman who had addressed me. There was a knowing look on her face. I knew their kind. The savvy, conniving street types. I thought of prostitutes. And this woman could easily be a handler of prostitutes.

"Did you ask me something?" I said.

"I was wondering if you'd fallen asleep. I've never seen anyone fall asleep while standing."

"I was meditating." I thought that this woman looked clever enough that if I wasn't cautious, she'd sell me in the Basantapur market next door before I realized what had happened.

"What type of meditation?"

"What?"

"Vipassana? Sahaja? Or something else?"

"What are you talking about? It's just meditation."

I looked past her at the other women. One dark woman was sitting against the wall, her head buried in her knees. She could have been sleeping, or in despair. One woman was staring out of a small window at the sky; another leaned against the wall, humming. A transvestite with a bruised face was softly crying. The cell was at the end of a corridor, and I didn't see anyone in the hallway. If no one showed up shortly, I was going to call out. Perhaps I should shout Bhagirath Lamichhane's name, so that they'd think I knew someone here, that I had a connection.

"I attended a Vipassana meditation camp once," the woman said. "It was a ten-day retreat: meditate all day and remain silent. It was hard, but at the end of the ten days I felt refreshed, as though a new person had awakened inside me. Alas, it didn't last long. After a week or so, my mind was back to its monkey tricks."

"What are you in here for?"

"I'd rather not say."

Then why are you blabbering to me about all kinds of nonsense? I thought. But I didn't want to engage her more than necessary, so I moved away.

She followed me. "In some prisons they are starting medication programs now because they have discovered that meditation makes balanced prisoners."

"I see."

"The food is terrible here. But today I think we get transferred to another jail, somewhere in the outskirts."

I approached the cell door again and shouted gently. "Anyone there?" Conversation and laughter sounded in the distance, toward the front office.

"Can someone come here, please?" I said again, a bit louder.

The woman stood next to me, looking in the direction I was. "I think they'll come only in the evening, unless another prisoner arrives."

"I can't wait until the evening." I was about to say that I had a business to run, but restrained myself.

The woman gave me a sympathetic smile.

"Bhagirath Lamichhaneji! Bhagirath Lamichhaneji!" I cried.

My loud voice woke the woman on the floor, who shot me a nasty look.

In the evening a few policemen came, handcuffed us, and led us away. I asked for their forgiveness for my behavior that morning. They remained silent as we were led out and herded into a van. A few yards away, some Japanese tourists were taking snaps of the nearby temples.

Inside the van the windows were not only small but also covered with mesh screens, allowing only a small amount of light to filter in. By now my employees at Kailash Construction would be beside themselves trying to locate me. "Did madam have an appointment somewhere today?" they'd be inquiring of one another. The office would be in shambles; I liked to run a pretty tight ship, and the staff constantly looked up at me for guidance and authority. By this time, of course, they'd have called the house, and Kailash would be worried. Never had I vanished for an entire day like this. I'd not been out of touch with my family or staff even for more than a couple of hours—I was constantly on my mobile, texting and emailing and dialing and answering and confirming and negotiating and hectoring. My mobile, which the police confiscated this morning, must have rung all day.

Ramesh. I was so caught up in my own situation that I hadn't thought about him for some time now. Had he also been taken to the same place we were being transported to now? Was I going to be reunited with my son?

But it was quite possible that Ramesh had already been released, perhaps last evening, not long after he was taken to the station. I knew that many political protestors were detained for a couple of hours, then let go. It might be the same with troublesome youth, I guessed: seize them, cage them for a couple of hours, then discharge. For all I knew, Ramesh, after being released, could have slept over at a friend's house the previous night, as he frequently did these days.

"What are you thinking?" the woman, who had let me know that her name was Sita, asked me. The van was racing through the streets. I could only view a portion of the sky, the crisscrossed telephone and electric wires.

"Nothing."

"That's impossible," she said. She was sitting across from me. The dark woman crouching had her face covered with the end of her dhoti. A policeman sat next to her, his eyes half closed. "It's impossible not to have any thoughts inside your head," Sita informed me.

"It's possible for me."

"Why? Because you're so special?"

Her voice had no rancor, so I said mildly, "Maybe."

"Because you own a big construction company?"

Earlier when this woman, Sita, had asked me for my name, I'd only given my first name. Now it was clear that all along she had known who I was. The devious conniver! But I didn't want to give her the satisfaction, so I looked at the floor of the van.

"Anamika Gurung," she said.

Nothing was more depressing than the fact that this low-life woman not only knew my name but also was addressing me as though I was a petty commoner.

"I am your friend, Anamika," Sita said. "So you can tell me your thoughts. Anytime."

After traveling for close to three hours, the van stopped. The road we'd been on had frequently been uphill, and quite bumpy, so my body felt battered. The door opened and we were commanded to exit. The policeman who stood by the door as we climbed out of the van looked somewhat senior than the others, even in the dark, so I appealed to him, "Bhai, there has been a mistake."

"Keep on moving!"

"But bhai, please listen."

His subordinate struck my shoulder with his baton. A brutal, stinging pain coursed through my left shoulder, cascading down to my ribs and hips, all the way down to my toes. I sucked in my breath and limped ahead.

Sita walked alongside me toward the building where we were headed. "It's pointless to talk to them," she whispered. "Did it hurt?"

Hobbling, holding my arm, I didn't respond to her.

Load shedding had darkened the entire area, but a policeman was at the door of the building, holding a bright lamp, saying, "This way, if you please," and we were taken inside to what was clearly a jail: narrow rooms with bars facing a corridor. The women were being pushed into these cells in twos as we went along, and because Sita was next to me, we ended up together. They bolted the door from the outside.

"At least they have beds here," Sita said in the manner of someone inspecting a mediocre hotel room for its amenities. There were two bunk beds fastened to the wall, like in a train compartment. I wondered if I could request a different roommate, perhaps the dark one who hid her face and didn't say anything. Pain was shooting up my thigh and back, making my body crooked, but to sit down right now seemed like giving in, so I remained standing.

"Top or bottom?"

I grimaced.

"Do you want the top bed or the bottom bed?"

Any moment now, I thought, *they'll come to get me.*

"There you go again, lost in your thoughts."

"Top or bottom doesn't matter." I could barely speak.

"Then do you mind if I take the upper bunk? I've always wanted to sleep on top. One of my cousins lived in a hostel, and when I visited her, I remember thinking what fun it'd be to sleep so close to the ceiling and look down upon people." She clambered to the top bunk and sat cross-legged.

I had been dying to urinate since the morning. At Hanuman Dhoka an open toilet had sat in the corner, but there was simply no way I could have crouched in front of all those women to pee.

"I know you need to pee," Sita said. "It's not healthy to hold it in. Don't. I won't look."

I ignored her, but the pressure building up in my crotch was too much, and I had to go to the corner and squat. I stared ahead at the wall, where someone had scrawled some initials I couldn't decipher. Nothing came out. I squeezed my eyes shut and imagined that I was at home, in my own fluffy-toweled bathroom, but when I did I immediately thought of Kailash, how panicked he must be by now. He could also be thinking that I had left him.

"You're lost in thoughts again," Sita said. "You need to focus on the task at hand."

I concentrated hard on the initials on the wall. After a while the letters began to resemble shapes: a monkey's mouth, a crooked house, a flower petal. But still nothing came out; it was as though a rod was clamped across my pelvis, like I was wearing a chastity belt.

"Focus on your breathing," Sita said.

Without wanting to, I became aware of my breathing.

"In and out, in and out."

I could feel a movement in my abdomen, and along with it a slight loosening.

"On the out breath, let everything go."

I exhaled deeply, and a drop escaped. Another exhale, a small trickle. Slowly, bit by bit, I peed with Sita's guidance, thinking I looked like a child suffering from constipation who is gently coaxed by her mother. Toward the end, when I began to experience relief, I glanced at her and found her still in the seated position, her hands on her knees, her eyes closed.

A week passed. We were taken out of our cells to the dining room for lunch and dinner. In the evening after dinner, which was served early, we were allowed in the small courtyard in the middle of the prison. There were about twenty women in this prison. It must have been quite expensive to maintain it, what with the guards (about six, from what I could see), the food, and bedding. A dhoti, made of cheap coarse fabric, had been provided for each of us, so now all the women wore the same beige-colored garb, effectively making it a type of prison uniform. At times I thought they resembled the Padma Kanya college girls who all wore the same saffron sari. I still clung to the sari I was wearing when I was dragged in here, and it was beginning to give off a slight odor.

But everything around me had a smell: the cell, the dining room, the corridor, even the courtyard, which on some days had garbage piled in the corners. The only thing that didn't give off a smell was the prison dhoti. It was either brand-new, or it was washed and ironed and starched (most likely the latter), and I frequently held it to my nose and inhaled its freshness. Sita laughed when she caught me doing it. "It looks like you've elevated that dhoti to the status of a fancy perfume," she said. "The kind of perfume you used to wear, I'm sure."

Sita was the most cheerful of all the prisoners. She sang songs to herself—she had a surprisingly melodious voice—sometimes clapping her hands together. I didn't recognize any of the songs; they were folk tunes and had the language and diction of the hills and mountains, of young, demure yet clever lasses and seductive men whose main goal was to shatter their hearts into pieces.

Sita chatted with everyone. She knew all the prisoners by their names, and often she brought gossip home—to our cell—after our time in the courtyard. She related these juicy bits to me as though we were roommates in a boarding school, the kind I had attended as a young girl. It was a one-sided conversation, with her going on and me listening.

I barely talked to anyone; I had lost my voice. One time, I told a guard super politely, "Babu, it would be nice if I could send a message to my family."

"Political prisoners don't have that facility."

"Political?"

I had mustered up the courage to speak to him right as we were being steered into the dining room, with Sita walking next to me.

"Is your roommate dense?" the guard asked Sita.

"She's in a state of shock, Amrit. She'll come around."

"You better teach her, Sita. It's common knowledge that there can be no transfer of messages."

"She'll learn soon enough."

The dining room was basically three tables put side by side, where all the prisoners sat, crammed tight.

"What was that about political prisoners?" I whispered to Sita.

"Who knows?" she said. "I know zilch about politics, apart from the names of the parties—Ehmaley, Maobadi, Panchey, Cangressi." Then she came up with other made-up party names, "Hatteribadi, Gayegujrekobadi, Nakkacharey Dal, Machhikney Party," which elicited laughter.

Sita was such a presence in the prison that, as the days began to roll by, I wondered what it would be like in here without her. There'd be none of that clapping and crooning and yes, also dancing, although one had to be careful about dancing because while the guards tolerated some noise, dancing would have signaled a level of happiness that defeated the purpose of the prison.

That was what Sita told me in our cell as she danced and eyed the door to make sure that a guard wasn't peeking in through the opening. There were days when Sita performed just for me. "For you, my sweetie," she said, and she danced. Her dances were not varied. They all involved the same gestures and movement: spread the arms wide, tilt the body at an angle, and rotate clockwise, then counterclockwise as she twirled her hands in the air. It was a dance she'd learned in her village, a dance I'd seen hill women perform during the Teej festival.

When I asked Sita where her village was, what it was like, what was its name, she said, "All the villages are the same—the same village pathways, the same poverty, the same suffering. So what difference does it make what my village is called? God, it has been so long, I won't be surprised if its name actually begins to slip away from my mind. Actually, what's the name of my village?" The women around the table tittered. "Oh, look at me, I have become such a shameless hussy that I don't even remember what my village is called."

"A shameless hussy," someone said.

"What is it called, though? Is it Durgaon? Is it Dandakanda? It is it Bhakundo Khola?"

That had the women in stitches.

One day, I cited stomachache and didn't go for dinner, and when Sita returned she found me lying in my bunk, weeping. She sat next to me, put her hand on my arm, and started to sing in such a soft voice that it sounded like she was crying. She stroked my arm, and I said, "I can't, I can't."

She consoled me by saying, "I know." She lay beside me, and, tears streaming down my face, I made room for her. She took my chin in her hand and sang a song about the beauty of the hills and the dappling sunlight on the purest stream that one finds north of the Gangetic plains. She leaned over and kissed me on my forehead. I snuggled against her, the odor from her armpits making my nose crinkle. She kissed me on my nose, then softly on my lips.

• • •

From then on Sita and I slept together on my bunk bed. She sang to me, held me, and I thought, *God, I'd die without her.* Every day my need for her got stronger, and soon I was always clinging to her. There was nothing sexual about our relationship: it was only holding each other in bed, nuzzling, and occasionally, light kissing. I still hadn't regained my voice, but in this intimacy I had begun to smile a little, especially when she sang to me. Her songs transported me to a place and era that was so far removed that my throat swelled with longing. I closed my eyes and imagined myself in the places described in her song, and I momentarily forgot where I was, or why I was here.

After dinner, Sita sometimes braided and oiled my hair in the courtyard. We weren't allowed creams or lotions or oil, but she had managed to coax Amrit into bringing her a bottle from his wife—for what price or favor returned, I didn't know. We sat in a corner of the courtyard with the other women forming a circle around us to block us from the guards' view. As Sita worked on my hair, the women talked. The conversation ran the gamut, from the cloudless sky above to analyses of the guards' personalities. The women talked about their childhoods, their favorite foods, the festivals and the melas they'd attended, their best teachers, their worst teachers. I listened with great pleasure. It seemed to me that my life hadn't been that interesting, or at least that my likes and dislikes paled in comparison to these women's, or that even if I thought some details about my life were interesting (my love marriage with Kailash, for example), if I tried to tell them, I wouldn't find the proper voice for them, and they'd sound dull. So I was perfectly content to listen to these women.

Once or twice someone said, "And what about you, Anamika? Why don't you also say something?" I blushed and shook my head.

Sita took my chin in her hand and said, "Feeling shy, dearie?" I turned my face away, and they all laughed in delight.

"These days she's like a bride for you, Sita," a woman said.

There were nights I couldn't sleep. I thought of Kailash, of Ramesh, but they came to me as though they were people I'd known a long time ago, perhaps when I lived in a distant, mad country. The construction company that I ran single-handedly—now I knew that I wouldn't have the confidence, or the skills, to work there as a simple typist. When I recalled the bigwigs I met and made deals with, people like Mr. Pathak, I was struck with amazement as to how I accomplished what I did. It couldn't have been me, could it? No, it couldn't have. It was another woman who led that life, who went out every morning to face the world and to make a difference. This sense of alienation from my former self made me anxious.

I squeezed my eyes tighter to feel more fondness for my husband and for my son than I did. The harder I tried, the more they drifted away. In my mind the woman I saw with them was me, but she was also not me. She was stockier (I had lost significant weight in the prison) and possessed a more imperial appearance. She spoke in sharp, assured tones, whereas I could barely speak without blushing or hesitating.

"Any day now," the guard said one afternoon, the same guard who supplied Sita with bottles of hair oil.

A revolution was brewing outside—that was the report. "Political prisoners are being freed," the guard had conveyed in a whisper. In the past, too, there had been rumors, creating commotions among the women. Some time ago, there had been frenzied whispers that we were about to be executed, perhaps even beheaded. A couple of women wore handkerchiefs around their necks for protection.

Another time the news arrived that some male political prisoners were being brought in to mate with us, that those who refused to comply would be lashed. One woman put her hand on her crotch and said, "Bring it on! This cunt by now can take not only one cock but a dozen." But most of us were petrified. We walked around in a huddle, our ears alert for the voices of strange men at the main entrance. I clung to Sita, who patted my head and consoled me.

"I won't be able to take it," I told her.

"I won't allow anyone to touch you."

She talked to Amrit, who said, "If it happens, I won't be able to protect any of you, not even you, Sita, let alone her."

"I'm not worried for myself," Sita said, "but she will die."

"The most I can do is pair her up with a man who looks the most harmless, but even that I'll have to do surreptitiously." He lowered his voice. "The senior guard has been after me for a while now, ready to pounce. It's a dog-eat-dog world in here, I tell you, so I have to be extra careful. But for you, you know." He looked suggestively at Sita.

Sita put her hand on his arm. "You know the kind of reward that'll await you if you can do this for me."

I didn't know what Sita was talking about, for she was never out of my sight. We slept together, ate together, skipped rope together in the courtyard (the warden wanted us to exercise more). When did she have time to do anything for the guard? Was she doing things behind my back, even though I didn't know how that could be?

This secrecy between Sita and Amrit made me jealous, and I became more watchful of their interactions. Amrit could be getting his reward right under my nose, and the fool I was, I was not seeing it. I became more vigilant, observing every move that the two, especially Sita, made. But I found nothing.

Then I wondered if Sita was returning Amrit's favors in another way. Every night before going to bed, Sita meditated cross-legged on the upper bunk. I waited for her until she was done so we could sleep in each other's arms. But now I wondered if she was making herself sexually available to Amrit through meditation, through some kind of mental transference. So when she had her eyes closed, I watched her face for evidence of sexual pleasure. But she only had a tiny smile, like she did even when she wasn't meditating.

Ultimately, no strange men came to sleep with us.

That's why at first we thought that the rumor about a revolution occurring in the outside world was just that, a rumor. But one day we heard the main gate clang open, and soon marched in a small, chubby man in military uniform who resembled the midget comedian Mukri. "All the political prisoners, come out and form a line against the wall!" he shouted.

The guards unlocked our cells, but we were afraid to move, for if we heeded his command, we'd be admitting we were political prisoners. We weren't sure whether political prisoners were the heroes or the enemies in this revolution. The military man could line us up and instruct the guards to shoot us. As we were pushed out of our cells, I noticed red stains on the wall, which I had always thought were stains from paan that the guards had chewed and spat out. But now I wondered if they were something else. Others, too, noticed the stains, and we all edged away from the wall.

The military man turned to the warden. "Isn't this a prison for political detainees? Am I losing my mind here?"

The warden whipped his stick in the air. "You heard the colonel. Line up against the wall!" He raised his stick as though to strike us on our shoulders, but the colonel stopped him and whispered something. I caught the word *accountability*.

We lined up against the wall. The colonel walked past us slowly, the fingertips of his hands together, saying "Hmmm" as if appraising us for a ragtag militia he was forming. Finally he stopped, cleared his throat, and said, "Ladies and gentlemen, the revolution has arrived, and I am happy to report that we are on the side of the victorious and the righteous. There is a new spring in the air, a new dawn, a new beginning, and an awakening. The masses have arisen, the sleeping dogs are no longer lying, the tiger has roared awake." He paused. "Your contribution to this revolution, for the days you've spent here for your beliefs and convictions, is immense. The state recognizes it, and we—the army—recognize it and are grateful. Know this: your sacrifice will not be forgotten." He lifted his chin and sniffed the air. "I can smell our bright future." A more significant pause. "As of this moment you are free."

There was confusion. The prisoners moved away from the wall, then some moved back again. No one even dared to utter the word "free." I whispered to Sita, "What does he mean?"

She stroked my chin. "I think he means we can go home now."

"But why? Why?" I cried. My fingers were clasped with Sita's, and I dug into her palm with my nails, making her let out a small yelp.

After the initial shock was over, a couple of women began to weep openly. One prisoner ran into the courtyard and began to run in circles, spreading her arms like an eagle spreading its wings. Some were babbling about what they'd do once they were out in the open. Sita began to snap her fingers and croon softly about the rolling meadows and sweet-running streams and lambs and baby goats following their mothers. But today the pictures she presented appeared deceptive. I ran back to my cell.

Sita soon followed me. "Anamika?" I was on my bed, lying down, facing the wall. She sat next to me. "Don't be like this. Today is a day of jubilation."

My voice was muffled against the pillow. "I don't want to go."

She stroked my back. "Why be so afraid?"

I turned to her and waved my hand in the air. "And what about all this? What about this thing we've built in here? Is it simply going to vanish? No more?"

She didn't respond.

"And who is going to braid my hair from now on? Who's going to sing to me?"

She wiped my tears and sweet-talked me into sitting up. "We can't fight this, Anamika. This thing is bigger than us. If we don't accept it, then we are the ones who'll suffer."

I was still crying softly when she helped me gather my stuff—what did I have, though? Nothing, apart from an extra dhoti, a comb, and a half bottle of oil that Sita had given me.

Clutching their meager belongings, the women had formed a line in the corridor. The colonel led the way, marching in the front, his buttocks twitching. We went out the front door toward the gate. I had not seen this gate since I came to this prison nearly a year ago. I'd only heard it clang open or shut. At the gate we were given plastic bags, and when I looked into mine, I found my mobile and my purse.

I held the mobile in my hand—it felt like an alien apparatus, one that I had heard much about but never had a chance to see and touch. As I held it in my palm, it seemed as if it could start ringing at any moment, although the battery was surely dead. Someone from my family could call me, or someone from Kailash Construction. What would I do then? How would I account for all this time that I had lived apart from them?

I handed the phone to Sita, who asked, "You don't want it?"

"No," I said.

She put the phone to her ear and pretended to answer a call. "Allo? Allo? Yes, this is Kailash Construction. Yes, Anamika Gurung speaking. Oho, Bimalji! Mailey ta kasto nachineko! How are you? Everything well? No, no, that shouldn't be a problem at all. If you give us the dimensions of that plot, we'll build a nice home for you there. Yes, yes, with a swimming pool and a theater and all that jazz. You want two houses? One for your wife and one for your mistress? And one for the little boy who lives down the lane? No problem, no problem. You can have as many houses as you want. Why not? You've worked hard for your money, your father worked hard for his money, your grandfather worked hard for his money. It's your money to splurge. Arre, let people talk! Why worry about what others say? Do you think countries like America and Singapore progressed by worrying about what other countries say? Yes, a solar panel, a garden portico, why not? A pleasure room? That can be done, too. Yes, yes, with a massage table. Arre, who will I tell, baba? Why would I tell your wife? This is my bread and butter also."

Sita sounded so much like my former self that I was blushing with embarrassment as the others clutched their stomachs in laughter. Now the women were getting excited about what lay beyond the gate. Sita was gazing at my face. My eyes welled up.

"And?" she asked.

"I can't."

"What choice do you have?"

We observed each other for a while.

"Okay, I'll take you with me," she said. "But I'm a vagrant. I don't really have a home."

The gate groaned and clanged open, and we were told to exit.

The prison was on a hill, and the scenery before us was of a valley below in the great distance, where the city was. "It's about a half a day's walk from here," the guard at the gate said. "There's a great celebration down there. If you all stop your jabbering, you might be able to hear it."

We stopped shuffling and held our breaths and listened. What the guard had said was true: a soft din rose from the city, and if you remained pindrop still, you could even hear the sound of drums like a faraway heartbeat.

AMERICA THE GREAT EQUALIZER

At first Biks, too, hadn't understood what the fuss was all about. The guy had robbed a store. Biks had seen the grainy video in which he had shoved the Indian shopkeeper out of the way and walked away with the cigars. Even in that video he appeared mean and scary looking. Why were people now going on as if he were a charming, dimple-faced young boy who got shot by a racist cop?

He said so one evening in a Nepali gathering in Skokie, and he found many in agreement with him. "These blacks," said a girl who worked at a computer firm and made tons of money, "they'll cry racism at the first opportunity they get." There were a chorus of yeses, and an elderly woman said, "They play the race card, ke, race card. Bujhenau?" It was obvious she relished saying "race card." Others gave examples from their own lives about how the kaleys were lazy, took advantage of the system, and possessed criminal minds.

Biks became silent and watched them. Half of them were very dark people themselves—*As dark as I am*, thought

Biks, self-consciously—yet they referred to the blacks as *kaleys*. The computer girl was darkish. The fat married man from Bhairawa and his silent wife and two children were so dark they looked like some ancient aboriginal people. The young engineer wearing the I LOVE NEPAL T-shirt was dark.

Yet here they were, calling other people dark. Of course, they were using *kaley* as a racial identifier, not merely as "black skin," but it still sounded hilarious when dark people from one part of the world used "darkie" to put down people from another part of the world. When he'd started the conversation about Michael Brown, he'd not anticipated that it'd so quickly devolve into talk about the inferiority and criminality of blacks.

Fools, he'd thought, all of them, people who had no sense of history. Biks knew this history; he'd studied it. Over the course of the evening, as he heard his compatriots speak as if blacks didn't deserve this country into which they'd been brought as slaves, in chains and packed together like sardines in ships, a type of understanding dawned on him. The smaller truth might be that Michael Brown was not a victim, but the larger truth was something else.

That night he called Seema. It was early in the morning in Nepal. A man picked up the phone, presumably her father. Biks hung up. He checked her Facebook page. She'd never been a heavy Facebook user; her last entry was three months ago when she'd written about a social activist who'd passed away. Biks had offered his condolences beneath her post, but she hadn't "liked" it, so he'd sent her an email, knowing she wouldn't respond, just like she hadn't responded to the other emails he'd sent.

In the past, after failing to reach her at home, he'd tried her mobile, but a woman's annoying automated voice always informed him that the number was busy: "Tapailey dialgarnubhaeko number ahiley byasta chha." It did the same tonight, so he tried the home number again.

A woman picked up after a number of rings. It sounded like Seema. His heartbeat quickened. "Seema?" he said.

There was a pause. "She's not here."

It was Seema, he was certain, but then he thought the voice could belong to a servant. "Do you know when she'll be back?"

"Don't know."

He waited, hoping she would talk more so he could ascertain her identity, but when the voice said nothing further, he said, "Could you tell Seema that Biks called and tell her that I need to talk to her? Either on Skype or on the phone? Here, take down my phone number." He paused, then said again, "Seema?" But the other side had hung up.

Fall semester started. He began getting into heated arguments at Nepali gatherings. "You all are racists," he told them.

Now every time he spoke, he imagined Seema watching him, like an eye hovering above him. The third eye. What would she think of him now, getting all riled up about this thing? She'd probably say, "What's wrong with you, Biks?" He imagined her thinking, *You've turned into a loser.*

Yes, I might be a loser, he answered her back in his mind, *but what's going on is also not right.* What all these people said about blacks was not right. They feared blacks, discriminated against them even as they themselves were targets of discrimination in the white world where they worked. A middle-aged woman who worked at Jewel Osco complained about her white customers yelling at her because they couldn't understand her accent. "You come here and take our jobs," her customers said, "and you can't speak English."

A young man who sold used cars in a dealership said that he was the constant butt of jokes of his white colleagues. They mimicked him, sometimes feigning "bad smell" when he was near them. The manager once told him, "Maybe that sales pitch works in the Third World—don't use it here."

"You all are immigrants," Biks told his compatriots, gesticulating with a beer in his hand, "and you're prejudiced against people who've lived here for centuries."

"You arrived here yesterday," someone said, "and you judge us."

"I may be a newbie," said Biks, who was a second-year graduate student in political science at Northern Illinois University, "but I know more about this country's history than all you yokels. Slavery doesn't matter? All that lynching doesn't matter? Have you hillbillies heard about Jim Crow? Segregation? You think all of this is happening in a vacuum?"

Biks recalled his early days at Northern Illinois. In the cafeteria, he'd find himself sitting next to students who were

Pakistani or Indian, sometimes with the occasional Nepali. The white students sat by themselves, and the black students formed their own clusters. A couple of times, he'd sat at the black table, but it had been an uncomfortable experience. It seemed like the black students didn't know why he had joined their table. He thought he heard someone mutter "faggot" under his breath, and he saw a couple of them kicking each other under the table. He exchanged a few words with the student next to him, but the student had a smirk on his face, and the others said something to him, something Biks didn't catch, in rapid English—some sort of a black dialect, Biks had thought at that time. The experience had left him slightly depressed and insecure.

"I don't need your history lesson," said a restaurant owner from Des Plaines to Biks. "I've lived in this great country for twenty years." He put out his hands in front of him. "See these? All these burns and cuts? That restaurant I built with my own two hands."

"And you'll take my restaurant only from my cold dead hands," said a young man whose hairstyle could only be described as a mohawk.

The restaurant owner held up his hand to quiet the laughter. "That so-called Michael Brown was a thug, like most of these kaleys are. I know because I've tried working with them. It's in their genes. And I'm glad he got shot. End of story."

"Khel khattam paisa hazam," someone else said. "But look at them, acting like animals, robbing and looting."

They sympathized with the Indian store clerk who had

been manhandled by Michael Brown, even though Indians often didn't feature well in the conversations at these gatherings. "These kaleys don't want to work, but they rob decent people like us who want to work," someone said. Another person expressed irritation with "all this talk about race-face" and suggested that they play cards. A group immediately sat down on the floor and began to play Flush, and the hostess hurried to make tea, and someone opened a second bottle of whiskey.

Biks went to a corner with a beer. Purushottam Uncle came up to him and said, "What has happened to you these days? Why do you get so agitated? I thought there was going to be a fistfight."

"I was ready for a fight. We all need to fight ignorance, Purushottam Uncle, don't you understand?"

"There's slavery in Nepal, too," Purushottam Uncle said. "Isn't our kamaiya system of bonded laborers slavery? Why do you have to talk only about American slaves?"

"Oh, so because slavery is still alive in Nepal, it's okay?"

"Let it go, Biks," Purushottam Uncle said. He taught English at a community college but still carried a pronounced Nepali accent. Biks had often wondered if his students made fun of him, like students did of Chinese professors at NIU who taught math or computer science in incomprehensible accents. A relative of Biks's mother, Purushottam Uncle was a green card holder who'd lived in Chicago for years, and had promised her that he'd look after Biks in America. "I need to talk to you about something," Purushottam Uncle now said. "In private."

The two pushed the screen door open and went out to the deck. In a corner, a couple of girls and a boy huddled together, but when they saw Biks and Purushottam Uncle, they quickly disengaged and went down to the large backyard, leaving behind them a waft of marijuana smell.

"This new generation can't party without ganja," Purushottam Uncle said in dismay. "Hettiraka! What has this world come to?" He took out a pack of cigarettes and offered one to Biks. "One of those girls"—he pointed to the group that was now smoking near the bushes—"her father is Dr. Gupta, that neurosurgeon, but look at her, smoking ganja and whatnot. I hear she is . . ." He looked at Biks meaningfully, but Biks ignored him. He was still thinking of retorts he could have used on the restaurant owner.

The two smoked in silence. Finally Purushottam Uncle said, "So I'm assuming you haven't heard?"

"Heard what?"

"I thought so."

For a moment Biks wondered if something had happened to his mother—an illness, hospitalization, discovery of cancer. He hadn't called her in a couple of weeks. "What, Purushottam Uncle? Why are you being so secretive?"

"I'll tell you, but remember, Biks, okay, don't kill the messenger." He said "don't kill the messenger" in English, raising a finger as though he were admonishing school students back in Nepal.

Biks took his last drag and threw the butt toward the lawn. "Just say it. I need to go home soon."

"I've heard that she got married."

Biks put his hands into his pockets and stared into the darkness.

"It's a recent thing." When Biks didn't respond, Purushottam Uncle said, "Biks?"

"Who is your source?"

"Why implicate people with names? My source isn't the type to spread rumors."

"Okay, thank you for letting me know," Biks said. "Thank you," he added for mock emphasis and went back inside. Standing against the wall, he watched the card game, taking long swigs from his beer. Purushottam Uncle also came back in and stood in the corner, watching him.

"Aren't you going to play Flush, Biks?" the hostess asked.

"He's still worrying about slavery," a player said.

"Fuck you," Biks said to him, but he sat down to play. He played hard, taking risks he normally wouldn't. At one juncture he tried to bluff his way through a lousy hand, but the other person wouldn't relent, and at the end of that round he lost about fifty dollars. Soon he got up and left the party, catching a ride with someone who was headed in his direction, to the house he shared with two Indian roommates on the edge of the campus.

He called Seema that night. He first tried the home number, then her mobile number. No answers. Marriage preparations, he thought. He thought of the banker, the one he'd seen at the hotel where she worked. Biks had gone to her hotel one day to surprise her, and there was a tall, handsome man in a suit chatting with her near the reception.

The man was laughing and leaning close to her, and Seema was smiling. The man caressed her arm. She saw Biks by the door to the lobby, and an expression of alarm passed through her face. Later he learned that he was a successful banker, the son of her father's colleague.

Biks called Ira, Seema's friend. Ira had occasionally hung out with Biks and Seema, and Biks had her mobile number jotted in his address book.

"Arre, Biks!" Ira said when she picked up, sounding pleased. "Long time no hear. How is America?"

After some chitchat he asked about Seema.

Ira became quiet.

"So what I've heard is true," Biks said.

"What can I say, Biks?"

"Did you go to the wedding?"

"I'm finding it difficult to talk about this with you."

"Nothing difficult. It can't be that hard to say whether you went to the wedding or not."

"Yes, I went," she said, barely audible.

"How was it?"

"Biks."

"Please, Ira, tell me how was the wedding?"

"You want to punish yourself? It was bhavya."

"Bhavya?"

"The grandest wedding I've attended."

"Where was it held?"

"At the Hyatt Regency, in Bouddha."

Ah, of course. Seema's parents wouldn't have it any other way.

"Who did she get married to?" Then, before Ira could answer, he said, "Wait, don't tell me, but do tell me whether she looked happy?"

Ira didn't answer.

Something changed in Biks after that night. It was as if he stopped caring about the world or his place in it. Things no longer made sense. He stopped going to classes. It was very hard to get up in the morning. When his roommates tried to wake him up in the morning, Biks curled over to the other side and waved them off. Around noon he got up, drank some coffee, then smoked a joint, after which his thoughts became manageable. He watched TV for an hour or two, first CNN, then FOX, then CNN again. News about Ferguson saturated everything. *Racists, all of them*, he muttered to himself.

Toward late afternoon, after the effect of pot wore off a bit, he drank some beer. As part of his graduate assistant-ship, he had evening duty at the media center, where he worked for a few hours. But he stopped going to his job, too. There were phone calls. A secretary from the depart-ment called and left a message on his machine, asking him if he was sick, if everything was all right. He didn't respond to any of them. His money was running out, but he no lon-ger cared about that. When Purushottam Uncle called, he pretended he was too busy with schoolwork.

Rich girl. Pretty girl. Fair Seema. No wonder she had rejected him. Not only was he very dark, his hairline was already receding. He thought of the word *rejection* when he realized what she'd done, and it generated in him a feeling of shame and anger. For the first time it occurred to him that she had rejected him not only because his family wasn't as established and wealthy as hers but also because of the color of his skin. The realization startled him, for he had not thought this way before. She had never given him a reason to think this way. In fact, she had always professed that she loved his dark skin. She'd run her finger over his face and say, "My kalu Biks, how I love you so." In the past he'd loved to hear her say, "My kalu Biks," but now he recalled a teacher from the seventh grade who'd always demonstrated antipathy toward him.

The teacher would run his index finger down Biks's cheek, then inspect his finger and say, "This one is such a darkie, I'm afraid I'm going to get coal smeared all over my finger."

Watching the anger over Ferguson brought back the memory of his first day on American soil, an incident he'd discounted until now as part of the ritual of entering America. At Chicago O'Hare airport more than a year ago, the immigration officer had looked at his passport and asked, "Is Nepal an Islamic country?" Biks said no. "Then why does your passport have a green cover?" The officer repeatedly looked at the passport and the I-20 and at Biks's face. "Do you have relatives in yo-yee?" When Biks expressed confusion, the officer said, speaking slowly, with controlled hostility, "UAE. United Arab Emirates. I'm asking if you have family in UAE." When Biks said no, the officer asked what the purpose of his visit to Dubai was. The

Dubai trip was for a conference paid for by the travel agency in Nepal where Biks had worked. "What type of travel conference?" the officer asked. Biks couldn't think. Much of the time he'd spent at the hotel pool, drinking beer, talking to Seema on Skype. The officer waved over a second officer, who escorted Biks to a room in a corner of the immigration area.

After half an hour, he was escorted farther inside and grilled by a woman officer with high cheekbones: "Are you of Arab ancestry? Do you have a criminal record in Nepal? What's your father's occupation? What was the name of the hotel you stayed in Dubai? Do most Nepalese look like you, with curly hair? Don't they have, uh, different skin color?"

He'd become afraid that he'd begin to speak to the inter-rogating officers in Nepali, as if he were addressing cops in Nepal: *Ke ho yesto? Timiharule jathabhavi garna pauchau? America jasto thauma pani yesto annyaya?* Instead he said in a calm voice, "The American consulate in Nepal checked all my documents and gave me the visa."

The officer interjected and said she had the right to deny him entry. "I have the power," she said. He was escorted to the outer room again and asked to wait. Biks noticed other passengers in the room: a red-faced white man who was speaking fast to a teenager in what sounded like a European language; a family of small-bodied Muslims, the woman in a burqa, the man wearing a skullcap, with two children, one of whom was watching Biks with her thumb in her mouth. Biks observed the baggage claim area through the glass win-dows and didn't recognize any of the passengers from his plane, which meant that they had all left. From a corner of the terminal came a crowd of new passengers, and workers in loud voices directed them to proper lanes.

After an hour the officer returned, handed back Biks's passport and documents and said, "Welcome to America."

In mid-September Biks ran into Saurav when returning from a bar, The Thirst, one late afternoon. Saurav, who was active in a Nepali organization in the Chicago area, was the first Nepali Biks had met when he landed. He had picked Biks up from O'Hare and had helped him get oriented those first few days. Then they'd lost contact.

"What's up with the beard?" Saurav asked.

"Just like this, yaar," Biks said, caressing his bushy growth.

"Diusai dankayera ayeko jasto chhani, ke ho?"

"Just a glass or two, yaar. At The Thirst. I was feeling bored."

They ended up in Saurav's apartment that evening, drinking. Lisa and her baby had gone to her mother's house in Toledo for a couple of days. Saurav was pursuing his PhD in physics at Northwestern, had been working on his dissertation for years now. He'd met Lisa in a bar. Lisa had told him she couldn't be sure who the baby's father was.

Biks finally told him that he'd quit school and was now short on funds. He told him about Seema. Saurav sympathized, kept saying, "Tragedy has befallen you." But it was not good, Saurav said, that Biks had abandoned his studies. "That might be a bigger mistake than the tragedy that has befallen you," he said.

Biks said he agreed, but that there was simply no way he could focus on academics right now. "I don't know where life is going to take me from here," he said. As they got drunker, Saurav made an offer: Biks should move in with him and Lisa. They had a room meant for the baby, but the baby slept in the same room with Lisa and Saurav anyway. When Biks said that Saurav should first consult with Lisa, Saurav dismissed his concern. "Maybe you can help with the groceries," he said.

"But I don't have any money," Biks said.

"I'll get you a job," Saurav said. With an exaggerated accent that could have been Middle Eastern or European, he added, "You will be rolling in bread, my dear friend from the mountains."

Lisa wasn't pleased when she returned to find Biks occupying their spare room. She and Saurav argued behind closed doors in their room while Biks sat in the living room with a beer and the TV on, watching protestors shout "Arrest Darren Wilson" at their elected leaders in a county meeting in St. Louis. His phone buzzed. Another text from Purushottam Uncle: EVERYTHING OKAY? WHY AREN'T YOU PICKING UP THE PHONE? Biks didn't respond.

The argument inside seemed to die down, and Biks heard the bed creak and Lisa moan softly.

"She thinks I'm going to marry her, Biks," Saurav said a few days later when Lisa was out. "She wants to go to Nepal. Wants to have a Nepali wedding there. What do you think, Biks? Should I take her to Nepal, introduce her to Pitaji and Mataji? Ask her to do pranam to them?" He pressed his palms together and bowed.

"You're not serious about her?"

"I'm a playaaah," Saurav had said, but Biks knew that he liked Lisa, more than he wanted to admit. Saurav just couldn't imagine taking her to Nepal, especially to his aging parents who lived in a village in Parbat. His uncles had homes in Kathmandu, but even they would be aghast if he brought back a bideshi, not to mention an unwed bideshi with a baby whose father was unknown. Sometimes Saurav acted out the chaos that would ensue: his aunts, all super religious women, in a tizzy; his older uncle advising him in a grave voice that a liaison with a kuiriney would never work; his younger uncle, himself a Don Juan known for his extramarital affairs, telling Saurav laughingly what a fool he was for not understanding that these goris were good only for fun and not for marriage.

Saurav got Biks a job at a gas station about a mile from his apartment. Saurav knew the Indian owner, but Biks soon discovered that Saurav knew everybody and everybody knew Saurav. The Greek manager of Town Market where he bought groceries greeted him by name. The Vietnamese butcher gave him the special cuts of goat meat he liked. The Somali car mechanic did his oil change for free.

The gas station owner was a paan-chewing middle-aged man with a beer belly who called Saurav "dada." Biks was employed for the evening shift; he'd get paid six dollars an hour, which, Biks was told, was not bad for an illegal.

This is what my life has come to, Biks thought the first evening at the job. *There I was in Nepal, dreaming about spending my life with a woman as beautiful as Seema, and here I am working illegally in a gas station owned by an Indian whose mouth is always bulging with red-juiced paan. How could I not have seen my life's trajectory?*

His college friends in Nepal had been surprised when Seema fell for him. When she started coming to Biks's house, Mamu, an educated woman who taught school, had said, "How fair Seema is. Biks, how did you manage this? She is so fair and beautiful, she looks like a model. She's not going to end up deceiving you, is she?"

He'd scolded his mother for her questions but he'd also understood where she came from: she herself was a dark-skinned woman who'd faced taunts and comments, often from her own mother-in-law, who, Biks remembered in stunned moments of rage, was an illiterate hillbilly who had to sign documents by dabbing her thumb in ink. But he also knew that Mamu approved of Seema not only because she was gori-ramri but also because she came from a well-to-do family with old money. Mamu went out of her way to cater to and please Seema. Biks had thought it was a bit excessive, Mamu's fawning, but he had also been secretly pleased. Once he and Seema got married, he'd mused, there'd be no friction between his mother and his wife.

But that time never came. Now it became clear to him that Seema never had intentions of introducing him to her family, let alone make a case that she ought to marry him. No wonder she'd not objected when he'd initially talked about his desire to go to America for further studies. Not only had she not objected, she'd encouraged him to apply. And he had assumed that his going to America was part of their future together, perhaps even an investment in it. He'd imagined that even if he were to go alone, she'd soon follow him within months, and they'd solve the problem of potential irreconcilability between their two families. What was America if not the great equalizer, the eraser of differences, of caste and creed?

By the end of the first week, Biks had come to hate his job. There was a pervasive smell of gas that infiltrated his nostrils even when he was inside, behind the counter. He made mistakes when he sold lottery tickets. The customers became irate for small reasons: for the store not carrying their brand of cigarettes or beer, for it not having an air station for their tires, for the line at the counter being too long. Whenever a cop car showed up, Biks felt like he should duck or go into the back room, but that'd have made him look even more suspicious.

As the days started getting colder, he became convinced that Seema had rejected him because of his dark skin more than because of his family status. "Do you want to live with someone as dark as him for the rest of your life?" he imagined Seema's mother saying to her. Her mother would stroke Seema's hair and say, "Such a fair, beautiful daughter I have. I can't think of someone this fair and beautiful with someone like him." Seema's father would be somewhere in the background, mumbling about dark men and their dark hearts. "Look, chhori," Seema's mother would say.

"The banker is tall and handsome. And look how goro he is, totally matching your skin color. You two would look so good together. Plus he's successful, has a name, comes from such a reputable family."

This was all too exaggerated, of course. There were moments of inactivity at the gas station, especially after ten at night, and Biks's mind went off on a spin. He got off around midnight, walked back to the apartment and curled into bed. He slept until noon, woke up depressed, then drank some cheap beer.

One day Purushottam Uncle showed up at the gas station, and there was a mild argument as Biks served customers. Purushottam Uncle said that Biks was ruining his life, and Biks said that he was an adult and didn't care for Purushottam Uncle's guidance. Purushottam Uncle appeared hurt. "Your mother," he said, "has faith in me, that I'd keep an eye out for your well-being. How can I fulfill my duty if you don't even talk to me?" Finally Biks promised him that he'd keep him updated, and that he'd also call his mother regularly. In return, Purushottam Uncle sadly and reluctantly agreed not to inform Biks's mother that he was now an illegal.

In October, Ferguson exploded around him. It was on the news all the time. *Of course, of course*, he thought. *This has been going on for centuries.*

"This country is hopeless," he said once at a Nepali party. His beard had grown so much that Saurav now called him a bushman. The gas station owner had asked him to at least trim his beard so that the customers wouldn't think he was a terrorist. "Arre, dada, you're looking more and more like Osama bin Laden," the owner said.

Go fuck yourself, thought Biks. A type of recklessness had come over him. These days when he crossed the street, he did it slowly, causing irate drivers to honk at him. Once he was taking his time crossing the street on his way to work when a group of young white men with crew-cut hair—possibly frat boys—shouted, "Move it, nigger," and sped past, laughing.

At home, when he caught his reflection in the mirror, he didn't recognize himself. *You look scary, nigger.* He wondered what Seema would think of him now. He imagined her running her fingers through his beard, saying, "So sexy, Biks."

As November rolled in, everyone was discussing what the grand jury decision would be for Darren Wilson. *It's a white man's world,* was the refrain among his black customers. "That white cop was acquitted even before he shot Michael Brown," one customer said.

In the apartment, it was exactly the opposite. "That habsi robbed a cigar store," Saurav said one Saturday. He was rocking the baby in his arms. "You don't think that's relevant?"

"Yes, he was no angel himself," Biks said. "But did he have to die? If he were a white boy, he'd have spent a night in jail, then let go. But no, a black man has to be put down. We're all niggers. That's how this system is. This is the history of colonialism. Coolies. In India, in Africa. That's what this uproar is all about."

Lisa came from the kitchen, shaking a baby bottle. "Do you know how dangerous these blacks are?" she said. "My uncle was a cop in Memphis. Every time he went into a black neighborhood, he didn't know if he'd come back out alive."

Biks was going to respond, but now Lisa had taken the baby and was trying to feed her. The baby was gurgling and squirming in her arms, and it seemed wrong to have such a heated discussion with a mother feeding a hungry baby. But it was Lisa herself who continued railing against blacks, or "African'ts," as she derisively put it. She blamed affirmative action, which she said discriminated against whites. She said that she had attended a mostly black school in Gary and had been constantly harassed and taunted for her skin color. "By the time I graduated, I hated who I was," she said as she rocked back and forth to calm the baby. "It wasn't until I went to college that I finally came to terms with being fucking white." She pointed a finger at Biks. "You're speaking out of your ass." The baby, mouth and throat moving as she sucked the milk, was watching her mother intently. "You didn't grow up here. You're clueless."

"And you're an ignorant white—" Biks stopped himself before he could complete the sentence.

"White what? White what?" The baby still in her arms, the bottle still in the baby's mouth, Lisa moved toward him threateningly. "Spit it out, motherfucker."

"Lisa," Saurav said.

"You say one word defending him," she told Saurav, "and I'll kick both your asses out of this house."

Biks went to his room and shut the door.

A couple of hours later Saurav knocked on Biks's door and asked him if he wanted to go to The Thirst. At first Biks said no, but Saurav persisted, and the two friends went to the bar. After a couple of beers, Biks asked Saurav what attracted him to Lisa.

"Come on, let it go, yaar," Saurav said.

"No, no, I'm just curious, that's all." And it was true: Biks had often wondered about it. Saurav the physicist, who with his advisor had co-authored an article for the *American Journal of Physics*, who was referred to as "brilliant" by many, both Nepalis and Americans. And Lisa, who had barely passed high school, whose idea of reading was flipping through *Vogue* magazine, who called Obama a Kenyan, a Muslim, a communist, a community organizer, always referring to him by his full name, "Barack Hussein Obama," with a long hiss on *Hussein*. She listened to Rush Limbaugh on the radio in the afternoon, volume high, more often after Ferguson, more often now as if to taunt Biks.

"Tell it like it is, Rush," Saurav sometimes said more out of amusement than any conviction as Limbaugh's hectoring voice filled the house. One time, when Limbaugh made a derogatory comment about a caller with a pronounced Indian accent, Saurav laughed and, when Lisa was out of earshot, said to Biks, "Isn't he such an idiot? Maharushi!"

"Lisa's easy to be with," Saurav said now. "I don't have to prove myself with her."

"Prove what?"

"Prove anything."

"What are you going to say to your parents? To your uncles?"

"About what?"

"About Lisa."

"I'm not going to say anything."

"You're going to keep her hidden?"

Saurav laughed.

"For how long?"

"As long as I can."

"And? Once it's out in the open?"

"Dekha jayega."

"You're going to declare your love for her?" Biks asked.

"I'll have her do pranam to my family, like this." Saurav put his palms together in obeisance and bowed. "Pranam, Pitaji. Pranam, Mataji."

"I can't see Lisa doing that," Biks said. "She's too . . ." Biks sucked in his breath.

"Too what? White trash?" Saurav laughed.

Biks kept quiet.

"She is foul-mouthed, but I like her. I like her honesty." Saurav studied him. "What about you, muji? You're always judging me and Lisa. What about you?"

"What about me?"

"Are you going to sit around moping, saying, 'My Seema, my Seema, why hast thou forsaken me?'" He was quite drunk by now, glassy-eyed, swaying a bit on the barstool. "Or are you going to call her and tell her you don't need her? Call her and say, 'Timijasta ketita yoh americama katti katti. Fairer than you, prettier than you.' Tell her that."

Yes, I might, Biks thought. *I might tell her that there's plenty of fish in the American sea.*

Later, as they made their way drunkenly out of the bar, Saurav slapped Biks on the back and said, "I'll ask Lisa to find someone for you. A whitey. Raaaamri, ok? Goooori, okay? Someone just like Lisa. That'll serve you right."

Biks started drinking right before he walked to work. Two or three beers, and he'd feel all right. *You're all right now*, he'd tell himself. He was especially chatty with his black customers. "Hey, brothah," he'd say. "Whaz happenin'?" The black women and girls who came in for a purchase he referred to as "sistahs."

Some of his black customers talked, some were surly, some gave him quizzical or bemused looks. One man in John Lennon glasses and tight jeans and a goatee, who Biks learned was a professor, paused with the change he'd received from Biks in his hand and asked tensely, "Am I your brother because we have the same mother, or am I your brother because you're African American?" Then he laughed and said he was just giving Biks a hard time.

One afternoon two white cops came into the gas station, and Biks heard them talk near the toilet. They were speaking in low voices, but he could tell that they were discussing Ferguson and he heard the word "Negro," which made him alert (*Who says "Negro" these days?* he thought); then he realized that it was said sarcastically. "The Negroes are up in arms," then a chuckle. The cop who said it happened to look toward Biks, and their eyes met. When the cop held his eyes, Biks looked away, heart hammering, convinced that his illegal status was about to be uncovered.

"Hey, boy," the cop shouted. "Don't you carry Minute Maid juice?"

Biks shook his head.

"This brand you got here sucks," the cop said. "Tell your manager. Or whoever the fuck is in charge."

"His dad," the other cop said, and they left.

Only after they left did it occur to Biks that the cop had called him a "boy," and he didn't know whether to feel angry about it or relieved that he'd not been taken away and deported.

Biks usually brought up Ferguson with his black customers. "This is outrageous," he said. "Look at that Darren Wilson's face. He was itching to kill a black man that day."

His customers usually nodded. Some said, "Yeah, postracial America." Some eyed him warily, as if they thought he was trying to trap them.

He struck up a friendship with a black man named Jacob who delivered soft drinks in a van at night. After Jacob restocked the drinks, the two stepped outside to smoke. Jacob was getting married in a couple of months and was eager to start a family. "I love kids, man," he said. He hadn't finished college but was into philosophy and was familiar with Hinduism and Buddhism. He listened attentively when Biks described Nepal to him. "I'd love to go see them temples," Jacob said and recited the names of Hindu gods: "Sheeva, Vaishnu, Ganyesh. Maybe you'll invite me when you get married?" He punched Biks on the shoulder. "You got a girl back in Naples, man?"

"Nepal," Biks corrected him.

"Yes, yes, Nepal. Well, do you? Have a girl?"

Biks smiled. "Maybe."

"Look at you, all smiling and shit. What's her name?"

"Seema."

"Seema," Jacob said dreamily. "Is she hot?"

"Very hot. Boiling hot."

"I bet. Indian women are so sexy."

"I'm not from India. I'm from Nepal." Biks pointed a stern finger at Jacob. "Don't ever, ever call a Nepali man Indian. We were never colonized by the British."

"No kidding!"

"And don't ever tell a Nepali man that Buddha was born in India. Unless you want to be lynched."

Biks cursed himself for saying "lynched," but Jacob laughed. "All right. You're funny, man." He asked if Biks had a photo of his "fiancée."

Cigarette in mouth, Biks took out his phone and showed Jacob Seema's photo. He had taken it in a café long before he boarded the plane to America, long before things went wrong between them. It showed her flashing a *V* with her fingers, looking with a half smile at the camera, her dark hair cascading down to her waist.

"Damn!" Jacob said and, looking away, stomped his feet. Then he grabbed the phone from Biks's hand and peered at the photo closely. "You're one lucky dog," he said. With an embarrassed but pleased smile, Biks snatched his phone back.

"You're bringing her over here?"

Biks nodded.

"You should get married here so I can come to the wedding."

A customer pulled up in her car, so Biks had to go into the store to attend to her. The conversation with Jacob had strangely buoyed him up, and he sported a silly grin.

He showed Seema's photo to new people he met at Nepali parties, saying she would soon be joining him. He did so when Purushottam Uncle wasn't around. One time, around mid-November, he and Saurav had taken a couple of new arrivals from Nepal, Jivan and Umesh, to the Indian district in Devon. They were sitting in Sukhadia, drinking tea. Saurav had gone to the bathroom when Biks, out of the blue, showed Seema's photo to Jivan and Umesh. They oohed and aahed. He told them that he was bringing her to America and they'd be married in the Hindu temple in Lemont.

When Saurav returned to the table, Biks changed the topic and began talking about the great sweets that Sukhadia had. "They taste better than Aangan in Kathmandu," he informed the newbies.

Later, when the four of them went to Navy Pier for an evening stroll, Umesh ended up mentioning Biks's soon-to-be-bride coming over from Nepal.

"There's no bride," Saurav said. "I'm trying to find a white dulahi for him here."

"But he showed us the photo in the restaurant."

"What photo?"

Biks took out his phone and showed Seema to Saurav. "This one, nigger."

"What is this nigger-nigger?" Jivan asked. "Isn't that a bad word? Used for kaleys?"

"We're all niggers," Biks said. He pointed at Jivan. "You're a nigger." Then at Umesh. "And you're a nigger." At Saurav. "And this one is a full-time nigger. But he thinks he's white."

"Why?" asked Umesh. "Because he's shacking up with a white girl?"

That evening in the apartment Saurav confronted Biks. "What was all that about?"

"What?"

"That I think I'm white."

Biks said nothing. He felt bad about what he'd said earlier in front of Jivan and Umesh but wasn't ready to take it back.

"It's not good, Biks, it's not good," Saurav said. Looking at the carpet, he shook his head as if he were contemplating a crop that had gone bad. "You think you're so progressive, enlightened, but you're no different." Lisa was in the next room with the baby, so he lowered his voice. "I know you don't like her, but you have to understand you're a guest here, and she is the host."

"I don't give a fuck who is a guest or who is a host. You think I give a fuck?"

Saurav watched him in dismay. "What's the matter with you? You've become so aggressive these days."

Biks waved his hand imperially in the air.

"And what is this nigger business? Why are you going

around calling everyone nigger? One day these kaleys will beat the crap out of you."

"Chances are," Biks said, "I'll get shot by a white cop."

Saurav shook his head slowly, sadly.

"Yes, I can see myself getting shot by a white cop," Biks said. "Will they shoot me because I'm a black nigger or because I'm a Nepali nigger? Or perhaps"—he caressed his beard—"a Muslim nigger? A terrorist, perhaps?"

On the evening it was announced that the grand jury had decided not to indict Darren Wilson, a group of high school-aged white boys dawdled by the counter at the gas station, using the word *Apu* in every sentence as they inquired of one another what they should buy.

"What about Starbursts, Apu?" one said.

"We need some Doritos, Apu," said another.

"Apu, Apu, what should we do tonight? Should we go to Steve's place, Apu?"

"Apu, what's your wife's name again? The one with the large eyes and the dot on her forehead?"

The boys were clearly making fun of him, but Biks couldn't tell how. The name Apu sounded familiar. A tune coursed through his head, then the singsong-y "The Simpsons" popped into his head, and it clicked. Apu, the Indian store owner with the pronounced Indian accent.

The boys—there were four of them—had put their purchases on the counter for Biks to ring up, but Biks pushed them to the side and said, "Sorry, you can't buy here."

"What?"

"I can't sell you those."

The boys turned quiet. Then one of them laughed and said, "Dude, you're not refusing to sell us things, are you? Why? Because we're white?"

Biks was feeling hot and cold at the same time. "You're disrupting the peace," he said, then immediately felt foolish. He felt like he could no longer speak English.

"Disrupting the peace?" They were doubling up with laughter.

"You fucking crackers!" he said. He didn't know where the word came from; he didn't know he even knew that word.

"Crackers?" one said.

"You mean honkeys?" another said.

They were laughing, jabbing one another.

"Oh, I'm so offended," one said. "Who you calling honkey, Mr. Curry Breath?"

"Where are you from?" another said. "Afghanistan?"

"He's Taliban," another said. "The beard. It's a dead giveaway."

Biks had a vision of himself coming out from behind the counter and fighting with these boys. He'd taken some karate in Nepal, and he wondered if the moves would come to him. But it was all so ridiculous. They were barely past their teens, even though all of them were bigger than Biks.

He rang up their items, and they paid him, not letting up on their mockery. "Thank you, Apu," they said. One of them put his palms together, bowed, and said, "Arigato, sensei."

After they left, he bolted the door from the inside and put up the CLOSED sign. He grabbed a beer from the cooler and sat on the floor, drinking, hidden from the door. Every now and then he was aware of customers jiggling the doorknob, then voices. "Why is it fucking closed?" he heard a man say.

After three beers, Biks took out his phone and dialed Seema's mobile on a lark. A female voice picked up at the other end. Seema. Or it could be a servant. "Seema?" he asked.

There was a pause, then, "Biks?"

He closed his eyes. Things were moving inside his body, like ants. "How are you?" he finally asked.

"I'm fine. How is America?"

On TV they were showing explosions in Ferguson. The police—or was it the army?—in riot gear faced the protesters. A woman was shown ranting into the night. "My studies are going well," Biks said. "I'm preparing for my exams." He kept going. "It's not easy here. You have to study hard. You have to write papers. You have to participate in class discussions. Expectations are high."

"Are you happy in America?"

"What's not to be happy about? How can anyone not be happy in America? This is America, not some piddly-ass Third World country."

She gave a soft chuckle. "Listen to you, sounding so American."

After a pause, he asked, "Are you—? What can I say? I've heard things."

There was silence at the other end. Momentarily, he panicked, thinking she'd hung up. "Seema?" he said.

"Yes, I'm here."

"Don't worry," he said. "Such is life."

"Such is life," she said.

"But you're happy?"

"I'm happy," she said, softly but firmly. "Very happy."

"Ah, you've always had a good attitude."

On TV, Sean Hannity was going on about the mob in Ferguson: "What about the dangers to our cops? What about the risks they literally have to take every day when confronted by these thugs?"

"I've grown a beard now," Biks said.

"Really?" Then, gently, her voice filled with sympathy, "Why? Has some tragedy befallen you?"

"I now look like a terrorist," he said. "They'll soon take me to Guantanamo Bay."

She gave a soft chuckle at the other end, and then they got disconnected.

He didn't want to stay in the gas station, hiding. And it had also become clear to him he could no longer work at this place. This was not the life he'd envisioned, being taunted by teenagers, called "boy" by white cops, trying to be blacker than blacks—"Blacker than thou," he muttered to himself—when his history didn't compare to theirs, the brutality, the dehumanization, the violence. He was a fraud, trying to pretend to be someone he was not. Perhaps Seema had sensed that in him. That's what Saurav, too, was trying to convey, although Saurav came with his own set of problems. "I am a pretender," Biks said to himself. "A poseur. An impostor." He sighed. "An impossible impostor."

He left a note for the manager, who usually came to

open the station in the mornings. *Dada, salaam!* he wrote, and continued writing in Romanized Hindi, borrowing the overly dramatic language from Hindi movies: *Aaj mai aapsey albida mang rahahoon. Mujhe maf kardena, Dada Don. Mai aapka pau ka dhool bhi honai ka laik nahin hoon. Albida! Albida! Albida!* —*Apka namakhalal Biks.*

Seeking goodbye, please pardon me, I am not worthy to be even the dust at your feet. Goodbye! Goodbye! Goodbye! —*Your backstabber, Biks.*

He turned off the lights, locked the doors (he'd hand over the keys to Saurav) and was on his way out when a semi truck pulled into the station. The station wasn't very large, so usually big trucks avoided it. The driver leaned out of the window and asked, "Is there a bathroom here, man?" He had a long brown beard running down his chin, like one of the guys from ZZ Top. He was even wearing dark glasses at night.

Biks was about to say no when ZZ Top said, with an impassive face but in a voice that broke, "Need to pee real bad."

Biks unlocked the gas station and got the key that opened the bathroom on the side of the building. As he waited for ZZ Top to come out, he lit a cigarette. Then he noticed the license plate on the truck. It said MISSOURI.

It made sense that he'd end up in Ferguson that night, at two o'clock in the morning, bleary-eyed yet insanely alert, as though someone had jolted him with an electric rod. ZZ Top had dropped him by the side of the road on I-270, in

Florissant, near a high school. "No way in hell I'm going in there," ZZ Top had said, pointing toward Ferguson. "That place is burning tonight. I'd say it's about a thirty-minute walk from here. Use Google Maps on your phone if you get lost."

Biks thanked him.

"Well, best of luck, buddy," ZZ Top said, and zoomed off.

So here he was, Biks, in Ferguson, after an hour walk in the dark through what appeared to be a largely residential area, wondering if a cop was going to stop him. Or a redneck in a pickup truck, elated by the grand jury decision, who might decide to take it out on a lone darkie who looked like an "Eh-rab." At one point in a street that was less well lit than the others, he had become anxious that he'd be lost and would have to spend his night roaming around these neighborhoods. Or, irrationally, that he'd be mugged. What the hell, Biks homie, he'd chided himself. Where do you think you are? New York City? Then, he heard voices and saw figures in the distance: people moving toward the action. Soon, he was no longer a solitary figure, and there were people, a pizza shop, Walgreens, a church, brighter street lights.

Now he was smack in the middle of the madness. There was a palpable, unpredictable energy in the air. People swarmed around him. A young woman wearing a colorful headscarf met his eyes and said, "It's so fucked up!" He responded, sickened by the wisdom in his voice, "Tell me about it." He noticed a few white people in the crowd, and some with Oriental features, but no one who looked South

Asian. He almost expected someone to get into his face and shout, "What the hell are you doing here? This is not your fight!" It was irrational, this feeling, yet it had returned, the earlier sense that he was an impostor.

In the distance he saw a large building that had been set on fire—it was glowing, bubbling. He moved toward it as though it were his lodestar. A group of people huddled near a grocery store whose windows were shattered: they were burning the American flag. A strong smell hit Biks's nostrils, as though flesh had been singed. "I'm tired, I'm so tired," a middle-aged black woman wailed as she crouched on the ground near Biks, her fists bunched in front of her.

Police in riot gear approached from the next block to meet the protesters.

The city exploding—the burning, the anger, the screams of murder and helplessness—was, in a way, like home. He could, if he wanted to, start shouting slogans in Nepali. So he did, gently mouthing, "Police atyachar, murdabad, murdabad. Peace and justice, paunai parcha, paunai parcha." He giggled. This could work.

The woman in the colorful headscarf was next to him, looking at the police with piercing eyes. "Damn!" she said. Some of the younger men around them were hurling stones and bottles at the cops, who were shuffling toward them in a tightly knit formation, flanked on both sides by what looked like small tanks. "You go home!" the protesters shouted at the cops. A series of small explosions sounded, like firecrackers. But Biks was entranced by the woman's earrings. Long and dangling down almost to her shoulders, they were made of tiny black and white beads that stitched together resembled dancing skirts. He was certain Seema had worn the exact same earrings one afternoon when she'd come to visit him. Well, I'll be damned, thought Biks now, and he nearly reached out and touched them. The woman noticed him staring at her and, with rolling eyes, moved away.

What craziness. Here he was, in the thick of it, and he was checking out a girl. *This will not do, my friend from the mountains.* A glass shattered, and suddenly a flurry of bodies hurtled toward him, chased by the police, and he was pushed to the ground. He struggled to get up, but his every attempt was thwarted by people trampling him to get away. There were clattering and clanking noises, then hisses. "Tear gas!" someone shouted.

Then it was as if Biks's chest had caught on fire. He nearly clawed his eyes out—that's how badly they burned. A searing heat entered his lungs, and he hacked and coughed and doubled over on the ground. He writhed, made "hah" sounds with his breath, called out his mother's name.

But even in the midst of this ridiculous pain, he knew ultimately nothing would happen to him, that he'd come out of this fight unscathed, at most only bruised. This realization brought some solace, and he closed his eyes tightly, feeling tears running down his cheeks. *Do it*, he told himself. With a concentrated focus, he encouraged his mind to rise above his body, and it did, bit by bit, until he was so high up that he saw himself like a tiny rag doll below, with other small figures running about, small globs of fire exploding here and there.

But he was already on the move.

Now he was sitting on the roof of his house in Kathmandu. It was evening time. He could hear the sounds of pots and pans one floor below in the kitchen, where his mother was cooking dinner. On the horizon, rising above the city's clutter, were those brilliant white mountains. He was sipping tea, with a strong flavor of fresh ginger, just the way he liked it.